FINAL WAR... IN T
stories written by B;
and early 1970s und

Books published the two collections as one half each of an
Ace Double, and they became Malzberg's first published
anthologies— his announcement to the world that he had
officially arrived and was ready to stir things up.

The *Encyclopedia of Science Fiction* described him as "a
master of black humour."

Brian Doherty in *Reason* magazine proclaimed
Malzberg's writing to be "incisive, heartbreaking, wildly
imaginative, and darkly hilarious."

Andrew Fox called him "My Science Fiction Rabbi": "The
tales Barry tells are tales of crushed dreams and choked
ambitions, but they are also tales of exciting intellectual
adventures, friendships both literary and personal, and a
fellowship of minds devoted to human progress, or at
least to warning humanity away from its most base
impulses and foibles."

And Harlan Ellison asserted that Malzberg "one of the
few writers in the world whom I will gladly, happily,
loudly declare is a better writer than I am."

Enter the world of Barry N. Malzberg...

FINAL WAR
AND OTHER FANTASIES
IN THE POCKET
AND OTHER S-F STORIES

BARRY N. MALZBERG

Stark House Press • Eureka California

FINAL WAR AND OTHER FANTASIES / IN THE POCKET
AND OTHER S-F STORIES

Published by Stark House Press
1315 H Street
Eureka, CA 95501, USA
griffinskye3@sbcglobal.net
www.starkhousepress.com

ISBN: 979-8-88601-117-3

Book design by Mark Shepard, shepgraphics.com
Cover art by Jeff Jordan
Proofreading by Bill Kelly

First Stark House Press Edition: November 2024

TABLE OF CONTENTS

Raising the Bar

By Barry N. Malzberg

These two initial collections, published in the format of Ace Doubles half a century ago sported introductions which even at the time struck me as callow and self-serving. Coming to science fiction for a concatenation of reasons after having failed as a graduate fellow to get work into the so-called "literary" market, I had come to science fiction as a kind of default. "I used to read a lot of this stuff" quoted my aspiration in the late 60s, "Maybe I can sneak my way into here." That turned out, somewhat to my surprise, to be possible and "Final War," sneaking into *The Magazine of Fantasy and Science Fiction* turned out to be close to the very first proof. I (consciously) knew its derivation from *Catch-22*, but caught in 1965 on a Shubert Fellowship at Syracuse the rising arc of suspicion, then revulsion surrounding Vietnam adventure and there was just enough ambiguity in the background to let Ed Ferman squeak it into *The Magazine of Fantasy and Science Fiction* where it created in the then closed category and created the mildest of stirs. Shortly followed in that market by "Death to the Keeper" (washed-up actor decides to re-enact 11/22/63 with himself playing the lead role and thus "purging national guilt") it confirmed Ferman's initial daring, opened the market, and in tandem with "Final War" pointed a path which I followed for decades. These two early collections both exploited and extended my familiarity with science fiction and so it goes and so it went. Over the next several decades I published at least 350 narratives of various lengths in a category with which I became increasingly proficient and also angry. (So much seemed possible then.)

I had a pretty good run, many of the stories derivative (subtly or otherwise), many of them not so such. An essay could be written surrounding many of them but can be particularly well supervised by a little roundelay I passed on to Gardner Dozois when both of us were a lot closer to five and twenty that we were subsequently to be. Our insight and progression early on were quite similar. "You know what?" I said to the very early version of the category's most outrageous, most courageous and most improbable editor, "You and I have made the same discovery ... if you throw in a rocket ship, a cast of aliens or some audacious future, you can get away with almost anything here."

Gardner, then immersed in his own entry and a few years younger nodded vigorously. "Exactly" he said. He was not merely humoring me as we both learned.

The publisher asked if I wanted to run the introductions to these two very early collections in the collection which follows and that would have been the easiest and fairest way to deal with the situation but on reflection "easiest and fairest" did not seem the proper attendance to these two collections; these were written not so much in exploitation as transgression and as I look them over more than half a century down the pike I opted for this somewhat wearier appraisal. "Final War" was a Nebula finalist and if I had known how to lobby (I am glad I did not) might have won; "Gehenna," the only work of fiction I ever wrote in a state of drunkenness is in voice and accomplishment utterly apart from the body of my work. "Death to the Keeper," the much-reduced version of a play written for the Shubert Fellowship, then novelized, then reduced to a novelette remains outrageous half a century after its original version. If you take this racket seriously which unfortunately I did most of the time, "audacity" or "outrageous" is how you play the game. I am still at the earliest point of internalizing that.

—August 2024: New Jersey

FINAL WAR
AND OTHER FANTASIES
BARRY N. MALZBERG

Writing as K. M. O'Donnell

For Edward L. Ferman and Donald A. Wollheim
with thanks
And for Harry Harrison and Kris Neville
with affection

FINAL WAR

"'Twas a mad stratagem,
To shoe a troop of horse with felt ..."
Lear, Act III

Hastings had never liked the new Captain.

The new Captain went through the mine field like a dancer, looking around from time to time to see if anyone behind was looking at his trembling rear end. If he found that anyone was, he immediately dropped to the end of the formation, began to scream threats, told the company that the mine field would go up on them. This was perfectly ridiculous because the company had been through the mine field hundreds of times and knew that all of the mines had been defused by the rain and the bugs. The mine field was the safest thing going. It was what lay around the mine field that was dangerous. Hastings could have told the new Captain all of this if he had asked.

The new Captain, however, was stubborn. He told everyone that, before he heard a thing, he wanted to become acclimated.

Background: Hastings' company was quartered, with their enemy, on an enormous estate. Their grounds began in a disheveled forest and passed across the mine field to a series of rocks or dismally piled and multicolored stones which formed into the grim and blasted abutments two miles away. Or, it began in a set of rocks or abutments and, passing through a scarred mine field, ended in an exhausted forest two miles back. It all depended upon whether they were attacking or defending; it all depended upon the day of the week. On Thursdays, Saturdays and Tuesdays, the company moved east to capture the forest; on Fridays, Sundays and Wednesdays, they lost the battles to defend it. Mondays, everyone was too tired to fight. The Captain stayed in his tent and sent out messages to headquarters; asked what new course of action to take. Headquarters advised him to continue as previously.

The forest was the right place to be. In the first place, the trees gave privacy, and in the second, it was cool. It was possible to play a decent game of poker, get a night's sleep. Perhaps because of the poker, the enemy fought madly for the forest and defended it like lunatics. So did Hastings' company. Being there, even if only on Thursdays, Saturdays and Tuesdays, made the war worthwhile. The enemy must have felt the same way, but they, of course, had the odd day of the week. Still, even Hastings was willing to stay organized on that basis. Monday was a lousy day to get up, anyway.

But, it was the new Captain who wanted to screw things up. Two weeks after he came to the company, he announced that he had partially familiarized himself with the terrain and on this basis, he now wanted to remind the company not to cease fighting once they had captured the forest. He advised them that the purpose of the war went beyond the forest; it involved a limited victory on ideological issues, and he gave the company a month to straighten out and learn the new procedure. Also, he refused to believe his First Sergeant when the First Sergeant told him about the mine field but sent out men at night in dark clothing to check the area; he claimed that mines had a reputation for exploding twenty years later. The First Sergeant pointed out that it was not twenty years later, but the Captain said this made no difference; it could happen anytime at all. Not even the First Sergeant knew what to do with him. And, in addition to all of these things, it was rumored that the Captain talked in private to his officers of a *total* victory policy, was saying things to the effect that the war could only be successful if taken outside of the estate. When Hastings had grasped the full implication of all of this, he tried to imagine for a while that the Captain was merely stupid but, eventually, the simple truth of the situation came quite clear: the new Captain was crazy. The madness was not hateful: Hastings knew himself to be quite mad. The issue was how the Captain's lunacy bore on Hastings' problem: now, Hastings decided, the Captain would never approve his request for convalescent leave.

This request was already several months old. Hastings had handed it to the new Captain the day that the new Captain had come into the company. Since the Captain had many things on his mind at this time—he told Hastings that he would have to become acclimated to the new situation—Hastings could understand matters being delayed for a short while. But still, nothing had been done, and it was after the election; furthermore, Hastings was getting worse instead of better. Every time that Hastings looked up the Captain to discuss this with him, the Captain fled. He had told the First Sergeant that he wanted Hastings to know that he felt he was acting irresponsibly and out of the network of the problem. This news, when it was delivered, gave Hastings little comfort. *I am not acting irresponsibly*, he told the First Sergeant who listened without apparent interest, *as a matter of fact, I'm acting, in quite a mature fashion. I'm trying to get some leave for the good of the company*. The First Sergeant had said that he guessed he didn't understand it either and he had been through four wars, not counting eight limited actions. He said that it was something which Hastings would have to work out for his own satisfaction.

Very few things, however, gave Hastings that much satisfaction, anymore. He was good and fed up with the war for one thing and, for another, he had gotten bored with the estate even if the company hadn't: once you had seen the forest, you had seen all of it that was worthwhile. Unquestionably, the cliffs, the abutments and the mine field were terrible. It might have been a manageable thing if they could have reached some kind of understanding with the enemy, a peaceful allotment of benefits, but it was obvious that headquarters would have none of this and besides, the enemy probably had a headquarters, too. Some of the men in the company might have lived limited existences; this might be perfectly all right with *them*, but Hastings liked to think of himself as a man whose horizons were, perhaps, a little wider than those of the others. *He* knew the situation was ridiculous. Every week, to remind him, reinforcements would come from somewhere in the South and tell Hastings that they had never seen anything like it. Hastings told them that this was because there had never *been* anything like it; not ever. Since the reinforcements had heard that Hastings had been there longer than anyone, they shut up then and left him alone. Hastings did not find that this improved his mood, appreciably. If anything, it convinced him that his worst suspicions were, after all, completely justified.

On election day, the company had a particularly bad experience. The president of their country was being threatened by an opposition which had no use for his preparedness policy; as a defensive measure, therefore, he had no choice on the day before election, other than to order every military installation in the vicinity of the company's war to send out at least one bomber and more likely two to show determination. Hastings' company knew nothing whatever of this; they woke on the morning of the election cheerful because it was their turn to take the forest. Furthermore, the tents of the enemy seen in the distance were already being struck, a good sign that the enemy would not contest things too vigorously. The men of the company put on their combat gear singing, goosing one another, challenging for poker games that night: it looked as if it were going to be a magnificent day. All indications were that the enemy would yield like gentlemen. Some of the company began to play tag, leaping through the abutments, comparing them to the forest that would soon be theirs.

Then, from all conceivable directions, airplanes came; they wandered, moaning, a few hundred feet above the surface of the cliffs and apparently waited. When all of them were quite sure that no others were coming (there would have been no room for them anyway), they began to methodically drop bombs on the company. Naturally, the pilots and crews of the airplanes were terribly excited and, as a result, they misplaced their fire quite badly, missing direct hits on the company more often than not. After a while, there was so much smoke around the vicinity of the cliffs that the pilots were unable to see at all, and they drifted over and peevishly sent excess bombs on the mine field. Hastings, lying on his back, guessed that the First Sergeant had been proved right because, just as everyone had been telling the Captain, the mine field did not go up. It took the bombs quite nicely, as a matter of fact, not heaving a bit. When every plane had released its bomb (some had to actually go over the forest and drop one on the enemy; there was no other space left), they flew off in a dazzle of satisfaction, leaving the largest part of the company choking with laughter. Those that were not choking were unable to because they were dead. The point seemed to be that here it was the company's day in the forest, and now their own or some other force had come in and had screwed everything up. In the distance, the enemy could be seen holding cautious formation and then, with no hesitation whatsoever, they put themselves into lines and marched briskly away from the forest, taking the long route back to the cliffs. The new Captain got up on an abutment and made a speech; he said that this had been the first step in a whole series leading to mass realignment. The company applauded thinly, wondering if there was any chance that he might have a stroke. Then everybody packed up and went over to the forest; all of them, of course, except those who were dead. Hastings stayed with a work detail and labeled all of them so that headquarters, if they ever sent anyone up, would know who in the company had failed to take the proper precautions and was therefore to be permanently removed from the master roster list and placed in the inactive files, never to be bothered by formations again.

It was the election day disaster that caused certain men in the company to begin behaving in a very bizarre fashion. News received through the First Sergeant that headquarters believed that the president had won re-election had no effect upon the decision of these men to take up indefinite residence in the forest; they told anyone who asked them that the whole thing was a futile proposition and the company was always going to come back there, anyway. They refused to make formations and had friends answer for them; they covered their tents with mud and pitched them in the shadow of trees; they washed their garments in the rain and, furthermore, they told everyone in the company that they were fools not to join them. One morning, lining up in the cliffs, the First Sergeant noticed for the first time that five men were gone. He became furious and said he would not stand for it; he told the company that he had been through four wars, not including eight limited actions, and there was simply no basis, ever, to performances of this sort. The First Sergeant said that he was going personally to lead the company back to the forest to shoot those five men. They were all prepared to go, looking forward to the objective really, when a misguided enemy pilot flew uncertainly over the forest and, perhaps in retaliation, dropped thirty-seven bombs on it, blowing every tree to the ground, leaving the earth quite green and shuddering and completely decimating his own troops. They were unable to fight for a week because the enemy had to ship reinforcements, and when they finally got back to the forest, they could find, of course, no trace of their five men at all; only a few belt buckles.

It was right then that Hastings decided that the matter of his convalescent leave had come to a head. He had had the idea and he knew that it was covered in regulations: *he was entitled to it.* Army manuals noted the existence of something called convalescent leave: if it wasn't for situations such as these, well then, for what was it? *They had to deal with it.* One morning, he carefully re-drafted his original request with a borrowed pencil on the back of an old letter from his fiancée and brought it again into the First Sergeant. Hastings reminded the First Sergeant that he had originally put this request in months ago. The First Sergeant, groaning, said that the Captain could not possibly look at it because he was still getting acclimated to the situation. But, the First Sergeant added, he had been talking to the Captain on and off and he had some promising news: the Captain had been saying that he would probably be completely familiarized by Christmas. It was only a matter of taking time to get hold of a situation. Hastings said was that a fact and, mumbling promises to himself, left the headquarters tent; he told the Corporal with whom he slept that he hoped to be out of this sooner or later. Most of the company were still gathering for hours around the belt buckles, looking solemnly, telling each other that it was a damned shame what the Army did to people. Hastings, looking it over again, decided that he had written a strong appeal: how *could* it be ignored?

Gentlemen (Hastings had written), listen: I am applying for

convalescent leave as I have already done because I have been in vigorous combat and, while adding little or nothing to the company effort, have driven myself to the ridges of neurasthenia. What fighting skills I do possess and what morale I have acquired through recommended reading materials have fallen to a very low point because of the discouragement involved in the present situation. We are capturing and capturing again one forest and some wasted hills. The forest is bearable; the hills are not, but in the exhaustion of this repeated effort, both have leveled to a kind of hideous sameness; *now there is no difference*. Indeed, everything has become the same, as is common now in cases of great tensions occurring under stress situations. Recently, I have had cold sweats, nausea, some vomiting and various nervous reactions including migraine of relative severity that has cut my diminishing effectiveness even further. Most of the time, I can barely lift a rifle ... and for all of these reasons, I am repeating my ignored request of three months duration that I be given convalescent leave for a period of several weeks to months for the purposes of renewed vision. Ideally, I would like to go back home, see my civilian friends, share my experiences with them, but if it is found that I cannot be sent there due to problems with transportation allotments and the like, I would settle for being sent alone to the nearest town where there are women and where it is possible to sleep. I would even be willing, if the nights were quiet, to go to a place without women; as a matter of fact, this might be the best action at this time. I am certainly in no condition for relationships, not even those of the fragmentary kind necessitated by copulation. Hoping that this request meets with your attention and approval; hoping that you will not see it as the frenzied expression of a collapsed man but only as the cool and reasoned action of the professional soldier under stress, I remain yours truly, Hastings, 114786210. *P.S.* I wish to note that my condition is serious; how serious only a qualified professional judgement could determine. If this request is not met with your prompt attention, therefore, or not, at least sent to a competent psychiatrist for an opinion, it is impossible for me to predict what the scope of my reactions will be: *I can no longer control my behavior*. I have been brought up all my life to believe that institutions are the final repository of all the good sense left in this indecent world; at this point in my life it would assume the proportion of a major disaster if I were to learn that the Army, one of our most respected and ancient institutions, were not to be trusted. *P.P.S.* Please note that the mines here are *already defused*; inform the Captain that they need not worry him.

On the other hand, the *first* request had been good, too. The day that the *old* Captain's reassignment to headquarters came through, all of the men in the company had come to his tent to stand around him, giving him notes and wishes of good will. Hastings had given him his request in a sealed envelope, and the Captain had taken it for another farewell message and placed it carefully in his knapsack; he told Hastings and the others that he was moved by their display of affection and he hoped that any of them who came into his territory later in the war would like to find out personally how everything was going. After all of this was over, the old Captain had crawled into his tent, saying, over his shoulder, that the company had given him an experience that he simply would never forget. The company smiled at the Captain's closed tent and wandered off to play poker. (They had been in the forest that day.)

Hastings thought that he would join them and then decided that this would not do; he would have to force the issue, and so he crawled, quite respectfully, into the Captain's tent and, finding him wrapped in an embryonic ball on his bunk, told him that he had a few things to explain. Hastings told the Captain that he had submitted a request for convalescent leave and not a good will message. At this, the Captain's legs kicked from the ball he had made of himself, and he told Hastings that he felt that he had very little consideration. Hastings said that this might all well be true, but he *was* a sick man and he then outlined the substance of his request. The Captain wrapped himself up intently and thought about it, said that he could court-martial Hastings. He added cheerfully that, since he was not legally in command of the company now, Hastings could be placed in the stockade for divulging confidential material to an outsider. Hastings kneeled then and asked the Captain what the proper thing would be to do, and the Captain said that he hadn't the faintest idea. He suggested that Hastings recall his request and, as a concession, court-martial proceedings would be dropped. He said that the appeal itself was unexceptionable; the new Captain, if one ever came, surely would approve it.

Hastings took his envelope and left the Captain, went back to his tent singing an Army song and fixed up his pegs neatly, but by the time he had all of them firmly in the ground, he found himself stricken with a terrible intimation. He went back to see the Captain, learned that he was in the officers' latrine, and waited outside there until the Captain came out. Hastings asked the Captain if headquarters or the new Captain might think that his request was a joke. The Captain said that he could not speak professionally but from what he had gathered from summation, he saw nothing funny in it at all; it seemed quite serious, quite to the point. Hastings said that the Captain might feel that way but, after all, he had been heading up the war, maybe at headquarters, they did not glimpse the urgencies. The Captain said that headquarters was filled with understanding people: they were people who had approved his own request for transfer, and they could be counted upon to comprehend the necessary. Hastings said a few unfortunate words about possible prejudice against enlisted men, and the Captain's face became bright green: he said that he suddenly realized that he had not finished his own business in the latrine. Hastings could not follow him in there, of course, but he waited two hours until the Captain came out and tried to pursue the matter. But the Captain, walking away hurriedly, said that he did not know what Hastings was talking about: he did not even know what this request was, had never heard of it in fact; and then he said that, upon consideration, he realized that he did not know Hastings either; surely, he had never seen him before. The Captain ordered Hastings to return to his proper company, wherever that might be. Hastings explained that theirs was the only company within two hundred miles, and the Captain said that Hastings was obviously an AWOL with energy. Then, he ran briskly away.

Hastings gathered that there would be very little point in following and instead went back to his tent. His tent mate was sleeping inside, and Hastings methodically demolished the tent, wrapped it around the Corporal, picked all of this up, groaning, and threw it into a tree. The Corporal hit with a dull noise. When he came out rubbing himself, he said that he was shocked at this; he did not know that Hastings was the type. Hastings shrugged and said that some men changed personality under stress. He wandered away, not breathing very hard, and bought a pencil from someone, took some toilet paper from the latrine and began a very serious letter to his fiancée. He had just brought matters through the Captain's second flight when the sun set violently, and he had to put everything away. He slept quite badly in the mine field that night (he did not feel like returning to his tent; not quite yet) and in the morning, found that his letter had been somehow stolen. Hastings had a good reputation as a letter writer, and men in the company were always stealing his correspondence, trying to get useful phrases. Hastings did not care about this particularly, except that lately he had begun to feel that he had only a limited number of things to say and they were diminishing rapidly. This theft, then, intensified his gloom, and he almost decided to seek another interview with the Captain but then he said: *The hell with it. We'll give the new man a chance. That is the least we can do.* Looking sadly at the enemy tents, Hastings again decided that he was in a highly abnormal situation.

Headquarters (wrote Hastings some time later on the back of a letter from an old acquaintance), I am forced to take this most serious and irregular action because of the prejudicial conduct of the recently installed Commanding Officer concerning my re-request for convalescent status. As you may or may not know, I originally placed this request several months ago and rewrote it last week because of the failure of the Commanding Officer to pay any heed, whatsoever. This Commanding Officer has subjected me to an exposure of terrifying inadequacy without precedent in a Captain of this Army and has imperiled my entire image of your institution. He has never confronted me concerning either request but has relayed statements through the First Sergeant (who is a war veteran with great sympathy for my position) that I am behaving irresponsibly. Headquarters, I ask you, is it irresponsible of me to request a convalescent leave? I have been fighting this war for a considerable period of time now, exposing myself over and over again to the same dreary set of experiences while around me the company ebbs and flows and the reinforcements creep in darkly. The reinforcements tell me again and again that they do not think that there is any sense to this engagement, and I am compelled to agree with them. This entire action has acquired the aspect of nightmare, I am sorry to say, and although I am not an unstable man, I have found myself becoming, not neurasthenic as previously noted, but truly psychotic. This is terrible ritual, gentlemen, terrible sacrifice, really deadly convolution of the soul. Also, they are stealing my correspondence. I have not been able actually to mail a letter for months, even to tell my fiancée that I have terminated our engagement. Gentlemen, I *like* my fiancée and what is more important, after two years of distance, I now wish to make an arrangement to spare her of me. What more significant proof can I provide of insanity? Hoping that you will give this request the most serious consideration and hoping that you will review the folder of the Commanding Officer here very thoroughly indeed, I am sending this letter out by and through devious and covert means. Yours truly, Hastings, serial number posted.

When he was finished, Hastings took the letter to the officers section and gave it to the First Sergeant, who was cleaning some bits of litter from the top of his desk. He gazed dully at the First Sergeant and asked if it could be submitted through special channels, around the Captain. The First Sergeant gave him a look of wonderment and said that the letter could not possibly pass: it was not written in code as all direct communications to headquarters were compelled to be. Furthermore, the First Sergeant said, he had received exciting news from headquarters: there were plans to start a newspaper which would be distributed by airline to the company; this newspaper would tell them how they were progressing in their battle. The First Sergeant said that headquarters considered it a major breakthrough in morale policy. And, in addition to all of this the First Sergeant whispered, there was one other piece of news which had come through from headquarters which he was not authorized to disclose but which the Captain would make the subject of an address to the troops on this day. The First Sergeant said that this would probably be a revelation even to Hastings, a real surprise from headquarters. Hastings, still thinking about the newspaper, asked if it would contain anything except statistics, and the First Sergeant said there would probably be some editorials written by military experts. Hastings said that he wanted to awaken the Captain. The First Sergeant said that this was impossible because the Captain was already awake; he was drafting his speech, and he was too excited to deal with Hastings now. The First Sergeant added that he agreed that this was a shame. Hastings said that he was at the end of his rope. The Sergeant said that things were getting better: he recommended that Hastings learn headquarters code if he was serious about the message and then resubmit it, and he handed him a book. Hastings saw that the book was really a folder containing sheets of typewriter paper, and he asked the First Sergeant what this was. The First Sergeant explained that this was a copy of his short novel detailing his experiences as a veteran of four wars and eight limited actions. Hastings asked what the hell this had to do with learning code or with sending his message, and the First Sergeant said that he was astonished; he said that Hastings was the only man in the company so far to be offered his novel, and he added that everything in it contained the final answer, if it was only studied. The First Sergeant then said that the convalescent leave business was Hastings' problem, anyway; he had never cracked the code completely himself, and he doubted if it were possible to solve it.

When he came back to his tent, still carrying the First Sergeant's novel in one hand, Hastings decided that he had reached a moment of major crisis. There were obviously no points of reference to this in his life; he was definitely on his own. All of the company were getting up one by one, discussing the push to the cliffs which they were going to make later in the day. Some of the reinforcements insisted that to achieve the cliffs would be to attain a major objective, but older members of the company gently explained that the battle was probably endless. When they heard this, the reinforcements sat tearfully and had to be persuaded to strike their tents. The First Sergeant came out after a while and called a formation, saying that the Captain was going to address them. When they heard this, the company, even Hastings, became very excited because the Captain had never talked to any of them before; he had always been at the end of the marches, saying that he had to be acclimatized. Now, apparently, he had completed his assessment of the situation, and everybody was very anxious to find out what he had learned. Also they were curious, some of them, about his rear end and figured that at one time or another they would probably be able to get a glimpse of it now. Standing in the ranks, Hastings fondled the First Sergeant's novel and his letter and made a decision: he would present both of them to the Captain just as soon as he had finished talking. He would wait until the end of the Captain's speech that was, only if the speech was very interesting: if the Captain had nothing to say or only detailed how he intended to further familiarize himself, he would go up to him in the middle and simply hand him the letter. At least, he would have the man's attention. This would be a new element in the situation, right away.

Preceded by the First Sergeant, the Captain came from his tent and, walking carefully, came in front of the company. No one could see his buttocks because all of them were facing in the same direction. The Captain stood there, nodding, for several minutes, making some notes in pen on fresh paper, beaming at the motion. Hastings found this frightening. He had never before noticed how small the Captain's face was; at this distance it was seen to be covered with a hideous stubble superimposed over the features of a very young boy. In spite of all this evidence, he had not been convinced, apparently, because he wore a wedding ring. The Captain backed carefully against a tree and leaned against it, smiling at the company. "Some of you," he said, "have brought it to the attention of my First Sergeant that you are unhappy.

"More than unhappiness. I know that you are vitally concerned. You're concerned because you see no point in what you're doing. You're concerned because you can't see how what you are doing affects anything or anybody else. You're worried about this. This is serious. It is a real problem.

"It's a legitimate matter of concern, all right. When a group of men such as yourselves cannot feel dignity in the work they do, cannot feel that what they do is important to a much larger number of people, they break down. They become nervous. They begin to function in a cold sweat, and sometimes they do not function at all. I have noticed this about one or two of you. But even those I do not condemn. In fact, I have all kinds of sympathy for men in this predicament; it is not pleasant. I know what it can be like. But now and for all of you, this part of your life is over."

The company cheered thinly. Hastings folded his letter and put it away.

"The situation, in fact," said the Captain, "is now entirely changed; more than you would have ever thought possible. *General war has been declared.* The enemy, who have become increasingly provocative in recent weeks, bombed one of our ports of installation last week, reducing it to a pulp. How about that? As a result of this action, the president of the country has declared that a general and total state of war now exists between the countries of the enemy and ourselves. At this moment, troops all over the globe are actively pouring in and out of our military installations; their weapons at the ready!

"*Now, what does this mean?* I'll tell you what it means. Gentlemen, you are the first. But, you are only the beginning. What you have gone through will be absorbed, will be a spearhead. And when we go out today, we go into these fields with the entire Army, with the country behind us. You are some lucky bunch of fellows. I congratulate you individually."

After the Captain had finished, he stood against the tree, apparently waiting for the company to disperse, so that he could return to his tent without anyone having seen his rear end. Hastings, weeping, drifted behind him, stood in a clearing, destroyed his letter. The trunk covered the Captain's behind from that angle, too. *I do feel better, already*, Hastings told himself, *I feel better already.* But when the Captain finally gave a cautious look in all directions and started backing slowly from the tree, Hastings took his bayonet and threw it at him, cleaving the left buttock of the Captain, bringing forth a bright scream.

"I still feel lousy," Hastings said.

The Captain had never liked Hastings. Hastings walked in the middle of formations, telling everyone as they went over the mine fields that they were absolutely harmless, a fraud. No one would have taken any precautions going over the mine field, if it had not been for the Captain running behind them. Some of the men picked up stones and threw them at each other; some men said the war would never end. When things got utterly out of hand, the Captain would have to shout at the troops, at distances of hundreds of yards he found himself bellowing and, even then, the company would not listen. All of this traced back to Hastings. He was destroying the morale of the company. The Captain suspected that, beneath all of this, Hastings was trying to sink the progress of the limited war.

In addition to saying that the mine field was just as safe as a playground, this Hastings was a letter writer. He wrote letters to everyone; now he had written a request to headquarters (which was peculiar enough already; the messages coming from headquarters now were enough to confuse anyone, let alone a Captain just trying to get acclimated), giving his situation and asking for convalescent leave; he cited obscure regulations. The Captain knew, of course, that if he forwarded this material to headquarters, two or three field grade officers would come out in a jeep, capture Hastings and place him in a hospital for mental cases, and the Captain wanted to spare Hastings this. He was governed, then, by common, if causeless, feelings of mercy but nevertheless, there was Hastings, insisting that his form go through. The Captain did not know what to do with him. In the first place, he had only been with this company for six weeks and he was having all he could do to get acclimated to the situation; in the second place, he badly missed his wife and the cottage they had had in officers' quarters on a small post in the Southern tier. Furthermore, the Captain found himself wondering at odd moments in the night whether the war effort would truly be successful. There seemed to be some very peculiar elements about it. The bombing was so highly irregular, and some of the pilots did not seem to be very interested; they dropped bombs on their own side and also flew out of pattern. In addition, some of the men in the company had become attached to a certain part of the terrain; they were maintaining now that the entire purpose of the war was to secure and live permanently within it. The Captain did not know what to do about this. Also, Hastings waited outside of his tent often, trying to find out what he was doing with the leave request, and the Captain found that his free rights of access and exit were being severely limited, above and beyond the Army code.

The Captain had nothing against the war. It was all working out the way the preparation courses had taught. Certainly, it had its strange facets: the enemy also seemed to be attached to the forest part of the map and fought bitterly for the retention of certain cherished trees, but things like this were normal in stress situations anyway; after a while, all conflicts, all abstractions came down, in a group of limited men, to restricted areas. The Captain had been trained to see things in this fashion, and he had also been given a good deal of instruction in the intricacies of troop morale. So, he understood the war; he understood it very well. There was no doubt about that. *However*, the Academy had neglected to prepare him for Hastings. There was no one like

Hastings at the Academy, even in a cleanup capacity. The Captain had taken to writing his young wife long letters on stationery he had borrowed from his First Sergeant (a war veteran of four major conflicts and eight limited actions), telling her all about the situations, adding that it was very odd and strained but that he hoped to have matters cleaned up by the end of the year, that is, if he was ever unleashed. Other than this, he did not write her about the war at all but instead wrote at length about certain recollections he had of their courtship, entirely new insights. In the relaxation of the war, he found that he was able to gather astonishing perceptions into the very quality of his life, and he told his wife the reasons for his action at given times, asked if she understood. *We will get to the bottom of this*, he often reminded her, *if only you will cooperate*. His wife's letters in return were sometimes argumentative, sometimes disturbed; she told him that he was wasting his energy in the forgotten wastes, and that all of his strength was now needed to become acclimated to a new situation. When he read these letters, the Captain found that, unreasonably, he wanted to cry, but his bunk was too near to that of his First Sergeant, and he was ashamed. None of the officers wanted to be caught crying by the First Sergeant, a combat veteran.

Meanwhile, the Captain found that his communications with headquarters were being blocked for days at a time, and also that his messages, when they did come, were increasingly peculiar. Sometimes, the Captain succumbed briefly to the feeling that headquarters did not truly understand the situation, but he put such thoughts away quickly. Thinking them or putting them away; it made no difference, he was almost always depressed. *Continue on as you have done, worry not*, headquarters would tell him three days later in response to a routine inquiry. Or, *we are preparing new strategy here and ask you to hold line while formulating*. Such things were highly disturbing; there was simply no doubt about it.

One morning near Christmas, the Captain went through a near-disaster, a partial catastrophe. The First Sergeant came into his tent and told him that Hastings was thinking of submitting a letter to headquarters directly on the subject of his convalescent leave. The Captain said that he could not believe that even Hastings would be crazy enough to do something like that, and the First Sergeant said that this might well be true but, nevertheless, Hastings had brought in some kind of a letter that morning and asked to have it forwarded. The Captain asked the First Sergeant if he could see the letter, and the First Sergeant said that he had told Hastings to go away with it but that Hastings had promised to come back later. The Captain put on some old fatigues and went out into the forest in real grief; he looked at Hastings' tent, which was of a peculiar, grayish shade, and he sighed. Hastings was sitting outside the tent on his knees with his back to the Captain, scribbling something in the dirt with a stick. The Captain decided that he was ill; he did not want to have anything whatever to do with Hastings. Instead, he went back to his tent intending to sleep some more, but when he got there, the First Sergeant was waiting for him with astonishing news. He told the Captain that somehow a message had gotten through on Hastings because some Corporal was up from headquarters saying he had orders to put Hastings away in the asylum. When the Captain heard this, he felt himself possessed by absolute fury, and he told the First Sergeant that he was running this company and he refused to take treatment like this from anyone. The First Sergeant said that he absolutely agreed with the Captain and he would go out to deal with the Corporal, but the Captain said that, for once, he was going to handle the situation the way it should be. He told the First Sergeant to leave him alone, and then he went over to a clearing where the Corporal sat in a jeep and told him that Hastings had been killed a few hours ago in an abortive attack and was being buried. The Corporal said that that was a rotten shame because everyone in headquarters had heard the story and was really anxious to find out what kind of lunatic this Hastings was. The Captain said that he could tell him stories but he would not and ordered the Corporal to return to his unit. After the Corporal had explained that he was in an administrative capacity and therefore not at all vulnerable to the Captain's orders, he got in the jeep and said that he would go back to his unit and report what had happened. He asked the Captain if Hastings had had any special characteristics which should be noted in a condolence letter. The Captain said that Hastings had always been kind of an individualist and forceful in his own way; also he was highly motivated, if somewhat unrealistic. The Corporal said that this would be useful and he drove away. For almost an hour, the Captain found himself unable to move from the spot, but after a while, he was able to remember the motions of walking, and he stumbled back to his tent and began a long letter to his wife. *I gave an order today in a very different capacity*, he began it, but he decided that this was no good and instead started, *I have become fully acclimated to the situation here at last and feel that I am at the beginning of my best possibilities: do you remember how ambitious I used to be?* After he wrote this, he found that he had absolutely nothing else to write and, thinking of his wife's breasts, put the paper away and went for a long walk. Much later, he decided that what had happened had been for the good; it was only a question now of killing Hastings, and then he could begin to take control.

The First Sergeant had nothing to do with things, anymore. He slept a twisted sleep, crawling with strange shapes, and in the morning, the First Sergeant awakened him, saying that headquarters had just sent in a communique declaring that a total-win policy was now in effect; war had been declared. When the Captain heard this, he became quite excited and began to feel better about many things; he asked the First Sergeant if he thought that it meant that the company was now unleashed, and the First Sergeant said that he was positive that that was what had happened. The Captain said that this would definitely take care of Hastings; they could work him out of the way very easily now, and he added that he had studied the morale problem of troops; now he was going to be able to put it into effect. Troops, he said, were willing to get involved in anything, but if they felt they were being used to no good purpose, they tended to get childish and stubborn. The Captain felt so good about this that he invited the First Sergeant to forget things and look at one of his wife's recent letters, but the First Sergeant said that he felt he knew the Captain's wife already and, besides, he had to make preparations for the war; he had real responsibilities. The First Sergeant explained that this would be his fifth war, but since each one was like a new beginning, he felt as if he had never been in combat before and he wanted to make some notes. The Captain said that this was fine, and then, right on the instant, he decided to make a speech to the company. He requisitioned two sheets of bond paper from the First Sergeant and sat down to draft it, but he found himself so filled with happy thoughts of Hastings' impending assassination that he was unable to keep still, and so he decided to speak extemporaneously. He knew that he could deal with the company in the right way. When he was quite sure that he was in the proper mood to make the speech, he ordered the First Sergeant to call a formation, and when the First Sergeant came back to tell him that all of the men were assembled, he walked out slowly behind the First Sergeant, knowing how good a picture he was making. He stood near a tree for shelter and smiled at all of the men, especially Hastings, but Hastings, looking at something in his hands, did not see the smile and that, the Captain decided, was Hastings' loss. It was one more indication, this way of thinking, of how well he had finally become acclimated. Everything, after all, was only a matter of time.

"You men," the Captain said, "are plenty upset because you see no purpose in this whole operation. In fact, it seems absolutely purposeless to you, a conclusion with which I am in utter sympathy. It is no fun when emptiness replaces meaning; when despair replaces motive. I know all about this; I have shared it with you over and over.

"Today, we mount another attack and many wonder: what is the point? it's all the same; it always was. We've been back and forth so many times, what the hell's the difference, now?

"In line with this, I want to tell you something now, something that will, I am convinced, change the entire picture in your minds and hearts. *Something is different*; things have changed. We are now in a state of war with the enemy. Our ports of installation were bombed last night; in return, our president has declared that we are now in a position of total war. How about that?

"Before we have finished our mission now, ten thousand, a million men will have shared our losses, our glories, our commitments, our hopes. And yet, because these began with us, essentially we are the creators of the war.

"Are we fortunate? I do not know. Such is our responsibility. Such is our honor."

After the Captain had finished, he stood near the tree for a long while, marveling at his speech. There was no question but that it had gotten right through to the middle of the situation; it left no room for any doubt of any kind. Surely he had, just as he had promised, become fully acclimated and now, now there was no stopping him at all. And it took care of that Hastings; it took care of him but good. The next step for Hastings was darkness. Therefore, the Captain was enormously surprised when he saw Hastings, grinning hysterically, come toward him, a bayonet shining in his hand. It just showed you, if you didn't know it well already, that there was just no predicting anything with enlisted men. Before the Captain could move, Hastings raised his arm and threw the instrument at the Captain.

"What are you doing?" the Captain screamed. "I'm your Commanding Officer in the midst of a war!"

"I still say I'm not crazy!" Hastings screamed.

"We're in the middle of a war!" the Captain said, dying.

But Hastings, apparently quite mad now, would not listen.

The First Sergeant had never liked Hastings or the Captain. Both of them were crazy; there was no doubt about it. Hastings, a Private, told everyone in the company that the mine fields were a sham, quite safe, really, and the Captain insisted that they were ready to fire. When the company walked over the mine fields, Hastings cursed to the troops that they were a bunch of cowards, and the Captain, his stupid ass waving, fell to the end of the formation and screamed at them to keep going. The two of them were wrecking the company, making the entire situation (which had had such potential, such really nice things in it) impossible. The war was peculiar, there was no question about this, but there were ways to get around it and get a job done. But the two of them, Hastings and the Captain, were lousing things up. The First Sergeant found himself so furious with their business that after a while he could not even keep his communiques straight: all the headquarters messages were getting screwed up in the decode because he was too upset to do it right and no one would leave him alone. There was no sense to most of the messages; they all seemed to say the same thing anyway, and the First Sergeant knew that headquarters were a pack of morons; he had decided this three days after he had taken over his job and began getting their idiotic messages. Meanwhile, the new Captain would not leave him alone; all that he wanted to talk about was Hastings. It was Hastings, the Captain said loudly to the First Sergeant, who was fouling everything up. He asked the First Sergeant if there might be any procedures to get Hastings to keep quiet, because everything that had gone wrong was all his fault. Over and over again, the Captain asked the First Sergeant to figure out a way to get rid of Hastings *without* giving him convalescent leave. All of this was bad enough for the First Sergeant but then, on top of all of this, there was Hastings himself hanging around all the time, trying to find out things about the Captain, asking if the man had yet initialed his request. All in all, it was just ridiculous, what they were doing to him. When the First Sergeant decided to do what he did, he had every excuse in the world for it. They were a pack of lunatics. They were out of control. They deserved no mercy.

One morning, for instance, around Thanksgiving, the Captain woke the First Sergeant to say that he had figured out the entire situation: Hastings was insane. He was investing, said the Captain, terrible dependency in an effort to become a child again and his functioning was entirely unsound. The Captain asked the First Sergeant if he felt that this was reasonable and whether or not he thought that Hastings belonged in some kind of institution. The First Sergeant, who had been up very late trying to organize some confusing communiques from headquarters in relation to the Thanksgiving supper, said that he was not sure but that he would think some about it, and if the Captain wanted him to, he would even check into Army regulations. He added that Hastings might have combat fatigue, something that he had seen in a lot of men through the course of four wars and eight limited actions; some men were simply weaker than others. The point here was that the First Sergeant was trying to be as decent to both the Captain and Hastings as any man could be, but there were limits. Later that day, Hastings found him sitting behind a tree and told him that he had figured the whole thing: the Captain was obviously mad. He suggested that the First Sergeant help him prepare a report to headquarters listing all of the peculiar actions of the Captain and asked for some clean paper to do this. Hastings added that he thought that most of the Captain's problem could be traced back to his shame over his rear end. The rear end made the Captain look feminine, said Hastings, and the Captain was reacting to this in a very normal, if unfortunate, fashion. The First Sergeant said that he didn't know enough about modern psychiatry to give an opinion on that one way or the other. Hastings asked the First Sergeant to simply *consider* it, and the First Sergeant said that he would do that. After a while, Hastings left, saying that the First Sergeant had hurt him.

In all of this, then, it could be seen that the First Sergeant had acted entirely correctly, in entire justice. He was in a difficult position but he was doing the best he could. No claims could be made against him that he was not doing his job. But, in spite of all the times the First Sergeant repeated this to himself, he found that, finally, he was getting good and fed up with the whole thing. There were, he decided, natural limits to all circumstances and Hastings, headquarters, the Captain and the war were passing theirs; after a point simply no part of it was his responsibility, anymore.

This, the First Sergeant told the officers who knew enough to listen, was his fourth war and eighth limited action, not counting various other difficulties he had encountered during his many years in the Army. Actually, this was not entirely true, but the First Sergeant had taken to feeling that it was, which was almost better. The truth of the situation, which the First Sergeant kept to himself except for occasional letters to his wife was that he had worked in a division motor pool for fifteen years before he had been reassigned to the company, and that reassignment had been something of a fluke, hinging on the fact that the company had, before the days of the limited war, been established as a conveyance unit, and the First Sergeant had absent-mindedly been assigned as a mechanic. That things had worked out this way was probably the fault of headquarters; at least, the First Sergeant did not question them on *that* score.

Early in the career of the First Sergeant, he had accidentally shot a General while in rifle training. The General, fortunately, had only lost an ear which, he had laughingly told the First Sergeant at the court-martial, he could spare because he never heard that much that was worth hearing, anyway. The General, however, claimed that the First Sergeant had had no right to shoot at him when he was in the process of troop-inspection, even if the shots had only been fired from excitement, as was the claim of the First Sergeant's defense. The General said that he felt the best rehabilitative action for the First Sergeant, under all the principles of modern social action, would be to be shot himself, although not in the ear. When the First Sergeant heard this, he stood up in court and said that for the first time in his life, he was ashamed that he had chosen to enlist in the Army.

When the head of the court, a Major, heard this, he asked the First Sergeant to stay calm and state, just off the record, what he wanted to do with his life. When the First Sergeant said that all he wanted to do was to make an honorable career and a First Sergeancy (at this time he had been considerably less, a Private in fact), the Major advised the General that the First Sergeant would probably have to be treated differently from the run of the mill soldier, and the General said that he found the First Sergeant's testimony very moving. It was agreed to fine the First Sergeant one month's salary every month for the next five years and send him to automobile training in the far North. The General said that he could think of some places right off the top of his head where the First Sergeant might do well, but he reminded him that he would have to remember to cut down very sharply now on all of his expenses as he would be living on somewhat of a limited budget.

The First Sergeant learned to live frugally (even now, he was still forgetting to pick up his pay when headquarters delivered it; he was always astonished) and repaired vehicles for fourteen years, but inwardly, he was furious. Because of his duties in the motor pool he lost out on several wars and limited actions, and, also, his wife (whom he had married before he enlisted) was ashamed that he had not been killed as had the husbands of many of her friends. As a result of this, he and his wife eventually had an informal separation, and the First Sergeant (who was by then a First Sergeant) took to telling people just being sent into the motor pool that he personally found this work a great relief after fighting one war and three limited actions. They seemed to believe him, which was fine, but the First Sergeant still had the feeling that he was being deprived of the largest segment of his possibilities. He moved into a barracks with a platoon of younger troops and taught them all the war songs he knew.

In September of his next to last year in the Army, the First Sergeant fell into enormous luck. He often felt that it had all worked out something like a combat movie. A jeep for whose repair he had been responsible exploded while parked in front of a whorehouse, severely injuring a Lieutenant Colonel and his aide-de-camp who were waiting, they later testified, for the area to be invaded by civilian police. They had received advance warning and had decided to be on the premises for the protection of enlisted men. As a result of the investigation which followed, the aide-de-camp was reduced to the rank of Corporal and sent to give hygienic lectures to troops in the far lines of combat. The Lieutenant Colonel was promoted to Colonel, and the First Sergeant was sent to the stockade for six weeks. When he was released, he was given back all of his stripes and told by a civilian board of review that he was going to be sent into troop transport. The head of the board said that this would extend his experience considerably, and told him that he would be on the site of, although not actually engaged in, a limited action war. Standing in front of the six men, his hastily re-sewn stripes trembling, the First Sergeant had been unable to comprehend his stunning fortune. It seemed entirely out of control. Later, getting instructions from an officer, he found that he would take over the duties of a conveyance First Sergeant in an important action being conducted secretly on a distant coast. As soon as he could talk, the First Sergeant asked if he could have three days convalescent leave, and the officer said that regulations would cover this; he was entitled to it because of the contributions he had made.

The First Sergeant borrowed a jeep and drove several hundred miles from post to a dark town in which his separated wife worked as a waitress. He found her sitting alone in the balcony of a movie house, watching a combat film and crying absently. At first, she wanted nothing at all to do with him, but after he told her what had happened to him, she touched him softly and said that she could not believe it had worked out. They went to a hotel together, because her landlady did not believe in her boarders being with other people, and talked for a long time; and for the first time, the First Sergeant said that he was frightened at what was happening as well as grateful. He had been away for so long that he did not know if he could trust himself. His wife said that finally, after fifteen years, she felt proud, and she told him that she knew he would do well. Later on he remembered that. But he never remembered answering her that only distress can make a man.

They went to bed together and it was almost good; they almost held together until the very end, but then everything began to come to pieces. The First Sergeant said that he would probably not be able to write her letters because he was going to an area of high security, and she said that this was perfectly all right with her as long as the allotment checks were not interrupted. When he heard this, the

Sergeant began to shake with an old pain and he told her that the jeep had blown up because he had deliberately failed to replace a bad fuel connection. She told him that if this were so, he deserved anything that happened to him. He told her that nothing he had ever done had been his fault, and she said that he disgusted her.

After that, both of them got dressed, feeling terrible, and the First Sergeant drove the jeep at a grotesque speed toward the post. In the middle of the trip he found that he could not drive for a while, and he got out and vomited, the empty road raising dust in his eyes, the lights of occasional cars pinning him helplessly against dry foliage.

When the First Sergeant came to the company, they were just at the true beginning of the limited war, and he was able to get hold of matters almost immediately. The first thing that he learned was that his predecessor had been given a transfer for reasons of emotional incompetence and had been sent back to the country as the head of a motor pool. The second thing he found out was that his job was completely non-combatant, involving him only in the communications detail. When the First Sergeant discovered that his duties involved only decoding, assortment and relay of communiques from division headquarters to the company and back again, he felt at first, a feeling of enormous betrayal, almost as if he had been in the Army all his life to discover that there was absolutely no reason for it at all. The Captain of this company communicated with headquarters from one hundred to one hundred and fifty times a day; he tried to keep himself posted on everything including the latest procedure for morale-retention. Other officers also had messages, and in the meanwhile, enlisted personnel were constantly handing him money, begging him to send back a hello to relatives through headquarters. The First Sergeant found this repulsive but the worst of it was to trudge at the rear of formations while in combat, loaded with ten to fifteen pieces of radio equipment and carrying enormous stacks of paper which he was expected to hand to the officers at any time that they felt in need of writing. In addition, his pockets were stuffed with headquarters communiques which the Captain extracted from time to time. It was a humiliating situation; it was the worst thing that had ever happened to him. When they were not in battle, the First Sergeant was choked with cross-communiques; it became impossible for him to conceive of a life lacking them: he sweated, breathed and slept surrounded by sheets of paper. He took to writing his wife short letters, telling her in substance that everything she had said was absolutely right. In what free time he had, he requisitioned a stopwatch and tried to figure out his discharge date in terms of minutes, seconds and fifths of seconds.

Then, at the beginning of the first summer, the First Sergeant had his second and final stroke of luck, and it looked for a long while as if everything had worked out that for the best after all. He stopped writing letters to his wife almost immediately after the Captain was called back to headquarters and a new, a younger Captain was assigned to the command. This new Captain was not at all interested in communications; he told the First Sergeant the first day he was in that before he got involved in a flow of messages, he had first to become acclimated to the situation. That was perfectly all right with the First Sergeant; immediately he saw the change working through in other things; it was magical. Messages from headquarters seemed to diminish; there were days when they could be numbered in the tens, and the First Sergeant found that he had more time to himself; he started to write a short novel about his combat experiences in four wars and eight limited actions. Also, his role in combat had shifted drastically. Perhaps because of the new Captain's familiarization policy, he was permitted to carry a rifle with him, and now and then, he even took a cautious shot, being careful to point the instrument in the air, so that there would be no danger of hitting anyone on his own side. Once, quite accidentally, he hit one of the enemy's trees (they were attacking the forest that day) and destroyed a shrub; it was one of the most truly important moments of his life. Meanwhile, the new Captain said that he would contact headquarters eight times a day and that would be that.

The First Sergeant moved into one of the most wholly satisfactory periods of his life. His wife's letters stopped abruptly after she said she had been promoted to the position of hostess, and he quietly cut his allotment to her by three dollars a month; no one seemed to know the difference. He went to bed early and found that he slept the night through, but often he was up at four o'clock because starting each new day was such a pleasure. Then, just as the First Sergeant had come to the amazed conviction that he was not by any means an accursed man, Hastings came acutely to his consciousness.

Hastings, who was some kind of Private, had put in for convalescent leave months before, during the bad time of the First Sergeant's life, but the old Captain had handled the situation very well. Now, the new Captain said that he had to be acclimated to the situation, and so it was the First Sergeant's responsibility to deal with Hastings, to tell him that the Captain could not be distracted at this time. For a while, Hastings listened to this quietly and went, but suddenly, for no apparent reason, he submitted *another* request for leave. From that moment the difficult peace of the First Sergeant was at an end. Hastings insisted that this message had to reach the Captain, and the First Sergeant told him that it would be forwarded, but the Captain refused to take it because he said that he was in an adjustment stage. So, the First Sergeant kept the request in his desk, but then Hastings began coming into the tent every day to ask what action the Captain had finally taken. The First Sergeant knew right away that Hastings was crazy because he had a wild look in his eye, and he also said that the Captain was a coward for not facing him. In addition to that, Hastings began to look up the First Sergeant at odd times of the day to say that the Captain was functioning in a very unusual way; something would have to be done. When the First Sergeant finally decided that he had had enough of this, he went to the Captain and told him what was going on and asked him if he would, at least, look at this crazy Hastings' request, but the Captain said that it would take him at least several months to be acculturated to the degree where he would be able to occupy a judgmental role; in the meantime, he could not be disturbed by strange requests. Then, the Captain leaned over his desk and said that, just between them, he felt that Hastings was crazy: he was not functioning like an adult in a situation made for men. When he heard this, the First Sergeant laughed wildly and relayed this message to Hastings, hoping that it would satisfy him and that now the man would finally leave him alone, but Hastings said that all of this just proved his point: the Captain was insane. Hastings asked the First Sergeant if he would help him to get the Captain put away. All of this was going on then; the Captain saying one thing and Hastings another, both of them insane; and in addition to this, the limited war was still going on; it was going on as if it would never stop which, of course, it would not. The First Sergeant would have written his wife again if he had not completely forgotten her address and previously thrown away all of her letters.

Hastings and the Captain were on top of him all the time now, and neither of them had the faintest idea of what they were doing. Only a man who had been through four wars and eight limited actions could comprehend how serious the war effort was. Three days a week the company had a *forest* to capture; three days a week they had the cliffs to worry about, and on Mondays they had all of the responsibility of reconnoitering and planning *strategy*; and all of this devolved on the First Sergeant; nevertheless, neither of them would leave him alone. The First Sergeant had more duties than any man could handle: he supervised the officers' tents and kept up the morale of the troops: he advised the officers of the lessons of his experience, and he had to help some of the men over difficult personal problems; no one, not even a combat veteran such as himself, could handle it. He slept poorly now, threw up most of his meals, found his eyesight wavering so that he could not handle his rifle in combat, and he decided that he was, at last, falling apart under the strain. If he had not had all of his obligations, he would have given up then. They were that ungrateful, the whole lot of them. Hastings, the Captain; the Captain, Hastings: they were both lunatics, and on top of that, there was the matter of the tents and the communications. One night, the First Sergeant had his penultimate inspiration. In an agony of wild cunning, he decided that there was only one way to handle things. And what was better, he knew that he was right. No one could have approached his level of functioning.

He got up at three o'clock in the morning and crept through the forest to the communications tent and carefully, methodically, lovingly, he tore down the equipment, so that it could not possibly transmit, and then he furiously reconstructed it so that it looked perfect again. Then, he sat up until reveille, scribbling out headquarters communiques, and he marked *DELIVERED* in ink on all of the company's messages to headquarters. After breakfast, he gave these messages to the Captain, and the Captain took them and said that they were typical headquarters crap; they were the same as ever. The Captain said then that sometimes, just occasionally, you understand, he thought that Hastings might have a point, after all. The First Sergeant permitted himself to realize that he had stumbled on to an extremely large concept; it was unique. Nothing that day bothered him at all.

The next morning, he got up early again and crept through the cliffs to the communications tent and wrote out three headquarters messages advising the Captain to put his First Sergeant on the point. When the Captain read these, he looked astonished and said that this had been his idea entirely; the First Sergeant led the column that day, firing his rifle gleefully at small birds overhead. He succumbed to a feeling of enormous power and, to test it, wrote out no messages at all for the next two days, meanwhile keeping the company's messages in a *DELIVERED* status. The Captain said that this was a pleasure, the bastards should only shut up all the time like this. On the third day, the First Sergeant wrote out a message ordering that company casualties be made heavier to prove interest in the war effort; two men were surreptitiously shot that day in combat by the Junior-Grade Lieutenants. By then, the First Sergeant had already decided that, without question, he had surpassed any of the efforts of western civilization throughout five hundred generations of modern thought.

Headquarters seemed to take no notice. Their supply trucks came as always; enlisted men looked around and cursed with the troops and then went back. They did not even ask to see the First Sergeant because he had let it be known that he was too busy to be bothered. The First Sergeant got into schedule, taking naps in the afternoon so that he could refer daily stacks of headquarters messages in the early morning. One morning, he found that he felt so exceptionally well that he repaired the equipment, transmitted Hastings' request for convalescent leave without a tremor, affixed the Captain's code countersignature, and then destroyed the radio for good. It seemed the least that he could do in return for his good luck.

This proved to be the First Sergeant's last error. A day later, a Corporal came from headquarters to see the Captain, and later the Captain came looking for the First Sergeant, his white face stricken with confusion. He asked who the hell had allowed that Hastings to sneak into the tent and thus get hold of the equipment? The First Sergeant said that he did not know anything about it, but it was perfectly plausible that this could happen; he had other duties and he had to leave the radio, sometime or other. The Captain said that this was fine because headquarters had now ordered Hastings' recall and had arranged, for him to be put in a hospital. The Corporal had come up to say something about a psychiatric discharge. The First Sergeant said that he would handle this, and he started to go to the Corporal to say that Hastings had just died, but the Captain followed and said that this was not necessary because he himself had had Hastings' future decided; he would take care of things now. The Captain said that Hastings was not going to get out of any damned company of his any way at all; he would make things so hot for that lunatic now that it would not be funny for anyone at all. The Captain said that he was in control of the situation and there was no doubt about that whatsoever. The Sergeant left the Captain's presence and went outside to cry for half an hour, but when he came back, he found the space empty, and he knew exactly what he was going to do. He stayed away from the Captain until nightfall and, as soon as it was safe, dictated a total war communique. In the morning, breathing heavily, he delivered it to the Captain. The Captain read it over twice and drooled. He said that this was the best thing that had ever happened to anyone in the entire unfortunate history of the Army. He said that he would go out immediately and make a speech to his troops. The First Sergeant said that he guessed that this would be all right with him; if he inspired them, it could count for something in combat.

The First Sergeant did not even try to listen to the mad Captain's idiotic speech. He only stood behind and waited for it to finish. When Hastings came over after it was done and cut the Captain's rear end harmlessly with a bayonet, the First Sergeant laughed like hell. But later, when he went to the broken equipment, wondering if he could ever set it up again, he was not so sure that it was funny. He wondered if he might not have done, instead, the most terrible thing of his entire life. Much later and under different circumstances, he recollected that he had not.

DEATH TO THE KEEPER

PIPER: The disastrous consequences of George Stone's live (?) appearance on the INVESTIGATIONS show of October 31 are, of course, very much on my mind at the present time. I can find little excuse or explanation for the catastrophic events which have followed so rapidly upon its heels: the gatherings which the press so helpfully informs us are "riots," the general upheavals in the national "consciousness" and that climactic, if ill-planned, assault upon the person of our Head of State last week. No American more than I, William Piper, deplores these events; no American is more repelled by their implications. It was truly said that we are a land of barbaric impulses; our ancestors were savages and our means consequently dramatic, that is to say, theatrical.

But at the point at which *I*, William Piper, become implicated in these events, implicated to the degree that responsibility is placed upon *my* shoulders, at the point at which I am held responsible for these disasters simply because I permitted the renowned and retired actor George Stone, for private and sentimental reasons, to utilize the format of our INVESTIGATIONS show to act out a dramatic rite which was the product of his sheer lunacy; it is at that point, as I say, that I must disclaim. I disclaim totally.

How was I to know? In the first place, I had not seen or dealt with George Stone for the past 14 years and, following his reputation as it curved and ascended through the media, thought him merely to be a talented actor, superbly talented that is to say, whose appearance on our show would function to divert our audience and to educate them well, that joint outcome to which INVESTIGATIONS, from the beginning, was dedicated. In the second place, although I was aware that Stone had gone into a "retirement" somewhere around the time of the assassination, I did not connect the two, nor did I realize that Stone had gone completely insane. If I had, I certainly would have never had him on *my* production, and you can be sure of that.

Piper is not an anarchist. Piper does not believe in sedition. While INVESTIGATIONS, product of my mind and spirit, came into being out of my deepest belief that the Republic had no answers because it was no longer asking questions, the program was always handled in a constructive spirit; and it was not our purpose to bring about that mindless disintegration which, more and more, I see in the web of our country during these troubled days. That is why I feel the network had no right to cancel our presentation summarily, and without even giving us a chance to defend ourselves in the arena of the public spirit.

And the recent remarks of our own President, when he chose to say during a live press conference, which no doubt was witnessed by some seventy millions, that the present national calamity could be ascribed wholly to the irresponsibilities of "self-seeking entrepreneurs who permit the media to be used for any purposes which will sell them sufficient packages of cigarettes," were wholly unfortunate and, to a lesser man, would have been provocative. Not only is Piper no self-seeker, Piper has nothing whatever to do with the sale of cigarettes. We sold spot times to the network; what they did with their commercials was their business. I have not smoked for 17 years, and had no knowledge or concern with what products the network had discussed during our two-minute breaks, being far too busy setting my guests at ease, and preparing to voyage even deeper into the arena of the human heart.

"Self-seeking entrepreneurs" indeed! The very moment the announcement of the thwarted attempt to enter the White House and kill our beloved President was flashed upon the networks, I prepared a statement urging the nation to be calm, and repeating the facts of Stone's insanity. It was William Piper, who in the wake of the hurried and inaccurate reports as to the size and true intentions of the invading forces, called a press conference and there offered my services to the Administration in whatever capacity they would have me. Is this the performance of a seditionist?

But there has been no peace. Ever since Stone's spectacular public plunge some seven weeks ago, ever since his convulsions and death (now, blame *me*; say that I gave him poison) it has been Piper, Piper, Piper. Had Stone lived, the accusation would have gone where it belonged: on his curved, slightly sloping shoulders, and *he* would have had much to answer, crazy or not. But because of his unfortunate demise, everything explodes upon the "entrepreneur" who happened to be merely helpless witness to convulsion. Is this fair?

But it is not the purpose of this introduction to be self-pitying or declamatory. Piper spits at such gestures; Piper transcends them. It is only, as it were, to set the stage for the revelations which follow; such revelations speaking for themselves and which publication will fully and finally rid Piper of this incipient curse. Thanks to the production skill and merchandising genius of Standard Books, Incorporated, I have been assured that this small publication will receive the widest distribution imaginable, being fully covered for foreign rights in all countries of the Western world (that is about all that one can expect) and with a fair chance of subsidiary, that is stage and motion picture rights, being taken up as well. The dissemination of this volume will serve, once and for all, to perish all doubts of Piper's patriotism and, as well, will free him, I am sure, of that threatened business for sedition which is now working itself laboriously (but successfully) through the network of the appellate division. They don't have any kind of case; my lawyer assures me they have no case at all.

Let me explain the background of this.

In the aftermath of that INVESTIGATIONS segmental during which George Stone, once a renowned actor, attempted to reenact the assassination of our martyred President and ended by dying before the cameras; in the aftermath of that it was necessary, of course, for his environs to be searched, his personal effects placed under government security, and the whole history of his psychosis, needless to say, to be traced. Because the performance occurred on those very premises where Stone had spent the last years of his tragic life, and due to my own heroic efforts to have these premises secured, government and military authorities were able to make a total inventory at once. Billboards were seized, posters, newspapers, political works, magazines, personal paraphernalia of all kinds, stray bits of food secreted within hidden places of the wall, and so on. Also found was the journal which follows.

This journal, kept by the actor during the week immediately preceding his appearance on the INVESTIGATIONS program proves, beyond the shadow of any man's doubt, that the actor was completely insane, that his appearance was plotted with the cunning of the insane for the sole purpose of assaulting the precarious balance of the Republic, and that William Piper and INVESTIGATIONS were, from the start, little more than the instruments through which George Stone plotted insurrection. Why then, you ask, was this journal not immediately released to the public, thereby relieving all innocent parties of responsibility and halting, before they began, so many of these dread events?

There is no answer to that. Our Government refuses to speak. Indeed it has not, to this day, acknowledged the existence of such a journal, stating over and again through its mouthpieces that the actor "left no effects."

The Government is monolithic; the Government is imponderable. Nevertheless, and due to these most recent events, the Government, mother of us all, must be profit from itself. A carbon copy of this journal, hidden in the flushbox of Stone's ancient toilet, was found by a employees of INVESTIGATIONS during a postmortem examination of the premises three weeks ago, and immediately placed into Piper's hands. Piper, in turn, hastens to release it to the widest possible audience.

Let me make this clear again: *this journal will prove without shadow of doubt that Stone was insane and perpetrated a massive hoax through the persona of the late President, and that all of us were ignorant and gloomy pawns he moved through the patterns of his destiny.* There is no way to sufficiently emphasize that point. It will recur. The hasty publication of this journal, with foregoing textual matter by William Piper, has led to disgraceful rumors within and without the publishing field that said journal is spurious, is not the work of George Stone, and was prepared by the staff of William Piper solely to relieve himself of present dangers. Having the courage of my format, I will come to grips with this mendacity forthrightly by acknowledging its existence and by saying that it is scurrilous. How could this journal possibly be spurious? It was found above Stone's own toilet seat. Besides, it exhibits, in every fashion, the well-known and peculiar style of this actor; its idiosyncrasies are his, its convolutions are the creation of no other man. Its authenticity has been certified to by no less than Wanda Miller who, as we all know, lived with the actor during those last terrible years, and was privy to his innermost thought. If *she* says it is the work of Stone, how can we possibly deny?

I therefore present, with no further comment, the journal of George Stone. Present difficulties notwithstanding, and with all sympathy for the embattled Administration, I must point out that this should bring, once and for all, an end to this business. How could I possibly have had anything to do with Stone's performance? I was merely the focus, the camera, the static Eye. The vision, the hatred, the pointlessness of all of it was Stone's own, as is the creation of all madmen. "Reenact and purge national guilt by becoming the form of the martyred President and being killed again!" Yes, indeed! Is such nonsense the product of a sane mind?

And now let it speak for itself.

STONE: Yes, here it is: I have it right here. I wrote it down somewhere and I knew it was in this room. Well, I found the little son of a gun. Right under the newspapers on the floor. I must remember to be more organized. Wanda won't like it if I don't get organized. She's warned me—rightly—many times about this. Live and learn, I say; live and learn. I WILL NOT SCATTER MY SHEETS.

Anyway, I've got it. The whole memory, just as I transcribed it yesterday. Or the day before. July 11, 1959. It is July 11, 1959, in Denver and Stone is acting Lear again.

He—that is, I—am acting him half on history and half on intention, trapped in all the spaces of time, the partitions of hell. Space is fluid around me, shifting as it does defined only by rows, by heads, by dim walls, by my own tears and tread. Sight darts crosswise. I act Lear as only I, George Stone, the flower of his generation, can, while the cast stands respectfully in the wings like relatives at a baptism, while lights twitch and hands wink.

For I, George Stone, *am* Lear. It is the Gloucester scene and old Earl, my familiar and my destiny, stands behind, laying mutely while I rant. He is fat, he is bald, he is in fact old Alan Jacobs himself, familiar as God, as empty as death ... but no matter; I am alone. I extract the words carefully, reaching inside to make sure that what they can mean is still there; *the burning, the burning*.

> "... I know thee well; thy name is Gloucester;
> I shall preach to thee, so listen ..."
> *And the burning leaps, the burning leaps.*
> "... When we are born, we cry that we are come
> To this great stage of fools ... this a good block;
> It were a madness to shoe a troop of horse
> With felt; so when I steal upon these sons-in-law,
> Then, kill, kill, kill, kill, kill kill!"
> *Do you hear me, Jacobs?*
> "Kill, kill, kill, kill, kill, kill!"

I wheel upon the bastard; I take old Earl by the shoulders, and I move to vault him on the sea. He trembles in my grasp, and I feel his false surfaces shake; he gasps and groans but no matter for I am beyond his objection: I drag him to the sheer, clear cliff and topple him over, send him shrieking ten stories searching for the ground until he hits with a thud and in an explosion of sawdust, his brains spill free and then, cotton as they are, turn green in the fading light. *So much for Lear*.

Sa, sa, sa, sa. For I can kill; I *can* kill and now, against that wooden sky I scream murder so that they can hear; so that all of them can hear. No more of this magic, I say; no more of these imprecations against the nailed skull: in Lear, no one kills; no one *ever* kills, but *let us have no more magicians*.

Attendants come.

They have detected something in the wings, something they were not supposed to see. Ah, here they are: eight of them in a row, carrying a jacket of mail for my arms, my legs. They are coming for the old King; greet the world. I flee.

From stage center to left I go, nimble as light, stuffed like a porpoise. The spot cannot pin me; oh, boy, I transcend vision itself. *Sa, sa, sa, sa.*

Stone is acting Lear again. In Denver, in the vault of the unborn, in all the Denvers of the skull, in the sun of the city itself while the Keeper walks straight through those who love him. Perpetual Lear; perpetual Stone.

He had such plans, he did, that no one knew what they were. But they would be the terror of the earth.

On the other hand, does this make much sense? All of this is fine for me, fine for Wanda: we know what's going on here, and that Jacobs business in Denver was just terrible (did I kill him?) prefiguring, as it did, so much which followed. But I am no impressionist; not me, not George Stone. Got to get the material in shape *circumspectly*; from one thing to the next, all in its place and at last to end with something meaningful. So let me structure the materials as I structured a role; let me resist that impulse which is simply to implode my own skull; sprinkle this stinking cellar with thoughts and curses. Where is Piper? He promised to be here three days ago. The profligate louse; you can trust him for nothing but this time I have the goods and he'll be here. My reputation. That alone makes it worth it. STONE RETURNS TO PUBLIC LIFE ENACTING HIS OWN CREATION BEFORE YOUR EYES. Yes, that should do it. He loves that. But why isn't he here yet? Oh, Wanda, Wanda; I'll grasp a proper grasp to show you what I think of you!

We need an organized journal. Part one, part two, but first, by all means a prospectus. Begin with the beginning:

THE BEGINNING

So. It began like this: it was, for me, as if the worst of us had risen to confront and destroy the best; that the blood ran free in heaven because the worst said *they wouldn't take it anymore; don't need none of this crap*. It was a shattering, because no body politic can exist forever in two parts. Oh, I had it figured out so elegantly. I had it made.

For me it was like this: it was benefit Friday for the Queens chapter of one league or another; the curtain was scheduled to rise at two, and at one I was comfortably settled in full costume, fully prepared with nothing to do for an hour but sit and get in some serious time on the gin which I had thoughtfully stocked at the beginning of the run. I sat there for a while, drinking like that, and listening to the radio, and after a while the Announcement came through. I shut off the radio and went down the hall, looking for the stage manager.

Oh yes, he had heard it too; he had a television set in his office, and now they had broken into all kinds of programs with the Word. Yes, he believed that it was true; someone like the Keeper was bound to get it one of these days, and besides, every man elected in the even number years ending with *0* since 1860 had died in office. He had known the Keeper wouldn't make it from the start. And it looked how he was right, not that it gave him any pleasure and not, thank God, that he had any idea what was really going on. I left the stage manager.

Back in my own room, whisk close the door, listen some more and came the Second Announcement. The Keeper was dead.

I corked the gin and put it away, put my feet up and began to think the thoughts I have mentioned above, the best and worst and coming together and all of that. They certainly made me feel better, because my legs got numb right away, and I was convinced that if anyone was part of the best, I was. Didn't the notices say so? *Everybody knows Stone.*

After a while, the stage manager came into my room, and said that he had decided to call off the performance. Would I make the announcement? "After all, it's your play," he said. "Nobody else should do it. They'll feel better if they hear it from you."

"Why not just pipe it in and let them go home? Much easier."

"Can't do that. Equity rules, you know. Anytime there's a major change in a performance, a member of the cast has to announce it, from the stage."

"This isn't a change, it's a cancellation."

"Fight it out with Equity. There's no precedent. You do it."

"Can't say I want to."

"Who does?"

So I did it.

Can one explain the barbarity of that occasion? The theatre was virtually filled, then, and the news did not seem to have come to the audience; they were all sitting there in a spray of contentment, waiting for the curtain to rise on the eminent George Stone in MISERY LOVES COMPANY (doesn't it?), and there I came as the house lights darkened, to stand before the curtain with the servile tilt of the jester. They quieted, and a spot came on me.

"Ladies and gentlemen," the jester said, "I have an announcement. I am most entirely sorry to say that this performance will be canceled."

That seemed to sit fairly well: a few stirrings but nothing drastic.

The jester, pleased with his success, decided, however, that they deserved in the bargain to understand the cancellation (not being caused by the jester's health), and so he hastened to serve them:

"As you might know," he said, "our Keeper has been shot in the Southlands, and it appears that he was killed instantly. While we await official notification, it seems certain in the interim that he is no longer with us. Our new Keeper is already at the helm, of course, and will serve us well."

There was a faint murmur, and the lights began to tremble upward again; the jester looked out into the full eye of the house and noted that they were confronting him.

They were confronting him.

"A most terrible tragedy," he said helpfully, "and I am sure that all of you could be induced to join in a moment of prayer for the departed Keeper."

Not a good ploy. There were no bent heads, no shared mutterings during which the jester could make graceful exit. Instead, they continued to look at him. *And look.*

And the jester had an insight then, in that moment when all of the barriers were down and that ancient and most terrible relation between actor and audience had been established, killers and prey ... the jester realized that they were staring at him as if *he* were the assassin. If he wasn't, why had he interrupted their revels with such news? What had he done? How long had it taken him and how, then, had he been able to return to this stage so quickly?

Well, he had given the news, hadn't he? He, the perpetrator, had made it known. So, then—

It was a difficult period for the jester, and it lasted several seconds until, by sheer heroic will, he compelled himself to take his handsome, if slightly gnarled, frame off the stage and into the wings. He hardly wanted to do so, of course; what he wanted to do—that is, what *I* wanted to do, what *I* wanted to say—was to confront them in return and have it out, lay it on the line. *Excuse me*, I wanted to say: *excuse me, ladies and gents, but I cannot be held responsible for drastic acts committed by lunatics in a distant place. I am, after all, only an actor, an occupation never noted for its ability to perpetrate with originality.*

That is what I might have said ... but, to be sure, I said nothing at all. The moment passed, the confrontation went under the surface to muddle with other things. They rose, and as I watched them—having decided that it would, after all, be a mistake to leave the stage—they left.

And, oh god, I hated them, then. I hated their greedy need for a perpetrator as I hated my own tormented and quivering mind; I despised them and shuddered at how close these had come to evicting some final ghosts. But they were right.

They were right, you see; it was as simple as that, and as deadly. Oh, it took me a long, long time to apprehend that knowledge which they had so easily and effortlessly assimilated. I was the killer. The killer of their Keeper.

You can imagine the effect that it had upon me; it was simply catastrophic. I was appalled. It was appalling. It shocked me to the core of my innocent actor's being.

What happens? I asked myself in the empty theatre, uncapping my bottle of gin; *what is going on, here? We must define some limits and stay within.* Easier methods by far to dispose of a Keeper; quiet strangulation or death by pater; poison in the tonic and leeches in the bed. *This was going too far,* I said. I sat before the media and wept for the whole three days, and shortly thereafter I left MISERY LOVES COMPANY.

I left the play, found myself a proper slut to bed and plan with; and a fortnight after that I came to my present quarters, this reeking, stinking abandoned theatre, once a whorehouse, before that a slaughtering mart. A rich, a muddled history: this building is descending into the very earth of the lower East Side of Manhattan; in two hundred years it will peep shyly through a crown of mud.

But that has nothing to do with me. I lie here content with my notes, with my intentions, and with Wanda; always Wanda. Together, then, we work out my condition, my final plan and the plan becomes fruition through the corpus and instrumentation of William Piper. Ah, Wanda, Wanda; I'll make my skull a packing case for your scents, for my waters. I'll toss you a touch to make the altar jump.

My condition. All of it, *my condition*. For the Keeper's death, too, was an abstraction, and it did what nothing else could have done; sped me gaily to the edge of purpose; found me a proper slut and a proper tune. And now, to be sure, a proper destiny.

For the secret shorn bare is this: *it made everything come together*. Without it I was nothing, a child trapped in dim child's games; but with it, *ah with it*, I moved to new plateaus, new insights on the instant. *No one ever killed a King but helped the Fool.* Focused so, with edge and purpose at last, I feel within me wandering, the droning forebears of a massive fate.

So endeth THE BEGINNING. We move forward jauntily now, a fixed smile on our anxious face; the old, worn features turned blissful and unknowing, toward the sun.

So, before the act be done, before Piper and his technicians come to unroll the final implements of purpose, chronologize a little; we explain ourselves. Writing this late at night as I must, I can make little order; the entries flickering in time and space would be the ravings of a madman were I not so sane. Barriers must be smashed in any event; fact and fantasy must be melded together. As the Keeper knew. Wow, did he know!

But one last terror remains in these rooms, then, and that must be this: that when it is all over and when police come for my belongings, find this and turn it upon a fulfilled, grateful world, these notes may be taken as clinical offering; may, indeed, be found by Piper and his troops themselves and disseminated as "culture." Oh, I know your tricks, Piper; I know the corridors of your cravening soul and you will try, you will, to reduce these to pure casenotes, more symptomology. But if this be so, be forewarned, Piper: I will not be a document, I will not be a footnote. *Not me, George Stone; I will purge the national guilt by being the Keeper and plunging, at last, the knife into myself; take that, you bastard, and I'll free you all.*

So, chronologize a little.

My name is George Stone. I am an actor. I am the greatest actor of my time. Read the notices. Look at my Equity card. It checks out.

I know more than that. Thirteen seasons ago, when I was young and full of promise, I acted in repertory theatre on the black and arid coast of Maine ... a cluster of barely reconverted buildings on some poisoned farmland, a parking lot filled with smashed birds and the scent of oil; those dismal sea winds coming uninvited into all the spaces of the theatre. From this, I learned everything I know about the human condition.

How could I not? Life, you see, is a repertory theatre; each of us playing different roles on different nights, but behind the costume, always the same bland, puzzled face. Oh, we wear our masks of so many hues night after night that the face is never seen: tonight a clown and last night a tragic hero and tomorrow perhaps the amiable businessman of a heavy comedy of manners, and next week ... off to another barn. But underneath the same sadness, the unalterability: the same, the same, the same.

And so I know: I know what you wore Thursday and what the stage manager plans for you Monday night; I know while you pace the stage this Saturday, all activity, pipe clenched firmly in your masculine jaws, that crumpled in your dressing room lies the faggot's horror. *I know you.* The power of metaphor is the power to kill. You deceive me not for I know all of your possibilities.

Enough, enough. As always, I move from perception to abstraction, from the hard moment to the soft hour. Oh, I must stick to the subject, *I must stay in the temple, the temple of the Keeper.*

Last night, I became 38.

It was a poor enough birthday for the old monarch. Wanda brought me a cake, Wanda cut a slice and I ate it, Wanda blew out the candles, Wanda gave me congratulations. She too ate some, let me give her a pat and then, reaching, we tumbled to the slats and made our complex version of love; the bloat-king's fingers tangling through her hair. It was not a bad birthday, but it was hardly a good one.

Here it is: I got it down just the way it happened. Word by word. Wanda and I had a talk, after my party, and several matters were discussed freely and frankly:

STONE: Wanda? Seriously, now. What do you think of me?

WANDA: How's that?

STONE: Do you think this idea of mine is crazed, Wanda? A little mad? This matters to me, you being my world and all, you know. Is this a sane conceptualization; my reenactment?

WANDA: I don't get it.

STONE: You go out of doors, Wanda; these days I never do. You have perspective. You know things. The national guilt is really bad, isn't it? They really need a purge, right? You haven't misled me into—

WANDA: What do I have to do after all this time to prove to you that I'll never betray you?

STONE: I know; I know. But seclusion under such pressure must lead to difficulties. I am so frightened—

WANDA: You'll simply have to trust me.

STONE: I do; I do. But I'm not a machine. I tell you, I am not merely an actor, I *suffer*.

WANDA: Of course you do.

STONE: You could hardly imagine the reach of my passion were you not living with me. Consider what I have taken upon myself. The burden of a nation. The lost Keeper. All of that.

WANDA: Sure.

STONE: I'm no martyr; my uses are concentrated into the fact of my *humanity*. You do believe in the reality of my quest, don't you? (Anxiously) You share, don't you?

WANDA: Always, George. Anything at all. You really should rest now. You're being overanxious again. Everything will be just fine when Piper comes, you can be sure of that.

STONE: (Cunningly) What's in it for you?

WANDA: Huh?

STONE: Surely there's something in it for you, isn't there? A fat contract. Notoriety. A contract for your memoirs. Even if national guilt weren't so terrible, you'd *say* it wouldn't you?

WANDA: I don't know how you can say that of me, George.

STONE: Oh, it's easy; I've lived in the world a long—

WANDA: I'm really insulted that you think so of me. In fact, I think I'm going to bed. Good night.

STONE: Wanda—

WANDA: You'll feel better in the morning, George. (Exits)

STONE: She's as guilty as the rest of them.

My little closet drama. Wanda is suspect as well, of course, but happily enough, I do not care; a fine and grotesque mutuality, this: conceived for purposes as limited as they are relevant. And, as always for the jester, things voyage to a conclusion now. Nothing is eternal—not even Wanda's delights—and this will end after all. We have outlived our possibilities, she and I. Perhaps my intentions were misguided. But I needed someone ... an assistant, we shall say. I shall *always* need someone so terribly. *Piper*.

Wanda is coming in now.

Later: time for metaphysical notation. For I am sick, sick of metaphor; Wanda fed me and combed my poor, tumbling hair and pressed my hands to tell me that Piper is coming tomorrow, tomorrow with equipment and technicians. The broadcast will be tomorrow night. There is no time, then, for constructions; we must go to the heart of the issue. For I will tomorrow kill the Keeper, and the last that can be asked is that you know who I am. *Curse you Piper, but I have my notes*. "He finds the whole concept fascinating, George," she said to me. "Particularly this feeling that the national guilt must be purged. He agrees with you there." I bet he does. Fortunately, Wanda has been intermediary from the first—I will have nothing to do with minor relationships, and everything is worked through her, my bland familiar—and the rich implications of Piper's agreement, viz., national guilt need never be explored. Only exploited.

There is so little left to me. Twenty-four hours from now, then, where will I be, after Piper's machines have wrung me through? I must do it now, now, I must make it clear; *I must somehow trace the origin to the roots, past the trickling brown earth and the green stems into the gnarled, poisoned bases of life themselves, the liquid running thick in them, bubbling and choked like blood*.

I first learned that genocide existed, in Europe when I was 10. My mother, a husky tart named Miriam—but we won't get into *that*, not here, not ever—told me that I might as well face facts beyond the neighborhood: Jews were being killed in Europe by the millions while she hustled and I froze, and someday, if it and the Jews lasted long enough, I might find myself, someday, interceding for them. This news shook and grieved me for days; I wrote a long one-act play about an abstract, persecuted Jew; obscurely, I felt my mother responsible since, after all, she had broken the news.

But not long after that, I met for the first time two of the participants in my mother's vigorous scenario ... a mixed pair of Schwartzes, who tenanted and barely ran a gloomy candy shop on a nearby corner, put up a sign in the window announcing that they were members of a refugee organization, displayed scars which, they stated, were caused by beatings administered by the milder bigots, and generally made concrete Miriam's whispered injunction.

I was not moved at all.

I wasn't moved; I didn't give a damn. They were two raddled Jews; they raised prices in the store by a fifth, which was hardly justified by their curiously bland and self-indulgent tales of horror; even the exemplification was drab. The worst things had happened not to them but to people they had *heard of*. So one day, in a capitalistic outpouring of patriotism, I overturned the candy counter directly on Schwartz-pater's thigh, and ran. And I took my business elsewhere.

Was that the first inkling of my condition?

Call the Keeper.

Well, this then: once I took an acting course in a great university: I was 17 and wanted to understand why I was gripped by what has always possessed me. (As my obituaries will remind you, I left the course and the university at the end of the fourth week, but that is not the point. Nor is Miriam's reaction relevant.) The instructor warned us in an early lecture that the act of drama was but this: that it began in the particular and moved toward the general; originating as it did in the passion and moving later to the implications. We listened well; we took notes. *Remember*, he said, *when a role is acted, don't worry about what you mean; think about how you feel. Find an image and work, from that. Leave the meaning to the professionals. Just feel, feel.*

Ah, yes. Is there some way I can inform the gentleman that my most stunning roles—moving through the decades of my greatness and culminating in the Lear of Denver, the greatest and least human of all Kings, they called me—emerged from the most intricate, the least applicable convolution? Is there?

Does that inkle to my condition?

I call the Keeper.

And this too: I took a wife. The year was 1953. Her name was Simone

Tarquin. She was a designer in that repertory on the coast of Maine. She was 22, she was accomplished, she was lovely, my darling, in the rocks and curling waters. *How she rose to greet me—*

We met in July; I thought I loved her. She knew (she said) that she loved me in June, in all the springs of her life, and that was good enough for me; quickly, quickly, we chose to marry. I had had no time for women in those twenty-five Struggling Years; there was too much to do and too much to flee, and the conceit of having one of my own, at last, to play with for as long and lavishly as I chose was a pretty, pretty, pretty one. In the fall I had a contract at a university theatre; Simone would undertake graduate design on the other side of the country. So, our maddened lover's plans went like this: she would telegram her resignation and join me in the Midwest to type or file in a reconverted barracks; in the night we would build and fondle until a summons came from the East, saying that our time was up; we had transcended suffering. We might even have a child during the struggling period, just to fill out the picture. That was the way it was; we had it figured out. Ah, God.

I have not said that I was a virgin in those days; so I was, but she was not. Solemn confessions were traded during the premarital experience, and agreed to be of no consequence at all. But we decided to defer consummation; after all, there was no reason to further dishonor her (my thoughts). One Saturday, license in hand, we were married before the cast and crew; we said farewell to them and with noisy enthusiasm went straight to the nearest motel, a gloomy, shabby structure four miles from the barns themselves. We parked the car. We removed our luggage. We checked in. We entered our room. We placed down our luggage. We undressed. We had at one another.

And, yes, I can block the scene; yes, I can dredge through the channels of memory for the perfect, frozen artifact; yes, it is there like a horrid relative, ready for resuscitation on all necessary occasions and sometimes unbidden between. Yes, yes, yes, *it happened this way:*

SIMONE: Well, here we are.

STONE: Yes.

SIMONE: Naked, too.

STONE: Indeed.

SIMONE: So, come here.

STONE: Yes. One second.

SIMONE: What's wrong with you, anyway? You look kind of funny.

STONE: (Opening windows, inhaling deeply, fanning himself and knocking a fist against the wall) Kind of warm in here, wouldn't you say?

SIMONE: Silly. They have air conditioning. (She hugs herself.)

STONE: Probably isn't working.

SIMONE: Anyway, there's plenty of air now. Why don't you come here?

STONE: One minute.

SIMONE: What's wrong? You seem kind of cold all of a sudden.

STONE: Nothing is wrong. *Nothing.*

SIMONE: (Showing herself) Don't you like me?

STONE: What a question …

SIMONE: (Some unprintable, if not untheatrical gestures) Well?

STONE: Of course I like you. I love you. You look lovely.

SIMONE: So then …

STONE: So, I love you.

SIMONE: Why are you lighting that cigarette? Stop it!

STONE: Well, it's already lit, so that's that. Might as well finish it now. Be right with you. (He puffs grotesquely.)

SIMONE: (After a pause) I don't like this, George. What do you think I am, the blushing virgin? I *told* you, I've been around. I'm no teenager and I know what's going on. Now either get that miserable cigarette out or …

STONE: (Trying to be cheerful) It's almost done now.

SIMONE: *What's wrong?*

STONE: Don't be dramatic, Simone; I'm the actor here. Nothing's wrong. I love you. I'm just a little warm—I meant to say cold—in here.

SIMONE: Then come here. (More theatrical gestures)

STONE: I'm coming. Coming now. (Disposes of cigarette) See?

SIMONE: Closer.

STONE: Like that?

SIMONE: Not quite. More like *this*. And *this*. And *this*.

At this point our curtain falls chastely for some moments or hours; the scene behind is as predictable as it is monolithic and dull but there are limits to this playwright's gift for metaphor, and one has been reached now. Of course, one could do this scene in mask and symbol, showing Simone gripping a large, earless rabbit, but such is too tasteless even for that commedia dell'arte the sensibility likes to play in the vault in that noon of dreams. No, no: better to let the curtain fall. After some period of time—perhaps allowing audiences to think about matters and even to do some experimentation of their own—it rises.

SIMONE: (In a state of some agitation, twisting to her side of the bed, holding the sheets closely around her and looking wildly toward the corners of the room) What's wrong with you? What's wrong with you? What's wrong?

STONE: Ah—

SIMONE: Oh boy, do I see it now!

STONE: Ah—

SIMONE: It figured. Goddamn, did it figure!

STONE: (Really speechless; this ingratiating and benevolent presence unable to make connection with his audience for one of the few times on record.) Ah—now, look Simone. Ah, Simone—

SIMONE: *Actors!* You keep away from me!

STONE: (He can respond to that.) You bet I will.

SIMONE: Are you crazy? What's inside there?

STONE: I don't know. Nothing's inside, all right? Nothing. Is that what you want to hear?

SIMONE: I want to hear nothing from you.

STONE: You won't! You won't then! But the others will. Everybody will hear of me. I'll fix them. (He is distraught.)

SIMONE: Wow. *Wow!*

STONE: Let's get out of here.

SIMONE: I'll buy that. I'll just *buy* it, friend. That's the ticket.

STONE: Go—ah—go into the bathroom and dress.

SIMONE: Turn your back. (He does so and she exits hurriedly stage left, gathering garments as she goes, exuding a faint mist, tossing various parts of her body.) And I want you ready to leave by the time I come out.

STONE: I'll be ready.

SIMONE: Good; *good* for you.

STONE: I'll be ready; I'll be ready. I'll be so damned ready you never saw anything like it in your whole life, you bitch!

The curtain falls. Or, it does not fall—for somewhere, right now, it is yet open, the actors staggering through the banalities; in all of the rooms of the world, the mind, it goes on right now. You as well as the jester have lived through it all too many times; all have dreamed its horrid possibilities on wedding eves; speak to me not, then of divisions in lives. For as it ends, it yet goes on, leaving nothing more to play: I have no interpretations, nor shade, nor form to all of this, nor perspective against which to place it: it is done but it is undone, for at this moment it is going on, it goes on right now; it goes on ...

Does that abate my condition?

Call; call the Keeper.

Only this, only this must be said, which is: that I wanted *all* women that night but not this woman, that I wanted all flesh, but not that flesh, that I wanted the mystery but not the outcome, and in touching that flesh—in touching Simone's breasts, those wonderful abstractions which had dazzled and goaded and seized me with groans as their clothed representation glided past me so many times—that when I touched them, I found those breasts tough, resilient, drooping bags empty of mystery and redundant of hope; they were flesh, mere flesh freed of that which entrapped it: say too that I found her arms of stone, her thighs of wood and her lips like clay, mere clay; and pressed against her, holding her like a tumbled doll, I knew that by wanting everything, I had taken nothing; by being possessed of the totality, I had lost the elements; by seeking God, I had lost my soul and that in the dream of all flesh, I had lost my flesh.

And so, I too had had a dream: I dreamed that in the wanting of the fullness, I had lost the oneness, and that entering the cave of time, I had lost the lamp of self and that the light, all of the light, was one. *Light, light, give him some light, give the old King some bulb of hell.*

But there was more, too: it took me a long time to see that there was something else as well, and in the years to come, I learned; I learned by dint of cunning to enter and haunt their channels; I learned with Wanda how to do it and I did it; I did it with luck and skill (by closing my eyes and making pretty pictures); and now, as I lie with Wanda again and again, I lie, afterward, shaken and empty beside her and wonder how it would have been with Simone. Because the secret was all in the pictures; once you knew how to make the pictures, everything else would fall into place.

Suppose I had done it with her, then; suppose I had found the way and had taken Simone shuddering in our night: *would I then have found a fullness in the oneness, instead of the oneness outside this fullness? Would I? Would I?*

Where are you now, Simone?

Where are you, my darling, absolved, annulled these many years and never to be seen again? I dream you then to be in a cave by the sea or in a paneled kitchen staring absently for the Time; perhaps you have become a dressmaker's doll, but it does not matter; it does not matter for you are gone and gone. *Gone, gone; lost, lost.*

It is done. Could you have saved me, Simone? Could you have rescued me through your flesh, through your wholeness from the noisome spaces of this tenement; the shape of my days, the flow of my disaster? Could I have held you, could I have found salvation in you? Could I?

Could I? What could I have done? *What there was to do I did not; what I did I should not have done.* Is there anything ever done that would make any difference at all? Oh God, sometimes, dear, I think that I cannot bear it any longer; this filthy slut, this horrible life, these raving notes, this pointless reenactment: oh, the twisted plans and the despair and the rage, I am so sick of it, I am so sick listening to my tinny, tiny voice reverberating in the chambers of self; my own voice imploring, wheedling, ranting, going to periods of cunning, apologizing, searching ... *I cannot bear it anymore.*

Oh God, to live through it again with Piper; to implode with him in the reach of the Eye, and to be done with it, to be no more, no more, no more.

Call the Keeper, I want the Keeper, give me the Keeper. Where is our Keeper? We have lost our Keeper.

Death to the Keeper, death to the Keeper.

Call the Keeper and give him death. Call the Keeper and give him dread. Let him know; let him know.

Let him know love.

Know love.

Love, love, love.

Death, death, death.

Love, love, love.

Death, death, death.

PIPER: That evening, on the INVESTIGATIONS format, George Stone, representing himself as the image of the fallen Keeper, reenacted the assassination, thereby seeking to purge his country of "national guilt." The dismal outcome, of course, made necessary the publication of his journal.

I am so sure that his journal establishes beyond controversy the sole responsibility of the actor for the grievous events of today, and the complete victimization of Piper that I will say no more about it; no more; no more. Only one last irony remains: Stone felt that his act would *purge* us of "national guilt."

Purge us? One can only say, from this lamentable aftermath, that the precise opposite was accomplished. The attempt upon the person of the present President was disgraceful, and the ragged shouts of the fanatics, scurrilous as their leadership was damning, should convince us of the opposite. Certainly, there are things which should not be meddled with.

Say I; says Piper: if there is poison on the shelf leave it there; leave it sit, fester, mold for the spaces of eternity; do not touch it for once touched, if the poison runs free, it becomes the communal blood and riots and danger and sedition trials and trouble with the press and loss of great sums of money and then they all go out to get you just like they've been wanting to get you for thirty years but this time they have the chance and so the rotten stinking bastard sons of bitches never give you a moment's peace but Piper doesn't care because Piper has the *truth* and as long as man tells the truth he will be free—that's what I say to them, the hell with them, the hell with all of you, just get off my back before I get you in real trouble, Piper mows, Piper thinks, Piper functions.

Piper, Piper, Piper, Piper, Piper, Piper

A TRIPTYCH

A SPECULATION: THE EARTH

Miller floats slowly, revolving hand to heels, pulling up his T-shirt to show the outlines of his stomach. "Lice," he says. Thomas tells him to stop this. I am working on the charts and therefore have no time to get between them but I can sense their hatred. It is cold inside the capsule and soon enough Miller replaces his clothing and his suit, while Thomas checks out the equipment.

INTIMATIONS FROM THE CENTER

Miller says that if the retrorocket refuses to fire, he will spend the last week of his life telling everybody down on earth exactly what he thinks of them. "Remember," he reminds us, "radio transmission will be unaffected. I intend to start at the beginning of my life and not stop until the present, and along the way I will make very clear that I know what they have done to me. Right down to the last detail. I will give them a sense of communal guilt that will take them seventy years to outlive. I will personally tie up the project until the end of the century by destroying public opinion. I find being a potential sacrifice unpleasant, you see." Thomas points out that all the tests indicate the rocket will fire perfectly; if not, this was something which we were well aware before the flight and we had said we could take the risks anyway. He reminds Miller as well that he is the commander and can bar this. To all of this Miller laughs. "We'll have television too," he says. "I'll point out a few things to them on the way."

A RETROSPECTION

Control has reminded us to conscientiously avoid obscenities or double-entendres while on the network and to stay properly dressed and disciplined during the television interludes. It has been made clear to us that we must do nothing to offend the huge audience which comes along with us; furthermore, misbehavior can set the project back irreparably. Thomas has assented to this enthusiastically and has dedicated himself to enforcing tight discipline in the capsule, but Miller says that he is only waiting until the time when the retro-rockets fail, then he will do what is necessary. "We cannot live our lives as if the bottom two thirds of them do not exist," he has said. "If we go out into space we carry the best and the worst of us all bound up together and we cannot behave otherwise." I too find the instructions from control exceedingly irritating, but, of course, they have precedent; no one, to the best of our knowledge, has ever uttered a public curse while transmitting from space. There are rumors that during one of the first expeditions, one member of the crew, who will be referred to as X, was refused permission to join the others on radio transmission because he had previously threatened to wish his wife a happy birthday in a most graphic manner. Of course X said later that he had only been playing and that there had been no right to deny him greetings from space, but the commander on that voyage had not thought the chance worth taking. It is not that space is aseptic—I am cribbing from Miller here—but that the impression it makes upon all of us is that we should be on our best behavior.

BEING ON MY BEST BEHAVIOR

We defecate and urinate inside our spacesuits; plumbing would be impossible at this primitive stage of the project, and similarly the idea of placing receptacles around the craft was vetoed at a responsible level early in the project; the resulting mess would leave a very bad impression for the recovery crews, although we, of course, sealed inside our masks for the most part, would be oblivious to it. At those times that we took off our masks, the odor might remind us of our origins. Nevertheless, the rules on elimination are very strict, and we are careful to void just before the television transmissions so that there will be no possibility of an accident.

AN IMPRESSION OF THE VASTNESS

Looking out the windows, through the haze and the ice, we can glimpse the slow spin of the universe itself, working back against the frozen earth and moon which, from this angle, are stationary and pinned against what seems to be an enormous, toneless tent. Vague flickers of light seem to move in the distance, but the stars are no brighter than on a cloudy night on earth; perhaps we have a bad vantage point or perhaps the illusion of the brightness of stars is just that. Most of the time we try not to look out although control, of course, is very interested in our impressions. Of particular interest are the comments Thomas makes on the appearance of the earth, its greenness, it's homogeneous tranquility when seen from this enormous height. "It seems impossible to imagine war or strife; it seems impossible to imagine how the children of mankind cannot live together in peace and harmony faced with the awfulness of space," Thomas says, and control asks him to repeat that; the transmission seems a bit unclear.

THOMAS SPECULATES ON OUR DESTINY

Away from the responsibility of the transmissions, not involved with challenging Miller, Thomas proves to be an entertaining relaxed man, full of the responsibility of being the commander but, at the same time, possessing that kind of humorous detachment which probably underlies his seniority. Surprisingly, I never got to know him very well at base; we are separated by ten years chronologically, and Thomas says that there is no way our generations can understand one another. Nevertheless, once the final flight plans were drawn and he came to understand that both Miller—whom he rather dislikes—and I would be accompanying him, he did everything within his power to establish a cordial relationship, including having Miller and myself over to dinner several times with his family, a dull, strapping group of people whose names, numbers and ages I have never been quite able to catch. Since Miller and I were not and never have been married or even keeping serious company, we were unable to reciprocate in that way. Now, in the capsule itself, Miller and Thomas rarely speak to one another, except during the broadcasts when a forced amiability must prevail; otherwise, they can get at one another only through me, Miller because he feels that by being his age I am an ally, Thomas because I have never made the kind of melodramatic threats which Miller has. Resultantly, Thomas must rely upon me for conversation, and since there is plenty of time for that—our tasks, despite all the publicity, are really minimal—I have gotten to know a good deal about him over the past few days; he believes that the importance of our mission is overrated because it really has nothing to do with solving the problems back on earth, and yet, at the same time, he says he understands that the project is meeting needs for people which nothing on earth could allow. "This is why I don't want any cursing on the broadcasts," he says, "aside from anything which control would order. We have to make a fresh start; we can't carry on and on this way, always and forever," giving Miller a sidewise look. "X was a nice fellow but he thought the whole thing was a game, a power game, an adventure game; and that was why he got himself grounded, not only because of the dirty jokes. If it were up to people like X, we would inhabit all the places of the galaxy, and all of them would turn out like this one—the same poison, the same corruption. I don't believe that we were born having to be this way; we just kind of evolved. There can be a counter-evolution in space."

Miller, hearing all of this—there is no way he can avoid it—turns to ask if what Thomas really has on his mind is the banning of sex in space in addition to any scatological references. "You know that isn't what I meant," Thomas says angrily. "Well," Miller replies, "the three of us can't have sex together, not with those gadgets switching us into control anytime at all and without warning, so that means we have a flying start. Isn't that right?"—and I have to make some remarks about course corrections in order to stave off the tension.

ALL IS NOT ADVENTURE: WE SLEEP

In the slow, turning night of the capsule, heavy and grasping under the load of Seconal they have insisted we take, I can hear beyond Thomas' slow, even breath at the watch the quicker, higher gasps coming over the radio; it is as if, lying in this entrapment, I were not alone but being surveyed by millions of eyes, all of the eyes frantic and burning, sunk in their lostness, trying to get a grip on me through the television receiver, trying to understand through the web of my sleep what separates my darkness in space from theirs on earth. It is an uncomfortable sensation to know what we are carrying on this voyage, and so I must spend the majority of my supposed sleep-time trying to count off the minutes and, for comfort, imagining that I am lying on a closely enclosed field surrounded by sheep.

MILLER'S VISION OF THE FUTURE

"As far as I can see, within fifty years, we'll have such misery and congestion on earth as cannot be dreamt of now; such corruption and breakdown as to stagger the soul and then, spread out on the aseptic boards of the planet and their satellites, will be small colonies populated by people like Thomas, living in shells at a cost of one million dollars per square foot of gravity. And they'll be in constant contact with the earth on a network of fourteen new television channels set up to receive each of the colonies; and in every barroom, in every living room throughout the nation will be a group of people sweltering in darkness, watching what is coming through on the sets and dreaming of a better end. And then there will be the riots, too; terrible riots when they'll try to seize the project and get hold of the transmitter and kill the personnel, but they'll always be stopped because the most real thing, the most important thing, will be what is going on in those colonies, and they'll do everything to keep it coming in.

"And the worst part of it is that they'll live on Ganymede or Jupiter just the way regressed patients live in a lean mental hospital: plenty of paint and projects and no connection at all. So what's beaming in will be worthless. That's the thing I really can't stand."

THE MOMENT OF CONNECTION

After we settle into the orbit, Thomas reminds us that transmission will begin in fifteen minutes. We start the cameras clicking off their pictures of the moon, and Miller puts his helmet back on. I can see Thomas working on his suit with a rag he has appropriated from someplace; into the rag pours the grease and rust which the rays of space have pocketed on him.

THE ATTEMPT TO BREAK FREE

The retro-rockets fire immediately and we can feel the power drive us back against the seats; Thomas half rises from his chair and takes off his helmet. "See, I told you," he says. "There was never any problem at all. The whole danger was concocted by control, just as a means of keeping their interest. Without danger, there's no fun; you know that. Have to give them their bread and circuses." But we can tell by the tone of his voice that Thomas too had questioned; if what he says is true, then it would have been even more logical for control to have arranged for us to stay there forever, a beacon and a monument, a symbol of the pride and death which intermingled are all we know of space. Miller too must understand this because says nothing. "Well?" Thomas says to him, "are you sorry that you lost your opportunity? It would have been a great performance, a really great performance. And I wouldn't have even tried to stop you; how's that for a secret?"

"I know you wouldn't have," Miller says, "and my secret is that I wouldn't have done it, I would have been too scared. Only the really strong can do the things that they must die to do, and I am not that strong. But you are, Thomas. You would have done it. And that's my secret."

I see then, in their laughter, that we have not been so far apart during this voyage after all; the distance was only a state of consciousness, not the terrible, drifting quarter of a million miles that we must yet go to return—to return to, what?

HOW I TAKE THEIR MEASURE

"... At the present rate, as I see it, by the year 2000 everybody is either going to be on welfare or administering it. I see no middle ground at all. Just consider the statistics ..."

Unit Supervisor
NYC Dept. of Welfare
January, 1964

I had to climb five flights to get the fellow. It was hell, believe me. There's nothing funny about these old-line tenements, particularly the carpeting they have on their stairs. It's at least a century old and it's slippery. Not to complain, however. Every job has its drawbacks.

I knocked at his door several times and heard mumblings and complaints inside. The usual routine; they hate to get out of bed. After a while I turned the knocks into real bangs and added a few curses. There's no sense in letting them feel they have the upper hand.

It worked. The door opened about wide enough to accommodate head and shoulders. He was a small man, alert, bright eyes, a little younger looking than I would have figured from the application. "What you want?" he said. Sullen. Cautious. The usual business.

I showed him my black book in one hand, the identifying card in the other. "Government. We're here to investigate your application."

"I only filed yesterday. I thought it took a week."

"There's a new procedure. We're trying to catch up on our pending applications, move a little ahead." That wasn't strictly true; the truth was that his application had interested me the moment service had put it on my desk. Even on my caseload, he was something out of the ordinary.

"All right, come in," he said and opened the door. I went in. The apartment was foul, absolutely foul. It is impossible to believe how these people live. Litter in every corner, newspapers, smudges of food on the walls. That kind of thing. Inexcusable.

He saw me looking at it. "I'm demoralized," he said. "Things generally get this way when the external disorder begins to correlate to the internal chaos."

Big shot. I nodded at that one, opened my book and very cautiously edged to the center of the room to take the interview. You never sit down where these people have sat. And you have to watch out all the time for rats and insects. That's part of the training.

"Want to ask you a few questions," I said. "First—name, address and so on, all as verified on the application, right? John Steiner, 36 years old, this address."

"You have all that. They took it down yesterday."

"But we have to make sure it's the same person," I said. "Sometimes they send someone down for them, create a whole fictitious background. We've got to protect the public." Before he could think about it I took out my thumbprint kit, opened it, took his wrist and pressed his thumb into the ink, then took the smudge on the paper inside and put the whole thing away. "Procedure," I said.

"It all fits," he said. "Total depersonalization of the individual, that's what it is. Don't you have enough regard to tell me what you're going to do first?"

"Some of them protest," I said. "They know they'll get caught." I opened to his interview record and compared the physical description with him; it dovetailed reasonably well. "Just a few questions now," I said.

"Mind if I sit down?"

"You're ill? You can't stand. You need to rest?"

"Nothing like that," he said. "I just prefer to sit when I'm spoken to."

"If you're sick enough we can probably get you in a fully reimbursed category. No difference to you but more money for us," I said.

"I'm not sick," he said again. "Just depressed. Not that there's much of a difference to *you* people." The *you* rang out. One thing that can be counted on, always, is this stolid hostility. If it were enjoyable, one would count it as a fringe benefit. I do. It makes a good definition of the relationship. There is no hatred without fear and respect, two qualities which I like to command.

He sat in an old chair in the center of the room. Moth eaten cloth, intimations of small life crawling up and through the upholstery and so on. He lit a cigarette for me and tossed the match out the window.

"No," I said. "No cigarettes."

"What do you mean?"

"I don't like smoke," I said. "People don't smoke in my presence. At least, not people making applications. Put it out."

"No."

"Throw it away," I said.

"I won't. I like to smoke." The whine was coming into his voice.

"Fine," I said. "I'm leaving. We'll call it *application withdrawn.*"

He looked at me for a moment. He could see that I meant it. After a time, he threw the cigarette out the window.

"That's better," I said.

"You really enjoy this, don't you?"

"Enjoy what?"

"The power. The assertiveness of your job. It defines your role-situation, gives you a rationale for your—"

"Enough," I said. "I don't need analyses. Now, we'll call it quits in one second if you don't can it."

Since he had lost the first battle, the second was no contest. His eyes dropped.

"Occupational training?" I said.

"Sociologist," he said. Of course. "I went through all that yesterday in the intake section."

"I told you, I'm conducting my own investigation here. Intake and unit are entirely different; as far as I'm concerned, you don't even exist until you prove it to me. Why are you making application now?"

"Why do you think? I'm out of work."

"How did you support yourself prior to the application?"

He looked at me, almost pleadingly. "I went through that," he said. "I told you."

"The field investigator is the sole determinant of eligibility as he interprets the manual and regulations on public assistance. The intake unit passes on applications to the field investigator for exploration and judgment. You want more quotes?"

"No," he said. I guess that is when I beat him. He seemed to cave in on the seat, his eyes turning inward, almost oblivious of the small things that seemed to be moving on his wrists. He had been easier to bring around than most of them; it was surprising in view of his credentials. But then again, everything considered, his credentials almost explained it.

"I was on the Blauvelt Project," he said, "for 15 years, ever since I took my undergraduate degree and became a fellow there. The Project just ended last week. So I have no means of support."

The Blauvelt was another one of those small government-created boondoggles; probably the major means of sustenance for the psychologists and sociologists. Even *I* had heard of it. They investigated genealogy, the expression of characteristics as revealed through heredity and so on. Most of it was concerned with going back through old records and making statistics, but Congress had finally decided last year that it was easier and cheaper to shove them all on assistance. That was Steiner's little life in a nutshell. Useless. Wholly useless.

"Have you made efforts to seek other employment?" That was the test-punch. There was only one answer.

Even Steiner knew that. He managed to grin at me. "Are you kidding?" he said.

"So now you want government assistance? *Public* assistance. Relief."

"Do you see any alternative?" he said. His voice moved up on the *any* a little. I had him sweating, there was no doubt about it. A perfectly routine investigation.

"There must be jobs open to a man who's been on the Blauvelt. How about unskilled labor?"

"The pools are backed up 10 years with the waiting list. You know that as well as I do."

I sure did. "Any relatives who might furnish support?"

"My parents are dead. My sister has been on relief for 18 years. I don't know where my ex-wife is."

"You were married?"

"I put all that down yesterday."

"I told you, there are no yesterdays with me. When were you married?"

"2015. I haven't seen her since 2021. I think she emigrated."

"You mean, she left the country?"

"That's right. We didn't get along."

"She didn't like the Blauvelt?"

He stared at me. "Who did? It was make-work. Anybody could see it. She couldn't take it anymore. She said I should either kill myself or get out of the country. I didn't do either. I thought the project was going to go on forever."

Well, I had thought so too until Congress had had their little convulsion last year. A lot of things that were going to go on forever weren't. I felt like telling him that. But I said, "I guess that's about it. We'll keep you posted."

"You mean I'm eligible?"

"I mean, I've completed the pending investigation. Now I have to go back and write it up—after I see a lot of other people—and make a decision. You'll be notified."

"But listen," he said, gesturing toward me, "don't you understand? I have no money. I have no food. I got this place last week by telling the landlord that I'd be on assistance soon. I owe rent. I can't even breathe."

"You'll have to wait your turn."

"But I haven't had a thing for three days—"

"You have running water," I said, pointing to the rusted tap in the corner suspended over a bucket. "That fills up the stomach pretty good. You'll hold." Then, because I really didn't want to smash him down all the way, I added, "You see, there are a lot of people I've got to service. You have to wait your turn. The need is general."

That turned him off. "Yes," he said, nodding, "the need is general."

"I'm just trying to do a job, you understand. Nothing personal."

"You've *got* a job," he said bitterly. "That's something to say."

"You know how much I often think I'd like to collect and let the people like you do the work? It's no picnic, believe me. The responsibility and the pressure. Not that anybody owes me any favors, you understand. But it's a very tough racket. I work 10 hours a day."

"I bet you love it," he said.

"What was that?"

"I said, I guess it's very tough. I have sympathy for you."

"Much better," I said. The interview was over and the fun was out of it. I had taken him, I supposed, to the best limits I could. I closed my book, put away the pencil, went to the door. "Any questions?" I asked.

"None. Except when do I start getting some money?"

"When I get to it," I said. My last perception of him was a good one: staring stricken at the closing crack in the door. A hand moved idly to his face, and I snapped off the image before it went to his eyes.

I went down the stairs three at a time.

In the street, I tossed my field book and kit into the glove compartment of my car parked outside and went down the way to have a beer before I went on to see the other bastards. A place named Joe's which I had often visited before was full of reliefers, and, of course, I had the bartender trained as well: he kept them coming and I kept my money away. One of the reliefers tried to talk to me and asked me if I could get him into the bureau, somehow: he was a full medical doctor and perhaps his services could be used. Just for the hell of it, I told him that we were full up on medical doctors at present but there was an interesting government project, something called Blauvelt, which was keeping lots of people occupied. I suggested that he pursue it, chase it hard. He must have seen what I was saying because he moved away and left me alone, and the drinking was so good and the respect in the place so thick that I forgot all about work for the rest of the day and got stoned and needed four reliefers to get me to my car. I gave them the address and one of them drove me home. He owed it to me.

They all owed it to me.

The hell with them.

OATEN

SOCIOTHERAPY: A process of cultural integration (See Structured Programming) 2. Popularized in the Antique Centuries; that process of assembling cultural data through the implantation of a participant-observer called a "Scout" who reenacted cultural processes at a level of credulity. 3. Later, institutionalized as a means of vicarious entertainment, archaic. 4. In disrepute, disgusting, as, "You sociotherapist!" (pejorative) 5. A discredited science.

OF THE GRABALZI: GLOSSARY
Windt 114 R.P.

To: Post
From: Hellerman
Contents: Top-secret, confidential, etc., etc.
Friends: On a shrewd, sociotherapeutic scout's guess, I would say that this planet's population, perhaps for all future generations, are hopelessly psychotic. A few minutes ago I met their "Chief" for the first time in what they called an "initiation ceremony" before a huge bonfire, dancing natives, flinging beads, etc., etc. This "Chief" is an imposing (for them) creature of some four feet six with blue scales and eyes the shape and color of rubber bands, not that I want you to think my xenophobia is coming to the fore at all. *Greetings*, I said to him in the prescribed fashion, just as the Elders had instructed me. *I do come in Wideness. May I be one of you?* All of this was said in Approved Basic so that the suit's pickup could get it, all of it was so gloomily transparent that even a paranoid would have fallen on his knees, relieved at last to find a contentious Familiar. The Codifier, just to be on the safe side, burbled all of this out in their hideous, glottal language, working on only a three-second lag, and I waited for the next event in the Ceremony which, the Elders had told me, was a handful of Chiefly grease in my face, followed by much dancing and their interesting indigenous wine made, they assure me, from the bowels of the Oaten themselves

Liar! the "Chief" said to me, so distinctly that even the Codifier blushed. *You come in corruption.* He rubbed his "fingers" in his scales and began to coat my face, not with what I had been assured was mild grease, but something which had the approximate texture and early effects of lye. *Evil!* he said. *Pretender! Diseased! Filth!*

Despite the fact that the circle of natives confronted me with the most whimsical and inoffensive of aspects, I decided, frankly and immediately, that I was beyond my depth. Seizing the Codifier firmly by its straps, I bolted past the Chief, through the bonfire (it singed me slightly but perhaps I will achieve a small reputation for miracles) and into the fields where I was able to make the ship, panting only slightly and securing all the doors. Washing my face, I discovered that I had been painted, in fragments, pitch green (surely there is such a color) above the neck with a substance that seemed to create dimples.

I am radioing, of course, for instructions. I have absolutely no objections to my position and the obligations it thrusts upon me. Nevertheless, I do not think that sociotherapy will work here. Perhaps all cultures at all levels force a kind of integration above the level of hostility (you see, I've studied the manual carefully). But the behavior this evening was peculiar; likewise the Oaten which are nervous, foul-smelling beasts which, although they are certainly the subordinate life on the planet, certainly do not occupy that position through merit but only, it seems to me, bad luck. "Chief" indeed! I think that he was an adolescent, put up to this. Frankly, I feel vaguely humiliated.

To: Hellerman
From: Walker
Sam: Relax. Take it easy. In the first place, we're circling you only 400 miles away and in the second place you are, as usual, panicking. I mean it, Sam, this is the last time. We're going to have to find another Scout if this goes on. Granted that a touch of neurosis is essential to the job, you're pushing things a bit far.

The Grabalzi (and no more of your phonetic jokes, please) are not only the clear dominant species on the planet; they are a race whose cultural integration in the face of the most limited resources and terrible deprivation has been one of the small wonders of the Galaxy— or at least that fragment of it which practices sociotherapy. No race has ever had poorer luck, to our knowledge ... congenital sterility, allergies to almost all bacteria on their planet, no metal, no opposing thumb ... and yet this little people have one of the richest interior lives of any in the Time of Man. (Not to be sentimental.)

Last night they were merely performing the Ritual of Test; one in which the Visitor is first primed for Exaltation, then exposed to shock and finally, restored at a level of Celebration; a three-part ceremony whose allegorical significance and parabular economy can only be considered remarkable, particularly since it works on at least 14 levels of Imagic intent, at least as far as we have disassembled their cultural traits. By your stupid and offensive behavior you not only proved yourself unable to work through the simplest acts of persistence and levels of action but stamped yourself to the Grabalzi, perhaps perpetually, as an inferior and panicky being, permanently barred from that inner circle of knowledge which, to them, is synonymous with their existence. And to think that you did this after all the training and explanation we invested in you. Granted, Scouts are supposed to be stupid—it is impossible to get a decent Measurement unless they participate at the most credulous level—this is too much!

Listen to me, Sam. There are millions invested here as well as countless light years of travel as well as the professional lives of half the crew here, the sexual problems of the other, simpler, half. If we are to salvage anything from your fiasco, it can be accomplished only if you return immediately to the Elders—according to our calculations they live 1.8 miles northwest of the cave of the Chief, no?—and explain that you were merely trying to point out a new moral to the Test Ritual and, feeling that you might have offended them, would like to participate now in a more conventional way. That at least gives us a chance to recapitulate the situation and possibly annihilate your own corruption. Permit the Elders to prepare and again take you to the Ritual and this time, Sam, *stand still and keep your mouth shut!*

You think that this is fun? It's a nasty job, preparing little documentaries for the pleasure of morons and the implications are frightening. But it's a job and we have a responsibility. So do you.

By the way, what in hell are Oaten? The Grabalzi are not only the dominant species on the planet, they are, to the best of all official knowledge, the *only* species. Is there something else down there? You better not louse this up, Sam, because we don't have the time, let alone the money. The Grabalzi have reason to be dour, even black; not you, though, not you.

To: Post
From: Sam
Contents: Top-Secret; Not to Be Divulged to a Living Soul; For Your Eyes Only; Watch Out For Spies; etc., etc.

All right, I did it. I did just what you asked. What the hell is sociotherapy, anyway? I'm beginning to question everything except my own suffering.

I don't like those remarks about my brain, either. Despite the fact that I have told myself over and over again that these are the outcome of mere spite because I am the only man within 400 square light years doing anything useful, I must say that your remarks are pretty inflammatory, Walker, and too damned personal. Remember, I didn't invent sociotherapy in the first place, much less try to make a science out of it. I'm just a working man.

At any rate, immediately upon receiving your offensive message, I took myself to the dwellings of the Elders which, as you say, are exactly 1.8 miles from the cave of the Chief but *due north*, you idiots. I deliberately left the Codifier in the ship, inasmuch as I have established perfect visual communication with the Grabalzi and any dolt over the age of two years in any culture can tell *exactly* what they have on their minds simply by observing what they *do*. I made entrance to the Den of Elders and made clear with handwaving, shouts and reasonable gestures, my intention to once again go through the Ceremony and indicated that I forgave the Chief for his impatience during the previous ritual. All of this was through the ten layers of shielded asphalt that you call a spacesuit, so you should understand that I'm really working down here. I expected that the Elders would hear (or watch) me out and then table the entire matter for a day or so to reorganize matters but to my astonishment, and disgust, they indicated to me that the Ceremony was still in progress and were I to return to the "Chief," things could pick up exactly where they were left off. Inasmuch as some three or four hours had elapsed I found this incredible but when the Elders led me to the site I found out that all was precisely true: the same circle of natives stood in the same paralysis, almost as if nothing at all had happened and, wonder of wonders, the "Chief" was in the circle, "fingers" locked into scales, gesturing at me. It was then, for the first time, that I began to feel distinct unease: having ascertained that 3/5 of the planet was insane, I was now beginning to see it as somewhat malevolent and personalized: *they were out to get me*.

"Greetings again," barked the chief in staggeringly fluent Galactic and began, once again, to lather me richly with his grease. Rather than being green, I found now, by hastily running my fingers over my cheekbones, that I was stark yellow and the stuff had a peculiar porosity. Nevertheless, and after the previous events, I was willing to be reasonable and stand my ground, which I did with much aplomb. "Greetings yourself," I said rather stiffly. "Is it necessary for you to take such an approach to a friendly human?"

"Necessary, Necessary!" the "Chief" said crisply, moving below my face now to work vigorously on the various coils of the suit which bunched tightly from the neck down. "This off too."

"Can't do it," I said, rather pleasantly, I thought. "It's protection."

"Why not protection all over?"

"The atmosphere is satisfactory. I can breathe your air. But they made it very clear to me that I must be dressed so as to appear to you as an alien, frightening being. Don't ask me why. I'd as soon be naked, quite frankly. When does the dancing begin?"

For some reason this enraged the "Chief". "Alien being? Who is 'alien being'?"

"That's what I am. It's all part of the process. That stuff smells, you know?"

"Oaten."

"What's that?"

"Oaten. You are Oaten. Oaten monster."

"Listen, Chief, I am not an Oaten or their monster. There isn't an Oaten within a mile of here. They're shy, patient animals that prefer their own company, being slaughtered only for the most necessary of reasons. I boned up on your whole culture. There is no need to act that way."

"That is it," the "Chief" said. I trust you will understand that all this dialogue is a mere approximation, given so that you will get some picture of the situation, but hardly precise word-for-word. Frankly, I was shaken. "Get off this place."

"How's that?"

"I said get off."

"How? Where? You think I *like* your two-bit planet? Hey, you aren't even supposed to know what a planet is yet, are you?"

And at that, things, as they say, deteriorated rapidly. I found myself surrounded abruptly by a circle of approximately 75 natives; as thin and pale as they were, with decaying scales and pleading eyes and consumptive aspects, I found the situation distinctly menacing. Neither pondering nor concerned with alternative, I gave a mighty spring and pushed myself through the group and then, at a dead run, made the ship once again; a dull feeling of *déja vu* descending upon me as I ran and ran, gradually shedding myself of certain bottom garments to facilitate speed. Behind me were the Grabalzi mumbling what seemed to be distinct curses in Galactic and despite their perilous condition, most of them proved to be fast enough as runners to bring me to the ship within an inch of my life. I scrambled up the stairs, bolted through the open porthole and secured all hatches, putting out some protruding armaments to give them the right idea just in case they decided to rush the boundaries.

So they sat down, still in a circle—what do they have with circles?—and lit fires and there they are right this minute, glaring at me through sick, weak, descending rubber eyes. Do I have permission to return to Post? I think we have reached diminishing returns, here.

To: Sam

From: Post

Listen carefully, Sam. The situation is, perhaps, a little more grim than you think, although it is nothing to get nervous about. Let's take things step by step. Stay calm, Sam, and you have nothing to worry about. Walker, by the way, has been shifted to other duties and hence I'm taking the mike. Don't worry about who I am, it doesn't make any difference. Walker will be soundly punished, Sam. Don't think that he'll get away with what he's done.

Now relax and try to follow this. It's very difficult for a man of even average intelligence and although Walker was uncharitable, he was essentially correct in his evaluation of your gifts. Scouts aren't supposed to be bright, Sam. At any rate, I have something very important to convey to you and you'll have to try to grasp it right off or there will be a great deal of trouble. *You are an Oaten.*

Those friendly, hardy beasts out there in the forests, Sam? *They don't exist.* They're projections of your subconscious mind, as warped by the Grabalzi. *You* are the Oaten and that is what they think of you.

I told you that this wasn't going to be easy, Sam, and you'll have to concentrate now. We have found out a great deal about this planet in the last several hours, not the least important insight being that we have absolutely no business here. These are deft, tricky people, their poor health to the contrary, and we've been able to piece together a good deal from the information you've given us and the materials available here.

I mean, they're deft, *dangerous* people, Sam; perhaps we would be the same way if we were allergic to everything on Earth and had been forced to adapt a culture in which 40 of our years was a rich lifespan and 17 hours sleep a day a dire necessity. Having little else to look forward to, these people have developed the concept of inner space.

What I am trying to say, Sam, is that sociotherapy is severely contraindicated with this people and we have decided that their particular resources not only make them poor subjects for our methods but place you—*you*, Sam—in actual, terrible danger. If they can have you, in something less than half a day, posting the whole concept of Oaten, as well as a series of intercultural relationships, they are a *menace.*

Some of us (although there is, admittedly, disagreement here) feel that the two "ceremonies" in which you engaged with the Grabalzi were not as benign as the malevolent Walker would have had you believe, Sam; rather than reenacting an abstract allegory or parable, they were structuring a fantasy of subjugation which would indeed leave you, as you so aptly put it, "stark green" or "brilliant yellow." The fantasy would, of course, work toward your flight and siege and the end might be in sight: there is some question as to whether or not the things you see outside are fires or merely what you *take* to be fires. As I say, there is much disagreement on this point, as well as the inherent nature of the Grabalzi, a people whose name and address we dug from obscure, secret files only through extortionary means. They were not in the "off-limits" sector of the bureaucracy for no reason.

At any rate, Sam, listen and read this very carefully. Lift off *now*. Push the button on the extreme left to activate your motors and then the EMERGENCY panel on the board, the one which has all the stripes on it and looks like a candy cane. That will take you automatically on a trajectory bringing you to within some hundreds of miles of our own and from there, we can recover you. Do it *now*, Sam.

Do it *now*. The button on the extreme left and then the EMERGENCY panel.

You are in real danger, Sam. You better get going.

To: You
From: Sammy
Contents: This is a Secret from Me to You.

My friends are outside. They are colored blue. They are colored white. They are colored orange. They are all pretty colors. They are waiting for me to come out and play. My name is Sammy. I am a little boy.

I am a *little*, little boy. I am going to open the door. See the pretty door. I am going to open the pretty, nasty door and go outside. I am going to play with my friends.

I am pushing on the door. See Sammy push. He goes push, push! The door is opening wide. Now it is open. I see my friends. The friends see Sammy.

See all the pretty friends. Here they come. My pretty friends are coming.

See Sammy and his friends.

See Sammy.

See Sammy.

See Sammy.

See.

THE ASCENSION

The implosion came from within as always the point of it was that the wave had crested early in the middle of the term and was now heading down, down, down; even the Inner Circle itself had to admit now that things were on the downgrade and likely out of control else why the cessation of press conferences and the cancellation of all but the requisite civil liberties? His face, His features, leaden as always but suffused with that warmth which had enabled him to carry all but two of the minor states looked stricken now when He came before the populace and His hands fluttered above as well as behind the lectern; otherwise, everything was as before only more so. Denial was the route of first possibility, of course, but He knew, He knew everything (had He not ridden to power on the crest of Referendum?) and there were rumors in the City that He was snappish in private; given to longer and fouler jokes, generally afflicted with a malaise whose origins He attributed to the burdens of state but which could have only one source and that source would have to be

THE INCREASING FRAGMENTATION WITHIN AND WITHOUT THE CELLS OF THE NATION, THE GRADUAL WORKING DOWN TOWARD

a point where communication itself would be reduced to jargon and catch-phrases (He was very aware of this, having coined some of the best) and the possibilities for dialogue would be entirely shattered; that was what it was all coming to and once that happened, all the signs would be clear. After the dissolution of Language (which happened often, every so often; it worked in convulsions, but there it was) would come the riots and the crowds moving about the streets at dawn, soon after that, there would be the Presentation of Demands and then there would be only one course, the Balcony itself, and He didn't want it. That was the point; He didn't want it at all; He was only 37 (they were getting younger and younger all the time) and He had plans, plans which He was only dimly able to focus; He had ideas, perceptions, too. Nevertheless there it was and

THE MAN STOOD ON THE BURNING DECK AND SAID

"how long can we hold it off? Six months? A year? The crucial thing is to buy time, we can turn the corner for sure if we can only hold it off for a little while."

"It won't work," one of His advisors said, "the forces are already out of control. They reach a point where there's nothing that you can do, where instead of cementing your purposes the media only tend to implode them and the very handles of the government turn against you and then—"

"You say we've reached that point," He said, lighting a cigar absently, feeling a trickle of sweat running down the space behind His left ear and moistening His collar, trying to get a careful look at this Advisor because it was very important that He keep a close, meaningful relation right through to the end; you had to touch the nerves of people. (He knew.)

"Yes, we've reached that point," the Advisor said. "Every speech only makes things worse now, every public act gives the opposition a fresh focus. I wouldn't think we had six months left; I would say it's more like one. I'm sorry."

"I'm sorry too," He said, and had His Advisor removed by the loyal forces stationed in and around the conference room and shot summarily in the basement, his corpse then being whisked to the highest levels of the building in the crematorium where it was fragmented and sifted like dust all over the city (there was no point in making martyrs). But He knew that it was merely a gesture; it was not the solution, the problem was not in the Advisor but had to be

IN HIMSELF, THE FRAGMENTED ID, THE VISION THAT HE HAD GRASPED WITHIN HIMSELF ON THAT LONG-FORGOTTEN NIGHT AND TRANSMUTED SLOWLY, PATIENTLY, THROUGH ALL THE DEVICES OF THE DAY UNTIL THE NIGHT-VISION HAD WORKED THROUGH ALL THE CORRIDORS OF TIME AND EVERYBODY KNEW THAT HE WAS WHAT HE SAID HE WAS; IT WORKED FINE UNTIL A CERTAIN POINT WHEN

the opposition presented its demands very cordially in the East Wing that morning; their Deputy of Public Information keeping his appointment precisely at noon, surrounded by his photographers (there had to be witnesses) and the men of the Media who were in on a contingent basis, having made pool arrangements previously and having agreed not to break certain details of the story until all details were known.

"We request you withdraw," the Deputy said.

"This a formal request?" He asked, once again scratching his left ear in that once well-beloved gesture which had recently become so noxious; summed up in the dead-center of the Referendum, the hateful, poisonous, corruption which had become the totality of His worth, posing gently on His toes, another beloved habit (being so youthful) which had now been turned, by the Opposition, into a certain manifestation of effeminacy which was so—*so basically against the principles upon which the Republic was bulwarked.*

"No," the Deputy said, "we thought it would be better to be informal, first. Want to get a good picture of me, standing next to Him, shaking hands? Will look good in the reels."

They took the picture. "This is not then a serving of notice," He said, coming down on his heels and trying to save the Consensus (when it was all too late) by forming His hands into the suggestion of fists and brandishing them, smiling, at the cameras. But no bulbs flickered. "Merely a preliminary."

"That is right," the Deputy said. "Hey, you're smaller looking in person than I thought you were from the TV. Do you want me to go down the list of grievances?"

"I thought you said it was informal," He said, nodding slightly and trying to look pleasant, thinking, inanely of His perished Advisor whose silt, perhaps, had settled upon the shoulders of these very men in the room, so it wasn't dandruff at all, merely another refraction of Himself, not that that would give him any damned comfort at all, you understand.

"Doesn't mean I can't read the grievances. The War is very bad. And your sons have been carrying on, that business with the automobile was really too much. And we don't like the way you look when you smile. Besides, there's still injustice, poverty, to say nothing of suffering. And you eat too much, you said so yourself. That's about it, then."

"I'm sorry," He said, feeling a trickle of dismay working through him because, in front of all these people, the Demands had made the case, had proved the point, there was nothing to say: the car business had been ghastly with two people nearly killed because Martin had been drunk and the War was very bad, not going well at all as even His advisors told Him and there was still poverty and injustice in the land. *It was true, it was all true, they had made their case* and

HE FELT SORROW WITHIN HIM FOR HE HAD NOT DONE WHAT HE SHOULD HAVE, WHAT HE DID HE SHOULD NOT HAVE DONE AND THE CAMERAS

caught this as it passed across His face, lighting His tired features momentarily with a wisp of pain and the Deputy said, "What do you know? Well, in that case, we better go on the record, after all. You accept the charges?"

"I don't deny them," He said, because He could not; He was old, old, and cremating advisors in the elevator shaft, it was a hell of a thing. "I simply can't deny them."

"Then let's get the media in," the Deputy said, taking Him fondly by the elbow, "and put all of this on the record, put the show on the road. You have a little body odor, too. It's funny; you wouldn't think it from a distance."

The Media came in and He accepted the charges and took the vow of Penance, dwelling somewhat excessively on the soul of His lost Advisor who He said, had been stupid, not that that was any excuse at all.

WHICH LED SHORTLY TO THAT MOMENT IN THE SUN, STANDING ON THE PARAPET, CLUTCHING THE ANCIENT BOOK OF VOWS IN HIS HAND, THE REST STANDING FROZEN BEHIND HIM AS HE LIFTED HIS HEAD SLOWLY, WAITING FOR THE CRACK, WAITING FOR THE

thud of the distant rifle, the cameras trained closely on Him, three or four hundred thousand watching Him from below, and His hands moved over the cracked surfaces of the book and He muttered, *it was my fault, it was my fault; if I had stayed with the polls and kept the Opposition close to me, it would have gone the other way; I might have held out six months, nine months longer, but it's too late, too late; I have failed; guess I wasn't after all, the Messiah, although once I thought—*

They shot him.

He fell back soundless into His wife's arms, His dead lips reaching her eyes (making a fine picture for the late afternoons, as well as a permanent remembrance of our Sacred Dead).

THEY INAUGURATED THE 47TH PRESIDENT OF THE REPUBLIC THE NEXT AFTERNOON AT THREE, THE SUN WAS VERY WARM AND THE PRESIDENT WIPED HIS FOREHEAD SEVERAL TIMES: BEING WIRED FOR SOUND, HIS FAINT MOANS OF PROTEST IN THE HEAT WERE HEARD BUT HE STAYED TILL THE END AND MADE HIS SPEECH OF COMMITMENT WHICH WAS, IT WAS ALL AGREED, THE MOST POWERFUL HEARD IN MONTHS; HE SAID THAT HE SAW A VISION OF

THE MAJOR INCITEMENT TO RIOT

was the death-mask in the town square, suspended several hundred feet above the crowd but of such a dimension as to be visible in every feature to the least of those who stared. Every mole and welt, shadow and hollow of the face of the departed Chief Clerk had been faithfully reduced; his mouth quirked as if it at the beginning of an obscenity, gave firmness and character to the otherwise static representation. The breezes, coming in off angle, west and south, that is, caused the mask to flutter and occasionally some part of it would be torn from one of the poles on which it was suspended; when this happened, one of the men would have to scurry up on a ladder and affix it once again with tape. But the tape was non-binding, of course, so the mask was always in the process of tearing free from one or another of its moorings and moving out casually to the countryside. The band music, piped through loudspeakers in the bushes surrounding the scene gave an air of not irrelevant liveliness and festivity although some of the older townspeople were heard to mumble that the Chief Clerk did not look as they remembered him and that there was something about the whole performance, perhaps, which was not quite right.

Warren Cleaver came to the square with his son, Roger, directly after a good breakfast. "We'll be gone for a while," he told his wife, Mary, and consoled her with a touch on the cheek, "the time has come to show Roger, here, what's really going on in the outside world; show him the happenings in our Square." And touched her a booming touch reminiscent of many nights until she released her grip on the boy and told him that he could go.

Roger Cleaver was 14. Before adolescence he had been a happy, sunny child much given to collections but now that the first knowledge of puberty had touched his face, he seemed to have opened up into a complex kind of woe, seemed to be attuned to griefs and rages that were in no way a product of his fine upbringing. Since his discharge from the School, he had spent the majority of his time lying on the bed in his parents' bedroom, reading magazines or staying with the lights turned off and the covers past his forehead. He was reluctant to leave the house and only did so on special errands for Mary at her urging; when he did there were often tears in his eyes and when he returned it was with an air of having suffered unspeakable things. Although Warren and Mary were both concerned about the boy they had decided not to send him for special training because, as Mary said, he was only going through some kind of a stage and there was the likelihood that once he met a nice girl and got laid a few times he would recover his formerly happy self.

The two Cleavers, young and old, walked slowly to the Square, which was less than a quarter of a mile from their cottage and as they went, Warren told Roger some of the interesting facts behind the display: the history of the tradition, the explanation and what events had gone on at the previous showings. Roger listened quietly, showing little interest, but when they approached the site and the boy saw the death-mask his face took on a rare expression of involvement. "That is something," he said. "That really is. That's one big mask."

"It took five men five weeks to construct," Warren smiled, and introduced Roger to two business acquaintances who were standing on the fringe of the crowd. Approving remarks about Roger were made and they both wished him well.

"He should enjoy it," Warren said, "it's the boy's first time you know." The acquaintances said that there was certainly no time like the present and after shaking Roger's hand, left, moving further in to get a better view. It was at that moment, for reasons never satisfactorily explained—despite the complex investigations that began almost immediately after the events and continued for many years—that the riot itself began. Perhaps it was only a panicky member of the populace stumbling into one of the poles and causing the mask to flutter violently, tearing its connections with a sound like glass as it floated down. Perhaps the mask was not dislodged by accident but was aided in its descent by a cunning insurgent stationed near one of the poles. In any event it fell slowly, gracelessly, toward the people, its dimensions sufficient to promise entrapment for several hundred and as they realized this, the squealing and the running began.

Warren was trampled to death by the first segment of the pelting crowd. Roger, however, managed to dodge that onrush and found cover under the podium which dignitaries had used during the launching ceremonies. It was for this reason that his life was spared. He stayed there for several hours while the night came down and the flames that had been set to the crushed mask roared and cindered, but the flames broke against the fireproof net of the podium itself. When Roger came out, near midnight, the square was empty of people and filled only with ashes: ashes the color of fire, of loam, of the earth; ashes the complex colors of discovery, all of them darting and winding in the absent winds that had turned to come in from the east.

THE MAJOR INCITEMENT TO
RIOT

was the assassination of the Chief Clerk. It happened at a large public ceremonial function between the main course and dessert when a fanatic stood from a rear table and hurled a bomb at the dais. Most of the guests of honor escaped with missing or expanded limbs but the Chief Clerk himself—he was, of course, at the very center—was killed instantaneously and severely wounded in the bargain, making restoration impossible. Only a mask could be constructed, the usual total prostheses being, it was agreed, impossible under the circumstances.

The mask of the dead Chief hung, therefore, in state for several days; it was then transported to the town square and suspended hundreds of feet above the populace on several poles. Parades were conducted and troops were reviewed as a part of the ceremony and the usual contests and feasts were held under the mask on the eighth and ninth days of the display, all according to ritual.

During the latter part of the second week of the display, however, one of the Opposition threw a bomb into the square while, at the same time, a trained army of snipers rained their deadly fire from surrounding rooftops and enclosed spaces. In the ensuing havoc, several hundred of the townspeople were killed, including many children, and the mask of the Chief Clerk was burned to unrecognizability by terrorists. This is the complete account of how the occupation of the town began; other details have been invented or interpolated by spurious sources attempting to take some of the credit to themselves. The distinguishing mark of the knowledgeable historian in relation to the calamity is his *paucity* of information. In regard to this tragedy only an absence of data can be trusted. We do suspect, however, that the Opposition was merely looking for a convenient instrument for their long-planned *coup d'etat* and the assassin of our Chief set in motion that unhappy chain of events.

THE MAJOR INCITEMENT TO
RIOT

was the speech given by the unhappy Chief Clerk at the testimonial dinner held in his honor at the Town Banquet Hall; his last public appearance. Remarks made were highly inflammatory and could have had no outcome other than the culminative riots which superseded the mad, physical details of his passing. According to members of the press and personal, trusted sources who were there, the Chief arose after the conclusion of the serving to make the customary gratuitous offering of thanks ... but turned instead to a vile denunciation only amateurishly garbed as reminiscence or geniality:

"My dear friends," he is reported to have said, "we gather upon this occasion to celebrate not only a unity of purpose but a furthering of vision and in that context we must ask not what can be done for our way of life but what our way of life can do for you; we must never suffer questioning but we must question without suffering; we must liberate the little framework we have so that we can keep pace with the years we have lived but all through this task we must remember that although we make our courses wholly out of our judgment, we must never forsake the judgment to make courses; I say to you that out of the fire and forge and testing of this time a new generation must come, one fired and forged and tested; we must not forge the fire but we must not fire the forge either; we must fire and forge together as we test and test, this being not a quality of insight but an insight of quality."

At this point the bombing began. Emptying of the hall was rapid, screams were plentiful, confusion was rampant. The Chief, hit squarely in the underside of his torso by the third of the grenades tossed crystallized, fell into the smashed crockery, littered with food particles. Enough of the face was left to permit construction of the mask. The death-mask hung in the town square for the ritual three weeks, during which the counter-revolution began. Killings and other losses were light to moderate in view of the heavy importance of the action. The complete text of the Chief's speech may be examined by permit at the Museum under security guard during hours as outlined in the brochure.

THE MAJOR INCITEMENT TO
RIOT

was Roger Cleaver. He had been more and more unhappy during this, his most dramatic year. Some nights he had felt so guilty and lost that he had laid in bed for many hours, trembling. For days he could barely maintain the pretense of a relationship with his family, let alone peers. All the people he knew seemed to have no faces.

When he heard the news of the Chief's death over the television, Roger Cleaver felt guiltily happy and relieved because someone more important than he with more to look forward to had gotten himself, somehow, into a worse jam. He hated to feel that way but it confirmed what he had expected early in this dreadful year: that everything should get as bad as possible and stay that way for a long time so that his suffering would have real reasons. He had never known the Chief Clerk personally anyhow, although his father and mother had met him several times during the campaigns and occasionally little pamphlets and letters came from him to their house.

When Roger went down to the square with his father to view the mask—which really wasn't so hot when you came right down to it; it was kind of morbid—he wandered around and just looked things over for a while. But when he came to realize that there was nothing to the outing at all; that his father had simply taken him there because it was something to see and would then take him home, an explosion of terror rose within him at the pointlessness of it and he said to his old man, loud enough for everyone to hear: "I don't even know why you took me here. It doesn't make a bit of difference; this man, the one up there, didn't have anything to do with me at all and it doesn't make any difference what happened to him. Don't you see that it didn't make any difference to anybody? You just fool around when you say that something's changed and it's always the same no matter who gets killed."

People in the square turned distressed faces toward him and at that exact point—the Opposition having calculated doubt to the last one tenth of a degree—the bombing and the terror began.

WHEN THE RIOT WAS OVER, HOWEVER,

standing in the empty square, watching the fire and ash, Roger found that he didn't feel so bad after all; much better, for instance, than he had felt yesterday. For one thing he had gotten rid of his father and for another, assuming that he had any ambitions that way, he had cleared the way for his progress toward being Chief himself. As a matter of fact, Roger thought, turning homeward to comfort his mother, that was a good idea; he could campaign for it: hadn't he been the one who, in a certain sense, had been the leader of the Opposition?

God damn, muttered Roger Cleaver, and thinking of the beauty and terror of the fires that had wrought and then destroyed the death-mask, he felt the pity rise fully within him; the pity that would become an uncancellable debt that only he could fulfill when, a quarter of a century later, he acceded to the position toward which he had so long striven. But that and the story of the many great deeds he did in office are a different matter altogether and must be discussed separately.

COP-OUT

The time has come. George and I feel surges of power: intimations from distant hollows, a certain convulsive twitching of the psyche. The usual preliminaries; where we are located they call it "nervous energy." It is, of course, time to begin again. Naturally, we are reluctant. Despite our background, our seniority, our periodic increments which have brought us to the highest level of Grade Nine there is always this dull resentment before we are hurled (literally hurled) into a new Process. Perhaps it is that the results are always so dismaying. But this is no matter. There is no point in being bitter and as Headquarters has pointed out to us time and again, our potential is limited, our prospects mixed and we are fortunate to be in hands which can make maximum use of our abilities. Enough.

In this cycle we are living in a dim series of furnished rooms in what they call the "West 70s," high enough to smell a dismal sea, inspecting damaged pavements, easing curtains against their poignant and dying "surf." It is unusually fetid in these rooms—which is not surprising, considering the amount of material we have conveyed there, to say nothing of the newspapers. There are newspapers all over, going back exactly twenty years. This is part of the security check. They verify the expected; we will be "originals." The growing realization that we will actually have to go through with it has, as usually, rendered George speechless over the past few "weeks"; I accept the matter more philosophically. Of course, it is a question of roles, as well. This cycle is George's turn.

"Well," says George—that is, he does the equivalent of saying "well"; it is quite pointless to describe how we communicate when we are alone together which is most of the time. "We might as well get with it. They want us to get going. I can feel them. Some day—"

"Don't be bitter, George," I say. "You have a tendency to procrastinate on these jobs. You know you do."

"I don't suppose I could persuade you to exchange roles."

"Not a chance, George. Straight switching, you know that. Your turn."

"It's just that I have a feeling—well, I don't know how much *conviction* I've got left in me."

"In a place like this," I say motioning, "who needs conviction?"

George mumbles something, kicks a few newspapers. "Oh, let's get it over with, then. It should be a simple job, anyway. They're not sophisticated here at all."

"Quite," I say encouragingly. "You should do very well, here."

George gives me a hurt look and I resist an impulse to apologize. After all, it is only the truth. Still, George will manage here. On this cycle, the difference in abilities is meaningless.

Primitives.

"Brooklyn Heights." It is an appropriate enough place to begin our formal actions. Not that we have any choice, of course. The instructions always leave no margin for free will. We set up unobtrusively, slip into robes and commence.

"Speak up, King," I say.

"I am not a King."

"Ah. Of course. You are a Prince."

"I am neither. I am in the hands of the Father."

"And *who?*" I say with flourishment, "would *that* be?" We have a small crowd.

"God, of course." Muffled gasps. No matter the cycle, this is a strong line.

"Hah!"

"Laugh if you must."

I do, indicating to the crowd that they may join me. Presently, we go to the wooden cross we have already set up in front of a sewer. As they gather our purpose, there are some giggles. George backs against the cross, confronts the sky rather dramatically. "It is finished; forgive them, they know not that my bones are drawn out like casting lots for help me to make the vestments."

Curtain. Routinely done, the first step, stultifying in its correctness and predictability. I show our permit—everything approved, everything in order—to the two patrolmen who have wandered over and I gently refuse the coins that a few have tossed. Our technique has been a little rusty—considering the usual transfer of roles—but it is a beginning of sorts.

We push on.

"Macy's." "Washington Heights." "Borough Park." "Rego Park." We are playing to an audience of ten or twenty of their "adolescents" who watch us listlessly from two cars parked in the "snow." I stop George in the middle of a line.

"Time for the next level, George."

Still deep in his role—George, really, is resistibly stupid—he says, "I'll take the Mountain."

"I said, it's time to move on, George. It's time to make contact."

"What do you want from me?" George says vacantly, his robes shifting gently. "This is fine. Why can't we leave it right here?"

"It's too slow, George," I remind him gently. "It all takes too long." I resist an impulse to kick him. Every other cycle, we go through this. Will he never learn? "We've got to do it from the top, George."

One of the hoodlums snuffles, honks his horn. "What you stopping the *play* for?" he asks. "How does it all come out? This is very interesting."

"I'll take the steps," I assure George. "Remember, it's my responsibility."

"Fine," says George absently. "But let's finish the play, right?"

We finish the play and the hoodlum throws George a dollar.

So, I meet Brandt in a bar, through contrived coincidence. In every cycle there is always a Brandt when he is needed, but this time is the easiest of all. I buy him a "Manhattan" and offer him some of our clippings.

"Nah," he says, pushing them away. "Forget them. I know your reputation. Frankly, I'm very glad we ran into each other. I've had ideas for you men."

"I thought you would. We need exposure."

"Fortunately, you've found the right man. I have great access to media. *Hell*, I *am* media. Not that I feel guilty about it, of course. Would you like a pilot?"

"Why not?"

"I think that an act of yours would go over very good in these times. Of course, you'll have to cooperate."

"Our pleasure."

"And no monkey business. You guys play for laughs and you'll be run up the river."

"No laughs. Would we be in this for kicks?"

"Dunno," Brandt says, studying me. "There are a lot of nuts, nowadays. Nevertheless, I am a tentative sold. I want you on the carpet for a Wednesday run through—if you want it."

"We want it."

"You realize that this is commercialized. You can't get into anything these days, you don't make certain concessions. After all, someone has got to carry that freight."

"I know. I'm very conscious of the situation here."

"So am I."

"And we need a large audience."

"So do I," says Brandt. "You guarantee your partner?"

"All the way," I say.

And I present it to George just that way; as a finalized proposition. Glumly he agrees that I have done very well although, perhaps, I have been a bit on the impulsive side.

"Heavens, was that quick," is what he actually says.

So, we show. First we go to costumery in the basement of a warehouse where I find the necessary equipment: maces, bludgeons, hammers and so on, along with some simple robes. George's problems, of course, are not in that area. We go, per Brandt's instructions, to an attendant who dresses us and then by limousine to the offices of the studio. Directed to an anteroom, we wait. George insists upon hearing everything so, of course, we do. In simpler things, it is best to cooperate with him. Someone flings a door open; we stand there on the sill. Brandt nudges us across and we lurch on, slapping ourselves.

"Show me something."

"Give me a sample. Can they synthesize? Look, they're in a block, already."

"Give them," says Brandt, "a Resurrection."

"We don't do the Resurrection," George says.

"*I know you don't do it. Did I ask you that? Give them a Resurrection.*"

I have said that George is not very bright. "We can do it," I say to him. "What's the difference?"

"Go to it," Brandt says. "*Now.*"

George sighs. I pat him. Tables and chairs are cleared and we are directed to the center of the room. George shrugs (a simple Class 9; understanding nothing, doing everything) and I indicate a tomb with my arm, clutch its vanished surfaces delicately, then go to a window and stare. As always, I try to find Headquarters in the "sky" but this, of course, is sheer sentimentality.

"I have risen," says George haltingly behind me.

My turn. "Sure you have. You have risen."

"As I promised, so I rise. Did you not believe me?"

"Bet your life I did."

"He rises" we say together. We walk past the table briskly (until George stumbles into a chair) and then through a door. Brandt claps his hands.

"Like it?" he says. "They really play it straight."

"Dialogue is stereotyped."

"Yeah, and it seemed too fast somehow. Too quick. Where's the technique? You could hardly get a hold of it and then it was gone."

"But sincere," Brandt says. "Very sincere. That's how you get your immediacy."

"I say again, where's the tie-in? What could you sell with it? Wine?"

"Anything. You can package anything. Try it on sustaining; you'll love it."

"Gentlemen," a heavy man says, "do you really believe in this?"

"Implicitly," I tell him.

"They sure do," Brandt says cheerfully. "Where else would they find the gall?" There is a rising-to-feet.

"I'll slot them," the heavy man says. "Regretfully, but what's the alternative? At least they're relevant."

"Are they ever," says Brandt.

"We'll make it Sunday. A Sunday, yes. That's a good night."

"That's just the spot I had in mind."

"Of course we'll need adpub. *Heavy* adpub."

"My pleasure."

"And some PR as well."

"Why not?"

"And finally," the heavy man says, "no carryings-on from the cast. You married men?"

"No."

"Pity. Oh well. You go into a quiet hotel until the package is on or off."

"With pleasure," says Brandt. "We'll keep them far from the night. These boys are exemplary anyway, I point out."

This much is true.

Some weeks in seclusion, then, the evening has arrived; freed permanently at last from George's neuroses, George's trepidation, George's small, deadly hesitations, I am tucked with him again into the limousine. We travel gnomelike into tunnels and at last into the studio itself. Brandt is waiting for us, leads the way to a large dressing room with mirrors.

"We've got an audience for you. Network figured it plays better with bottoms in the seats."

"Fine," I say.

"Just stay calm and do it right." It is peculiar advice from Brandt. He is sweating. Surprisingly, he leaves us and closes the door.

George sits. Heavily. "We're in trouble," he says.

"Everything's fine." I say, "have we *ever* had luck like this in any cycle? Don't I even get a bouquet, at least, for the fast action. This Brandt is one in a million."

"I don't know; I don't know. I tell you, there's something wrong. I feel it."

"That means you're really into the role, George."

"No, it's something else. I can't explain it. It's never been like this before. There's something—"

"Get to the point."

"I just don't like it. Of course, I'm only an employee."

"We're *both* employees, George," I say, patting him. "Believe me, if I had your opportunities this time around, I'd be a grateful man."

"Want the role? You can have it."

"Come, come. It's too late now. Besides, a working arrangement is a working arrangement. You know that."

George says nothing, stares at the floor. I notice that there is a bottle of "alcohol" jammed into a corner of the dressing room mirror and I consider it, finally decide to pass it up. In a way, it is an insult.

After a time, some technicians lead us to the stage. It is jammed with equipment: cameras, wires, men, etc. In dead center is an artificial garden; waxen fruits, a few speckles of grass.

"It's not big enough," George murmurs.

"That's the medium," says a technician. "Make an adjustment."

"They wouldn't even let us *rehearse*, here."

"Don't get sulky, George." For the first time, I am furious with him. His conduct is really inexcusable.

"Have it your way," he says then. He draws his robes around him.

Apparently, it is time now, for which I am grateful. Lights darken, and mild applause rises from spaces beyond. A voice in the ceiling gives our names and purpose and lights blink. More applause and then silence. A red light winks down on George. He raises his hand.

"I see no bounty," he says. "I see stone."

"Stone?" I say.

"Yes, yes; the stones are gray, they shriek in their huddled spaces; I tell you that we have come to the end of our time."

"Madness," I say.

"But yet, I will reflower these blasted spaces; for the stones have accosted the heavens and they have said: no more, no more. They parch; they cry for water."

"Madness!" I scream.

"*You* are mad," George says. His face shifts in the light. "You are corrupt; you are tormented; ah, I say to you that you have reached the end of our possibility. And so I come—" There is a shout in the grayness. It is very matter-of-fact, for all its volume. "Crucify him," it says.

"Why?" I ask reasonably.

"Crucify him!" The voice is piercing and this time it seems to be accompanied by others. "Put him right up there! I *dare* you!"

It is Brandt's voice, of course.

I look sidewise at George. He is listening intently. I shrug: it is not, after all, such a complex alteration of the Program but only brings us to our goal somewhat more rapidly. "How about a crucifixion?" I whisper.

"Why not? Go right ahead. Crucify me. Isn't that what you wanted, anyway?"

"I'll be careful."

"Sure, sure. Be my guest. Go right ahead."

"How about that small tree?"

"Suits me just fine."

"Well, then!" I shout, "go up there and perish."

"I'm not afraid. I'm not afraid of you, anymore."

There is more shouting in the distance and sprays of cheering. "Go to it!" Brandt calls. I back George against the tree and take some nails from my pocket.

"Okay," I say.

"My pleasure," George says. He spreadeagles awkwardly against the plastic tree and waits. I put the nails in with a thumb underneath his wrists.

"Put them *in!*" they are shouting. "All the way!"

Confused, now, and slightly alarmed, I drive another nail, this time into George's finger. He wriggles but makes no sound. I go for his feet, shove them into the trunk until he can balance only by clamping the tree with his wrists. All the time, I am trying to make clear to him by whispering and signals that, after all, we are only expediting matters. But he hardly listens. In fact, he begins now to really struggle.

"Now the flogging!" Brandt screams. "Now, now!"

I turn to the sound and put my palms up. "There are limits," I say.

"*Flog* him, damn you!"

"We have to draw the line somewhere."

"Oh, forgive them," George says behind me. "They do not know—"

"George," I whisper, "maybe we should make a run for it." All of a sudden, something has come over me; a fester, not of doom but of *fraud*. Almost as if—

A man—not Brandt—vaults to the stage, looks past me and runs into our garden. "You've got to do it right," he says. His eyes are very clear.

"Better watch it," I say.

"Can't fake it," he says determinedly. He snatches a hammer from his pocket and begins to beat George, screaming. George screams back. Helplessly, I look for aid, but there seems to be none in sight. In fact, other people with weapons are leaping on the stage, vaulting from all directions.

I turn to George who is lying, bleeding, on the floor. I shrug. "What can I do?" I say. I pause. "What can I do? I didn't think it would end this way. Still, I've got a contract to protect. We're property, George. I can't risk myself, it wouldn't be fair to Headquarters. The insurance—"

And delicately but hastily I run to a wing. Now I hear curses and banging and I back away from the hands which are reaching toward me, dodge into our dressing room and slam the door. All the way down, I hear the screams.

No one follows. After a time, I take the bottle from the mirror and begin to work on it seriously, careless of the consequence. George, after all, was a partner. Furthermore, I am wondering just what I am going to tell Headquarters. It is a thorough, embarrassing mess; there is no doubt about this. I am still trying to figure out exactly how I am going to explain this when Brandt comes in, his face streaked, and stands behind me very quietly.

"Well," I say, without bothering to turn. "This is all your fault. I hope you stand thoroughly prepared—"

Brandt says nothing. I turn on him. "I hope you're ashamed!" I say.

Still, he says nothing. Instead, he extends his hands.

"You don't have to be so damned supercilious about it," I say. Then, I lose control and break the rule of Headquarters. "Thanks to you, we've botched our first job! What are we going to *say* to them?"

"Whatever you must," murmurs Brandt. His hands suddenly grasp my neck. "You played right into it." Almost detachedly, he begins to choke me.

Struggling in his grip, I see everything. From the first. *Why it was so easy. Why it came to this.*

"Damn you," I gasp (breaking another Headquarters' two rule), "you're from the Other Side."

"Precisely right," agrees Brandt, and begins to strangle me seriously. "You didn't think you'd get away with this forever, did you? We've had quite enough of your disgusting, cheap little operation and we're starting to take measures."

Then, there is a horrible twisting, and everything goes away.

When I wake up, I am in Headquarters, of course, and boy, are they ever mad!

WE'RE COMING
THROUGH THE WINDOW

Dear Mr. Pohl:

Unfortunately I, William Coyne, cannot send you a manuscript for consideration due to reasons very much beyond my control which you will soon understand. All that I can do in the very limited time, and with the limited opportunities available, is to write things down as best I can in the form of this letter and hope that you will be patient and understanding enough to see the great story possibilities in my problem. Perhaps after you see how important and unusual the situation is here you will consent to write a story out of it yourself and keep 50% (fifty per cent) of the proceeds, which seems fair enough because you don't have to think up any ideas. Or, if you find yourself too busy to write it, you might turn it over to one of your regular authors in which case he will do the same thing and I will allow him only 40% (forty per cent) of the sale price. But since this is a million-dollar idea as you will see, there should be plenty of money in it for everyone if you'll only *work fast*.

Last week I, William Coyne, invented a time machine. That is correct, *I* created from my own notes the first time machine. I, William Coyne, 29 years old, unemployed and presently living in very cramped quarters. I built it by myself in these three furnished rooms on the West Side of Manhattan, running back and forth between the hall sink and my bedroom because, like my own body, the mechanism is 85% undistilled water. The machine worked out very well, considering that I know next to nothing about electronics and the only science courses I have ever taken were for my high school equivalency diploma. I am not very advanced, as they say. Instead, I just kind of fiddle around and I guess I fiddled myself into the machine.

It is a very simple device, Mr. Pohl, and a very successful one; the only trouble is that its range is extremely limited. At the present time it will take me back only four months into time or forward seventeen minutes, it is poorly calibrated and at no time can I leave the actual time field, which embraces only five square feet. It is an early model and it will have to be refined then on part of the proceeds from the story you will write about me.

In spite of the problems though, it definitely works. Just last Tuesday

I shot myself back three months in time, found the newspaper of that date lying on my desk and my own humble form, the form of William Coyne, tossing fitfully upon the bed. It was an eerie experience meeting myself for the first time and it shook me up considerable. But when I came back to the present time, with the help of the machine, and before I could even look around, I was interrupted by the dashing appearance of my double who motioned me urgently and requested in a whisper that four minutes hence I would please go backward four minutes in time. Then he—me—vanished.

It was very frightening, let me tell you, talking to myself, William Coyne in my own rooms. But I counted off the four minutes and used the machine to go backward; then I met my earlier self and told him— me, that is—to go back four minutes in four minutes. Like that.

All right, Mr. Pohl, I know what you're thinking right now. You're saying that this is all old stuff for you and your writers (even though in my case, the case of William Coyne, it happens to be one hundred percent (100%) absolute true fact) and that you've seen it a thousand (1,000) ways. I read science fiction, too, or I used to read it before I got into this mess. But stay with me, Mr. Pohl. There are a couple of things I haven't explained to you yet which will make clear why this situation is 100% sockaroo for a good man like yourself.

You can imagine how I got the plans for the time machine, of course. That's right, a few months ago I woke up in the morning to find all of them written out for me in my own handwriting on my dresser table (that was what I did when I shot myself back the first time). I just used them. So I guess I didn't really invent it—or, that all of us invented it. But that is of little importance, Mr. Pohl, except to point out that I am not a creative genius and that is why I need help in my situation very, very fast.

You see the trouble is this: I told you that the machine. didn't calibrate exactly and every time I go back to the present I don't get to the exact present but instead a few seconds or minutes off in either direction. So now, every time I jump around, I always come back to meet myself, and if I jump back, and try to come in exactly on time, I just make more difficulties. The same thing happens every time I go back in time; I'm always meeting myself on the way.

Well, what it comes down to is this: I'm always coming across myself now and the more I try to straighten things out, the worse it gets. As a matter of fact, Mr. Pohl, I'm afraid to make any more jumps because the more I've tried to straighten out this situation, the worse it's become.

Well, the truth is that there are now about three hundred (300) of us in these rooms, Mr. Pohl, all of us fooling around with these small-time machines and none of us getting along very well. I mean, *I've* stopped trying to straighten myself out but most of the others haven't yet ... they have to learn the hard way and in the meantime there are just more and more of us. Right now there are about 310 (three hundred and ten) for instance, just in the few short minutes I've been able to borrow the typewriter from the other 53 of us who all are trying to write letters for help.

As a matter of fact, we're about to be evicted for overcrowding, Mr. Pohl, and in the bargain there's just no food or space left here anymore. And any time one of us goes out for food he seems never to come back with it ... not that it would do us any good because I had two cents (2¢) in my pocket when this all began and we would need several thousand of us to get enough food to feed ten of us if you see what I mean.

This is my situation, the situation of William Coyne. What can I (we) do? We need to make big money from the machine real fast, that's the point, but we can't get out of the field, so how are we going to make it? And then we just keep on meeting up with ourselves and having to explain things all over again and we're all dead broke. Please, please: would you have one of your writers, if not yourself, write a story about me (about us) and send the money just as soon as you can? We're all kind of desperate, here.

Hopefully,
WILLIAM COYNE
William Coyne
William coyne & ...

THE MARKET IN ALIENS

The first thing I did when I brought the alien home from auction was to plop him right into the tub. No sense in taking chances, even though they had assured me as usual that he was strong enough to exist out of the aqueous environment for several days. These were the same boys who had learned, only after a lot of trial and error, that they needed an aqueous environment in the first place, of course. The one thing I couldn't take would be an alien dying on me right off, and thanks to the liars and cheats who run these farces, there's a lot of precedent.

The next thing I did, after I established that he was going to lie there quietly, breathing slowly, turning the water their characteristic black, was to make a strong drink and call Intercontinental. I didn't even want to *try* making conversation with him; I had gone through that with the earlier ones, and it always came down to the same frustration, backed by whistling. Someday they're going to establish communication with them, and when they do, I'll be happy to talk. But until then, it's absolutely pointless. Besides, there is absolutely nothing an alien could say that would interest me in the slightest, not at this stage of the game.

I was lucky. I got Black, my contact, on only the fourth or fifth try at the switchboard—Inter is in administrative collapse like most everything these days—and after reminding him of all the favors I had done for him, I laid it right on the line.

"I've got one in the bathtub," I said. "A clean healthy male, in the pink of maturity, I'd say. All reflexes in order, highly responsive and probably as intelligent as hell; he's piping a blue streak. I just got him this afternoon."

Black shrugged, a common business technique, and then cut off his viewscreen. "Don't need it," he said. "We're already overstocked."

"You need this one. Prime of life and all that. Furthermore, I was able to get him reasonable, and I can pass that saving right on to you."

"Sorry," Black said. "We just don't need it right now. These things haven't been moving as well as we had hoped in the last month. People are tired of them, and I think there's a lot of guilt building up, too. What the hell, they may be intelligent with these space machines and all. Speaking personally, I think the bottom has fallen out of your craze."

"Never," I said. "You're talking about the whole appeal."

"You don't understand psychology. Not to get involved, though, and just because I'm curious, what would you want for it?"

"Five hundred."

"Five hundred what?"

"Dollars," I said. Black was my contact at Inter; I had sold him eight aliens at more or less fair prices. Nevertheless, all that sentiment aside, he could drop dead most of the time, as far as I'm concerned.

"Oh. I thought you meant five hundred cents. At that level, we might have something to talk about, for taxidermic purposes anyway. But I can't use it, Harry. We can't move the stock we got. I tell you, the word is out on these things, now with the research. We don't know what we've hooked into."

"Three hundred," I said, cutting out my own viewscreen, letting Black drift in uncertainty for a few moments, a legitimate business technique. "For you. Just for the turnover. Hell; I got him at 275 so you can see that I'm practically crying."

"No, Harry. Speaking seriously, I probably could take him off your hands at 150, maybe 175 if he shapes up. We could sneak it through. But I couldn't ask you to take a loss like that, could I? A friend is a friend. Try Franchise."

"I will if I have to. But I don't like Franchise. I consider you my closest friend in this business, Black. Just to keep that relationship alive, I'll let you have him at cost price. All right, say 250. Just to have the lines opened." I had bought the alien for 100, and the auctioneer had been practically begging for that figure; Black was right about the bottom having fallen out. Nevertheless, I hated to concede a point. It was the first step to losing money, and I hadn't lost a cent on the freaks yet. Not one. And not ever.

Black sighed and put his viewscreen on again, gave me a good view of some cigarette-work. "200," he said, "and you'll have to deliver, and the beast better pass."

"225 and you make pickup. And he'll pass. He was trying to sing me a lecture in there before."

Black showed me some smoke. "210 and I'll make pickup."

"Done," I said, and flipped on my own viewscreen, projected some sensitive profile-action. "How soon you be over?"

"We'll have a crew in about half an hour. You better get it sedated, Harry. Some of the crews are getting nervous about this whole business, now. I don't want any of that whistling."

"Leave it to me."

"Don't overdose him now."

"Don't worry about a thing," I said. "I treat them right. He's in perfect shape and he'll stay that way, and he'll be quiet as the tomb on the way over. You'll have the usual certificate for me, won't you?"

"Of course. You know how we do business. Personally, Harry, to loosen up a bit, I tell you that I don't see much of a future in this business for either of us, not with these latest reports. But I agree that you always came across with fair merchandise, and if he's a nice specimen, we might be able to turn him over to a lab, skip the zoo-route completely. I'll do this for old time's sake, but the lab pays only about 300, I want you to know, so who's taking the loss here?"

"Maybe the alien, is that what you're trying to tell me?" I said, and switched off altogether. The hell with them. Unctuous bastard. If anybody was going to get crucified first, though, it was going to be the Blacks, not me. I was only performing a service for a public demand, and I could prove it.

I went into the bathroom, feeling pretty disgusted with the whole conversation, and looked at the alien for a while. He was in a semi-doze, one of the usual comas, the eyes bright and fixated on me as he moved slowly on his back. His tentacles were twitching. No whistling, no gestures though.

"Only a few minutes for you here and you're gone, boy," I said. I always try to communicate with them; I never said they weren't intelligent. Deep inside me there is the belief that a bit of soul exists in everything. Hell, maybe they came to earth to cure us; how the hell do I know? When I see it, I'll believe it, that's all I know.

I locked the bathroom door and went into the den and watched television for a time, waiting for the crew to come. As usual, Black's boys were late. A bulletin came on saying that yet another of their ships had landed somewhere near Lake Michigan, the second in a week in that general area, and that the usual procedures were being followed. That relieved the depression a bit. It meant that if they were efficient there for a change, the auction would probably be ready to go by day after tomorrow. Detroit was a nice city; I hadn't seen it for a while. So I called United and booked flight, taking coach; no sense overdoing pleasure with business.

Sometime after that, just before the crew finally came, one of those damned scientists came on in an interview with the usual recent crap about mass guilt and stellar communication, and I switched that right off. The profit on the sale, less the airline deposit, left me with fifty clear and what I did was to call Ginny and take her out. We went to the zoo where I showed her the two specimens which were mine. On my own level, I'm very sentimental about the freaks.

BY RIGHT OF SUCCESSION

Oh God, it was a glorious day; indeed it was, fine and glossy high in the skies above. Even the motorcade—mark you, the *motorcade* came by exactly on schedule this once, proving the perfection of it all. As it passed under him, he heard the distant shouts, cries, the pounding of the cycles and then the procession itself: marvelous. Carson could hardly contain himself, it was all working out so perfectly. When The Car passed, he leveled properly, savoring the rightness and tightness of the stock high in his hands, the rightness and tightness of the ritual which Congress had in Its wisdom decreed ... and then he fired. Once. Twice. The true hit came on the second shot, just as predicted. Simple. There was nothing to the whole thing, once you had little organization, the right attitude. The cheering started immediately.

He worked his way down the Depository slowly, using the ladders, bowing gracefully at landings, remembering to keep his gaze straight, his hands busy. (*Stay in the role*, the instructors had reminded him.) At the fourth floor, he threw his hat into the crowd, at the third he chucked the rifle itself, watching it whirl, diminish, hit stones with a clatter. Someone cried *Carson!* and he smiled. When he came to ground level, two men dressed as police were already waiting, ready to take him by the arms and guide him safely to the car. Behind the barriers, people leapt, threw flowers. It was splendid, all splendid. *Thank you!* he said to the crowds.

It was all over, then. The only thing that had concerned him even a bit was being mauled or crushed as he understood a few had been; one had to pay the price of office of course, but not so gracelessly, so *publicly*. He eased into the cushions of the limousine easily, settled next to another policeman. In the front, an anonymous figure shifted gears. They moved rapidly then, doing eighty, perhaps ninety miles an hour between the barricades, toward the hospital. Carson felt fine, never better: no complaints, Lord, no complaints *at all*. Relaxed, content, joined utterly to himself for a change, all credit to the serenity of the operation. But, then (he reminded himself), that was understood to be part of the emotional reaction after the shots were fired; everybody felt great then. The question was how he would feel during the Inquisition. Most of them ran into trouble—if they were going to get into trouble at all, that was—during those intense moments. However ...

The policeman beside him bore a faint but interesting resemblance to the man Carson had just shot. That was all part of the process of course: great realism, great immediacy, identity and so on. They were clever. The important thing was simply to remember that the policeman was a robot, that all of them were probably robots excepting always those that weren't. The victim, for instance. Carson asked for a cigarette.

The policeman said no. "Don't believe in them," he added. "Just get a hold of yourself." That was to be expected, of course. Now and then you might find one programmed for amiability, he had gathered, but for the most part they weren't, which was probably just as well in the long run. Still, he felt exhilarated; he wanted to talk. "How we doing?" he said.

"What you mean?"

"We on schedule?"

"Five minutes ahead, maybe."

"Couldn't that be a problem?" Carson asked, feeling the first flick of anxiety. Five minutes ahead this early could mean trouble. It meant one thing for sure; he should have stayed with the crowds a little longer, met the public head on, pressed the flesh so to speak. It couldn't hurt when the bad times came. As they would. For that matter, perhaps he had shot too fast. Oh God, *if he had missed—*

"Don't mean a thing," the policeman said. "Always work out that way. We make up for it in the hospital by just sticking you in the anteroom a few minutes longer. There's so much dead time we can always pick it up there. Forget it; you're going good."

That was easy enough for the policeman to say; he would be quit of the game—dismantled, that is—in a matter of hours. Carson had to live with it, he reminded himself, had to qualify. "The crowd," he said. "I should have talked to the crowd."

"No point to that. They always overreact; makes them shaky. Don't worry about it; anything you do is applesauce from here on in. You placed the fire real good. I don't have cigarettes. I don't believe in them—"

"I enjoyed doing it. I enjoyed shooting him. You know—"

"This smoking's a harmful, dangerous habit. Shortens life, tightens the lungs. You take a tip from me and find another habit. You got a lot of responsibility now, what with doing so well and all."

"I'm doing okay?" Carson said. "Really?"

"Doing like almost all of them. The usual. No better or worse. How can you not flunk this, particularly when you say you liked shooting the guy? Trouble with all of you, you think you're the center of things. Well you ain't."

"Are you?"

"No more talk now. We've talked enough. We're not supposed to talk anymore and so I won't." The policeman closed his eyes. "Don't try to bolt, though; you do that and I'd have to make a move or something."

Carson settled for that, not that he had much of an alternative. Still, there were obvious limits to that kind of conversation. He pressed his spine into the cushions, feeling the sun refracting through the windows, whack into the panes of his face; the smell of turning autumn piped in through the air conditioner in the front. There was little communication these days for him, it had nothing to do with disobedient robots (who at best were only a symptom), but with the central things. Like, when you came right down to it, it was a pretty peculiar ritual. Past the exaltation now, he found himself thinking that there must have been a better way of qualification; even institutions could possess manners if not sense. He thought of bringing that up to the policeman just to see what he was programmed to respond in *this* situation, but before he could, they were at the emergency entrance of the hospital, doors flicking outward, shouts in the air. The policeman nudged him unpleasantly. "Out," he said.

"Couldn't we pick up the five minutes by just sitting—"

He felt metal against him. "Out," the policeman said, and Carson moved. He stood balancing awkwardly on the cobblestones, moving toward the entrance. "Not that way, you ass," the policeman said, slamming his back with a club. "The service entrance. You want to get knocked out right here?" Others came around them then: prostheses garbed to look like more policemen and press. Obscurely shamed, Carson scuttled through side doors. They tossed him into a huge, high room and closed the door on him, tossing a package of cigarettes and matches through the high transom, and he heard keys turning. Then, for some time, he stood in the dimness, smoking and watching the sun turn gray, turn brown, merge into the myriad colors of night. Just like the nation. Outside, he could hear screams, scuffles, clatters, a cry. He supposed that the worst part was coming now and he wondered if he was ready for it. Although he had been completely oriented, they had not made him realize how rough, how really rough, it could be toward the end. But then it would have to be. The materials, as they had told him, were central. That was the point.

After a time a functionary came in; an obscure, mechanical cross between priest, government clerical worker and footman; perhaps it was their technological mockery. "Well," it said, sighing and lighting a cigarette—this was a different kind of prostheses, obviously—"here we go again, I guess. This must be it, right now."

"Already?" Carson said. Despite the anticipation, the attenuated despair which had crept upon him soon to be allayed, the shaking, the wonder, the *responsibility* ... despite all of this he did not want it at finality. "Can't we wait?"

"Sorry," the robot said, and something close to sympathy lit its clenched features. *I am not a mere device. I suffer*, the cunningly realistic filaments of the eyes seemed to be saying. "We have to move ahead. We're actually running about ten minutes behind now, they picked up too much." It shrugged, moved in on him. "Mr. Carson, I must announce, with sorrow but with solemnity that due to the tragic death, etc., I must advise that you are the—"

"No," Carson said. "Oh, no. Please wait."

"You will have to meet the widow now, of course. She's outside, waiting for you; I'll bring her in. Mr. Carson, you are—"

"*Please*," he said. "*Please*."

But, it was too late. Oh, boy, was it ever too late. The robot said what it had to say then and the widow entered sneezing and all of them went to the airport together in a clutch and they threw him into the plane and inaugurated him.

And so he woke up then; woke up screaming in his coffin, screaming at the million eyes taped inside the wood. The eyes that peered at him knew better than anything else what was going on and he watched his reflection floating in the tank, thinking—in that first return to consciousness—*really now, there must be other ways to break in a public official these days; guilt is guilt, but this is too much, too much.* But they were coming at him from all sides, now, the technicians were running, running, clapping him on the back, pulling out the tensors and the wires and the cords and the needles and he was unable to preserve that cold moment of clarity; instead, as they unplugged him and let him loose like a doll from the tank he only sighed and straightened. And filled then, filled with the stimulants they were pouring into him, he allowed them to take him out restored and with more than a shadow of the old bouncing, bobbing, glorious confidence, he burst free alone into a full run, went back to the White House, went back to his office and decided that the price was almost worth the election, maybe, you never could be sure. At any rate, next week he would have finished six months in office and they would cut the treatments down to one a week. That was to hope for.

THE END

IN THE POCKET

AND OTHER S-F STORIES

BARRY N. MALZBERG

Writing as K. M. O'Donnell

For my daughter, Erika Cornell

IN THE POCKET

I will go into the core and, striking, take the sickness out. I will do this with humility because I am merely a Messenger. My enemy is metastases, my cause their expulsion, my sin is the vanity of pride, my future the casting of burdens. I am a messenger.

THEIR OATH

Yeah, they fill you full of that crap. Oaths, pledges, procedures, the mask of spirituality. By the time you get out of the Institute, if you're lucky, you can't think, much less feel. I'm one of the unlucky ones, of course. I don't believe a word of it.

No sir, I do not and I challenge anyone to tell me that this is anything other than a menial job, mere hand-labor and to hell with the pretensions. It's a vocational skill but, being the way they are outside, the less important you are, the more self-important they try to make you. It's a question of social control. The hell with them.

When I got through with lower school I had nothing to do, no mind to think with, no money to pay the difference. It was either the forces, of course, or tech training. I was wild for the forces—there's a whole incendiary MOS opening up which fascinates me—but my old man opted for the tech training. "Cure cancer," he said, "you don't have to be a slob all your life, you can make something of yourself. You'll be a professional if you're lucky enough to get into the Institute."

Lucky enough to get into the Institute! The Institute has a full-time recruiting staff doing nothing but scouring the inner cities for people like me; the Institute offers an enlistment bonus, no less, as my old man would have known perfectly well if he was, unfortunately, not literate. He found out, though. He appropriated the bonus himself and took off. There is some moderate justice in the world, however. He died of cancer not six months ago and due to my manipulations, he was refused treatment. I hear that it was an agonizing death. Although we are manual laborers, messengers have their small prerogatives to exercise.

So, I went to the Institute. For two years, emerging with a drill and a diploma. Learned to stand the reduction of the Hulm Projector, learned to move with cunning, a miniscule, hidden dwarf in the alleys of the veins, arteries, muscles, organs, etc. Learned how to burn it out, learned the strange quiescent beauty of the islands of metastases. Even took a little rhetoric and a little composition so that I could express myself decently. (But all the messengers, when they quit, are selling the rights to their stories. Too much competition. There's no future in this.)

The technical aspects were easy to master. On the psychology they fell down a little. I didn't learn until I went into the practice myself about the depersonalizing effects of cancer, the way the victim becomes merely an extension of the tumor and the burning-out is often an excision of self. When I told this to one of the interns he gave me a numb look, began to talk about my sticking to my function. A messenger is only a certain kind of orderly after all. But when you get down in the pocket, you begin to think: how can you not think?

Listen you: I know. I know the scars and souls, I know what afflicts. Body in your blood, form in your viscera, I have touched your dreary secrets, their dark possibilities, have wounded and restored them with the drill, have felt their convulsions, seen their thoughts swimming past me, clotted in the swollen blood. I know all there is to know about humanity: I wander into the intestines two or three times a day and, chuckling, dissemble. How can I not think? And the projection hurts. The body needs space to contain the soul, one does not contain two inches easily. This is a theory I have developed. How can one have a soul in tissue the component size of a small guppy? This too I think about.

This is the introduction to my story, the opening to my secret. Stay with me, with me. You will purchase second serial rights yet. I am an unusual messenger. I know all about the transference of guilt.

I want to tell you about Yancey if I may. Listen to me: Yancey is eighty-three, eighty-four years old, as shriveled without as he is porous within and not three days ago I myself, Blount, burned the metastases out of him, incurring the usual risks, the standard humiliations. I am entitled therefore to tell you about him, far more entitled than Yancey is to tell me about me. I have suffered. I am not your usual messenger. But Yancey talks interminably, irresistibly, the drenching flow making almost impossible the clean incision of silence. The bastard.

Ah, the bastard! He is full: full of statements, platitudes, small explosions of pique and all he must share with me. Mostly, they have to do with the newfound purity of his body (which, monstrously, he equates with a purification of soul). When he came in last week he had neither soul nor body but lay staring at the ceiling with eyes the shape of doors, working out the slow beat of his mortality, ignorant of what I was going to do for him. Those were the good times, of course, although I was not permitted to know that. I was his orderly as well and chose to ask him how he was and all he would whimper was "terrible, just terrible son, leave me sleep, leave the flesh crumple." But I woke up that morning in September and went before the projector, dwindled and went inside his inert form to clean him out right proper. It was in his liver, yellow and orange, busy as death. I took care of it. I took out the lovely silken metastasis, clutching it to my tiny chest and dropped it in the intern's tray. Now Yancey is full of rhetoric.

What does this prove?

It must prove something. This is what I hold to myself tighter than metastases: there is some purpose in this beyond what I see. But what can it possibly come to? He comes in, like all of them, even the women, riddled cheek-through-jowl and I take care of him nicely and all of a sudden I become an object of his reformation. As if an impure man could possibly perform my tasks!

I'm going to kill the son of a bitch.

There's no alternative to it. They permit me one death a year under the contract, possessed of an understanding that staggers me. We must kill to live. I thought that this was not true. But I see it now. One cannot excise without giving back to the good, gold Earth.

Yes, yes, I am his orderly and after hours tonight I may creep into his dark with the drill reversed, restore where I laid waste, restore a thousandfold. Then I will emerge, go before the projector again and sit by his side, waiting for the morning. When they come, they will see what I have done, clear it on their records to make sure that I have not exceeded my quota. (I have not, Yancey is my first.) They will remove the corpus. He has no relatives.

He's next. I think they know it already, these doctors and nurses and administrators, because they are staying away from me with a look that connotes surprised respect. They know when a messenger is about to go over that line. There have been no conversations in these halls today, no sarcasm, none of that easy, feigned viciousness with which the living (they think) discharge themselves from the dead (they hope). So they must know.

Yancey doesn't, of course. He lacks the intimation as all of them do, pre- or post-operative. Locked in his condition or its release. He calls it the "twitchings of recovery."

"Clean in God's hands, son?" he asks me, "or does the filth and decay of your function possess your soul; is your mind raddled and ruined? Corruption, corruption, but remember that the mind breaks first and only then the body; boy, you may be dying inside already with your filthy job and like that. Untenant your soul, throw away your drill, resign and let the breezes go free before you are incurable."

This is what he says to me.

(Knowing that: I know he is senile. I know. This has nothing to do with it. His cancer was not senile. It was bright, quivering, reaching for the heart's moon, full of joy and first seeking. I am not concerned with the condition of the container.)

Oh God stay with me. Oh God, I'm almost through it now and ready for the photographs. Listen, listen: it is night, darkest night. In that cunning I steal upon Yancey. It is late in his corridors as well, illuminated in the metastatic loss only by phosphorescent dust and faint refractions from quarters below. In his room, in his night littered with prefiguration and doom, murky to the sounds of his stirring, Yancey's gut is where I laid it last, turned slightly to the side. I hear murmurs. The blood's whiskey travels home. It bathes my knife.

I do it with the knife rather than drill-reversal; it is the soundest, most painful way. One thrust into the stomach, another turn past the arteries, finally into the pancreas itself hearing the shocked recession of the blood. When I am quite done I emerge, perch on the pillow, look at him. He has fallen heavily on his back, his eyes diminishing.

"Why do, son?" he says with what I suppose is his last breath. "Could you not escape your own corruption?"

I try to point out that it is the other way: that, in fact, it was my unassailability which broke *his* corruption but my tiny lungs resist as inflation takes over. By the time I can speak again he is dead on the floor. And I am pleased, pleased.

And then, from deeply within, I feel my own new tumor, full-come and dancing for joy.

For joy in the forever dark.

GEHENNA

a

Edward got on the IRT downtown local at 44th Street for Greenfield Gardens. The train stopped at 33rd Street, 27th Street, 17th Street and Christopher Circle. As it turned out, he met his wife at this part.

It was a standard Greenfield Gardens all-of-us-are-damned party; she was sitting in a corner of the room, her feet bare, listening to a man with sad mustaches play a mandolin. Edward went over to say hello to her. She looked at him with vague disinterest and huddled closer to the mandolin player who turned out, on further inspection, to be her date for the night. But Edward was persistent—in his youth his parents had warned him that his chief weakness was a lack of self-confidence and he had taken the warning to heart—and later that night, he got her address.

Two days later he showed up with a shopping cart filled with gourmet food and asked her if she would help him eat. She shrugged and introduced him to her cats. Three weeks later they slept with one another for the first time and the week after that the mandolin player and he had a fight at the end of which the mandolin player wished them well and left her life forever. Edward and Julie were engaged only a few days after that and within the month he married her in Elktown.

They went back to New London and started life together. He gave up mathematics and became an accountant, she gave up painting and took to going to antique shops once a week, bringing back objects every now and then. It was not a bad life, even if it had started out, perhaps, a bit on the contrived side.

Three years later, Edward opened the door and found Julie playing with their year-old daughter, shaking a rattle and putting it deep in the baby's mouth. The scene was a pleasing one and he felt quite contented until she looked up at him and he saw that she was crying.

He put down his briefcase and asked her what was wrong, she told him that their life had been an utter waste. Everything she wanted she had not gotten; everything she had gotten she did not want. She was surrounded by things, she told him, she had prepared herself as an adolescent to despise. And the worst of it was that it was all her own fault. She talked of divorce, but only by inference.

Realizing that the fault was all his, Edward said that he would check up on some suburbs, get themselves a nice-sized house and some activities during the day. And so he did—he did all of it—and they were very happy for a while if gravely in debt ... until he came home from the circus one night with his daughter and found that Julie, feet bare, had drowned herself in the bathtub.

b

Julie got on the IRT downtown local at 41st Street for Green Town. The train stopped at 32nd Street, 24th Street, 13th Street and the Statue of Christ. As it turned out, she met her husband at this party. It was a standard Green Town we-are-finding-ourselves-party and he came in late, dressed all wrong, his hands stretching his pockets out of shape. He was already very drunk.

She was there with a boy named Vincent who meant little to her but who played the mandolin beautifully and sang her songs of loss and love. If the songs were derivative and the motions a trifle forced ... well, it was a bad period for both of them and she took what comfort she could. But when her husband-to-be came and spoke to her she could see beyond his embarrassment and her misery that a certain period of her life and of the mandolin player's was over. He wanted her telephone number but because she didn't believe in telephones, she gave him her address instead while Vincent was in the bathroom. She felt very unsure of herself.

Three days later, while she was still in bed, he came with flowers and candy and told her that he could not forget. With a smile, she invited him in and the first time was very good ... well, it was better than it had been with Vincent. Edward was gone when Vincent came later that evening and she told Vincent that she had been lusting after gardens all her life; now, at least, she had found a keeper. Then she told him what she and Edward had done. He wept and cursed, he told her that she had betrayed everything of importance, the small reality which they had created ... but she was firm. She said that lines must be drawn for once and all between the present and the possible.

After that she saw nothing of either Vincent or Edward for a week. Then Edward came with a suitcase. He said he had moved out of his parents' home and had come to marry her. She did not marry him right away but they lived together for some weeks. One evening, just like that, she found a note in her mailbox saying that Vincent had committed suicide.

She never found out who had sent the note and she never told Edward a thing. But a week later they were married in Yonkers and went to a resort upstate where they were happy for a few days.

They came back and bought furniture for her flat, he dropped out of astronomy and became an industrial research assistant. For a long time, her days were simple—they were, as a matter of fact, exactly like the days she had known just before she met Edward—and the nights were good, pretty good anyway. Then she became pregnant in a difficult sort of way and eventually the child, Ann, was born ... a perfect child with delicate hands and a musical capability. Edward said that they would have to find a real home now but she said that the old life could keep up, at least until Ann was ready for school. But one night he came home early, very excited, and told her that he had found them a home in the suburbs. She told him that this was fine. He said that he was now perfectly happy and she said the same.

They left York Harbor for the suburbs and were content for a while what with car pools and bridge and whatnot, as well as good playmates and a healthy environment for Ann. But Edward, for no reason, began to get more and more depressed and one morning, when she awoke to find his bed empty, she went into the bathroom to find him slumped over the bathtub, his wrists open, blood all over the floor, a faint, fishlike look of appeal in his stunned and sinking eyes.

c

Vincent got on the IRT downtown local at 39th Street for the City of Greens. The train stopped at 36th Street, 31st Street, 19th Street and Christ Towers. As it turned out, he lost his girl at this party. It was a standard City of Greens look-how-liberated-we-are-now kind of party and it was a strange thing that the two of them should go separately since the 39th Street stop was the nearest to their two apartments. But she believed in maintaining her privacy in small, damning ways.

She was sad that night, sad with a misery he could not touch, much less comprehend; it had been a good time for both of them but now something was wrong. They had been going together for the four months since she broke off with his closest friend and he played her songs on his mandolin, promises of lost and terrible loves, promises of a better future, songs of loneliness, and she once had loved it. She had said that he gave her a soul in music.

So he was playing songs for her at the party this night, not even wanting to be there, hoping that they could go back to her flat and put the mandolin beside the bed while they made love, when he saw that she was looking at another man in the corner of the room: a man of a different sort from the rest of them, since he was not drunk. The man was looking back at her and in that moment, Vincent knew that he was quite doomed.

To prove it to himself, he left his instrument on her knee and went to the bathroom. When he came back they sprang apart and he knew that the man had her address. There was nothing to do, of course, but to leave the party and he helped her with her coat, put his mandolin over his shoulder and led her down the stairs. Halfway to the street he told her that she had betrayed them. She did not answer for a while, then murmured that she could not help herself, much less another person ... but she would make this night the best of all the nights she had given him.

And so she did, so she did all night and into the dawn while her cat stroked the mandolin, making wooden sounds, rolling the instrument around and around on the floor. In the morning he left her and took his clothing, and then he did not see her at all for a few days. When he came back there was a different look on her face and the man was in her bed, lying on the sheets.

He did not care—he had lost any capacity for surprise when she had come from his closest friend broken enough to need him. He only wanted to meet this man named Edward who might become his closest friend too, but the man did not want any part of this and there was a very bad scene, a scene that ended only when Vincent hurt the man and left him sobbing on the floor.

He never saw either of them again, victory or not. He had no need to; everything that needed proof had been proven. But he thought of her very often and many years later when he killed himself by leaping from a stranger's penthouse, his last thought as he felt the dry York City wind and saw the street coming at him was of his old mandolin, her solemn cat, and the night she had given him her best because she had already partaken of his worst.

d

The child, Ann—who had very sensitive and gentle hands—became a young woman who was drawn at odd moments to the windows of pawn shops in which she saw old mandolins, and once, for a week, she took lessons. But she had no money and less patience—those were her biggest faults along with a lack of assertiveness—and she returned the rented mandolin.

Now, she is going to a party in Greenwich Village. She does not know what will happen to her. The night is still a mystery. She is still young enough to hear screams in the wind ... tonight may hold some finality although one never knows. See her. She is in the Times Square station of the IRT; the engineer sounds a song in the density.

She counts the stops, smiling. The train stops at 34th Street, 28th Street, 23rd Street, 18th Street and 14th Street. Now she is at Christopher Street and Sheridan Square.

AH, FAIR URANUS

I

Coming in deep on the first orbit, looking at the gray and muddled surfaces of the planet which remind him of nothing so much as the insides of a grenade casing, Needleman has a pure moment of satisfaction: he has made Uranus. No matter what happens to him from this point onward, no matter how successful or disastrous the mission, they cannot say of him that he did not accomplish the primary objective which was to reach this fair and beautiful, this serene and floating outpost in the skies. *The sons of bitches thought I didn't really have it*, Needleman mumbles, shaking his head at the expanse of the plains, popping stimulants into his mouth, *well, this will show them*. It is only a pity that he cannot at this moment use the contacts to tell them what he thinks of them, how he can meet their contempt and hatred with a contempt of his own which goes far beyond even their capacity to assimilate but that would not be fair, of course, the contact, rare and valuable, must be kept open only for official communication and officially speaking the sensors alone have informed them of the orbit, the success, the connection. Everything else would be a superfluity, an extension of the already known and in any event, Needleman thinks, changing mental gears, he can show them by his silence that he is better than all of them, that he can meet contempt with grace, laughter with contentment, bitterness with humility. Everything is relative. It is all relative. It is a question of adjustments. Needleman closes all the visors, turns the phones to off and settles himself on the couch for an eight-hour nap to complete the first orbit. There is nothing to be done until he comes around again. Dreaming he thinks of sheep and flowers, trickles of water in the wood, the deep oaken sound of a stricken moose, calling to him from a departed hillside.

II

Needleman's mission is certainly rare and dangerous, his connection to Uranus is the last best hope of humanity and if he fails all of mankind will as well. The evil and dangerous L'Lar people, scourge of several galaxies, have been conducting raids upon the Solar System for the last fifty years, their intention clearly to expurgate humanity from the third planet so that all of Sol's system may be theirs to continue their terrible and inhuman path of conquest through the galaxy. They have already planted attack centers on Mercury and Venus, Mars and Jupiter, Saturn and most of the asteroids, avoiding in their terrible cunning actual contact with Earth which, lacking the proper technological devices, can only wait helplessly while the seeds of annihilation are sown, not being able to send its own courageous armies into space to fight the L'Lar at their source. For reasons best known to themselves (simple arrogance is suspected or perhaps their astronomers are incompetent), the L'Lar have left alone Uranus, Neptune and Pluto and it is to Uranus, the nearest unoccupied outpost, to which Needleman has been sent with his depth charges and cosmic bombs, dreams and terrible devices, to set up the counterattack upon the dreaded L'Lar. It was feared that the instant the ship was launched into space the surveying equipment of the L'Lar would have deduced both it and its purposes and have blasted it out of the sky but somehow the observation of the enemy seems inacute; Needleman has reached Uranus in three Earth days and nights without intervention. There is the question of terror of course and all the way past the orbit of Jupiter Needleman had sung songs, the songs which had been popular in his youth with certain side-excursions to the classical repertoire intermixed with an obscenity or two. But by Jupiter or two million miles beyond, when it became apparent to him for the first time that he might actually accomplish the goal of Uranus, all of Needleman's terror had dropped away like a cloak and now he dreams in silence, his pastoral imagery his emblem of courage or so he would think if he were conscious. Four tranquilizers have made sure that he is not.

III

The actual motives of the L'Lar were never quite deduced in the vast Center where Needleman worked and which was for various reasons the only institution on Earth thought capable of making such a judgment. The technological cadre talked much of entropy and simultaneous evolution and the finiteness of space but were never quite as convincing as the metaphysicians (in 2212, by Government edict, five metaphysicians had been assigned to the Center on a provisional basis and since then, through primogenitus and the Rule of Cultures had expanded to an appreciable if distinct minority) who wrote long treatises on the interweaving of Original Sin and Entropy which caused all kinds of difficulties in the National Councils since they raised certain issues which under no circumstances did the Council feel itself competent to solve. Needleman himself tried to think about it as little as possible; by the best calculations of the mathematical staff of the Center it would be at least thirty years until the deadly L'Lar made their actual attack on Earth proper and he figured that that was time enough to take care of his basic needs and even lead a satisfactory life, besides that he was on a twenty-year assignment to the Center and it was difficult in the nature of things to look too far ahead. Nevertheless, from the time that he found that the Mission devolved upon him and that upon his shoulders and no others might the fate of mankind rest he found that he had been thinking about it constantly. The least that could be asked of a man with such an important task is that he have a certain sense of perspective and history, the trouble was that the more he thought about it, the more Needleman thought that the metaphysicians were right and this was particularly disturbing because he was not even quite sure what Original Sin and Entropy (with a capital "E") was exactly about. "Don't worry about it," the Director had said, "your training is fundamentally technological and if you stay in that line everything will work out satisfactorily. The important thing is to make sure that the charges are set up properly, if we ever get you into orbit we don't want a lashback." Needleman had thanked the Director very much, it was certainly something to know that the Center would take care of the background if he took care of the actions but he was really not quite as simpleminded as he once thought he had been and the thing was that he could not get one thought from his mind: that possibly the L'Lar (looking at things from their side of the table) were right and that there might be good and sufficient reasons, in the universal scheme of things, for the Earth and mankind to be put out of action at the present time. All through the journey these speculations had stayed with him, had formed counterpoint to his popular songs, had shaped and structured even his fear, had worked their way into his dreams and now, even under the multiple dose of codeine, waiting with the more circumstantial part of him for the blind orbit to end, he cannot quite keep them out of his mind. *Why not?* a merry idiot voice has been asking Needleman for two hundred million miles, *why not indeed? They probably have their own problems. The L'Lar may have run out of space. They have a definite right to live too.*

IV

Like most of the employees in his niche in the Center Needleman has had a very controlled life; nevertheless he was permitted a Love

Relationship in the requisite time and circumstances and this Relationship left, perhaps, more of an effect upon him than was strictly provided for through the code. (On the other hand possibly not. He has no idea of the limits of approved behavior, precisely because, behaviorally speaking, he has always functioned as they told him to.) Wrapped with him tightly in the night, lurching toward an outcome as complex and involuted as any he had ever known, Needleman had felt himself on the verge of a vast understanding, had suspected that if he could sustain this lurching, these feelings, this connection for only an instant or so more he might get through and to the other side and see things as he never had before but time and again he would tumble through, wheezing, staggering to some climax that was more like an expectoration and then, inevitably, it would all begin again. He was told that he was functioning within normal limits and when the requisite adjustments had been made it had been taken away but to this moment Needleman is still not sure of it, not sure of many things, not sure as to whether what he touched was an extension of himself or something serene and finite, corporeal and mysterious, as far from him as the other side of Uranus, never to be known except in the pictures he made during the lurching.

It has affected his whole life, this mystery. He knows that it (and nothing else which the Center provided) has anything to do with the L'Lar who only came after the fact and as an unforeseen intervention but he cannot get over the feeling that all of it was, somehow, part of a scheme, a scheme which devolved upon him in personal and intricate fashion and which he will settle in one way or the other when the charges are lit. He does not know which way he will light them.

V

Coming toward the end of his orbit and the sleep, Needleman has another kind of dream although it may not be a dream, perhaps it is a hallucination or an actual contact with the L'Lar. The chief of that race stands before him, infinitely wise, infinitely patient, infinitely pained, wearing the robes of his high station and a crown of fire. "Forget this, forget all of it," the Chief says, extending a tentacle (or maybe it is a hand) toward him in an encompassing and gentle way, "all of it was vanity, the Center, the studies, the manipulation, the Mission, the whole nagging constancy of it nothing but a dream and now at last this space an awakeness. It means nothing, I tell you, forget that it ever happened, float around Uranus now and then turn the charges the other way because there is no point to any of this, no point I tell you, you see only a microscopic slant of the spectrum. We know things we can never tell you; we come from a scheme much vaster than yours, in that scheme all motive prevails and in that motive a kind of conclusion. Listen, be sensible Needleman, from your point of view we may look like the enemy but believe me, from ours, we're pure protagonists." The Chief winks, seems to shift in the light of Uranus then drifts backward and somewhat to the right. "Of course I have to leave it in your hands," he said, "the whole fate and outcome, I mean. If you want to set the charges against us you can blow us out of your sky and that's the truth. On the other hand you can do it the other way and inaugurate a new era of peace and progress, galactically speaking. It's all up to you, Needleman old friend, the decision has to be yours but I tell you this much, do not take it casually."

"You don't understand," Needleman says, trying to make it as clear as possible because he knows that this dialogue is somehow central to the fate of humanity to say nothing of his own life and if he does not get it right now he never will, "I mean I'm simply not made for these easy choices. I can't take it one way or the other way, all simple and clear. Besides, the charges might misfire either way and then what? I might do exactly the opposite of what I wanted to do. You can't talk me into one way or the other, though."

"Consider your training," the Chief of the L'Lar says, "and you'll find that if nothing else it counsels you toward easy dichotomies" and on that ambiguous statement he vanishes, popping into the air like a fine mist or the body of Needleman's lover when he felt the first seizures of his own climax and Needleman finds himself quite alone and quite conscious on the couch as the craft swings past the first orbit and into the second. Uranus, fair Uranus, coming through all the windows of his cockpit and it is lovely—ah, God, it is lovely!—to look at Uranus this way on this fine morning in 2315, no better place to be than circling Uranus with all the wonderful fate and testament of mankind riding on your back and Needleman stumbles to his feet and goes to the machinery, finds that the machinery is ready to fire, mumbles to himself in contentment as he sets the charges, then picks up the contact—the hell with power loss—to tell them exactly, precisely, definitely what he is going to do ... and as he begins talking the very walls of the craft seem to curve and attenuate, almost as if they were listening (as the whole damned universe must) to Needleman's analysis of the final sense of it and what a man must do to cope.

NOTES JUST PRIOR TO THE FALL

Simmons. Simmons the horseplayer. That horseplayer, Simmons. Let us consider him for the moment if we might: he is leaning against the rail at Aqueduct surrounded (he feels) by wheeling birds and doom, clutching a handful of losing pari-mutuel tickets in his left hand. His right hand is occupied with his hair; he is trying ceaselessly to comb it into place, a nervous gesture which caused one of his drinking companions (he has no friends) to call him years ago "Simmons the Dresser," a nickname which, unfortunately, never stuck since his other drinking companions knew his habits too well. It is 1:43 now, some twelve minutes before scheduled post-time for the second race, and Simmons Is desperately seeking information from the tote board. He has already lost the first race. The results posted indicate that the horse on which he bet finished third. Simmons did not have the horse to show or across the board. He is a win bettor only, some years ago having read in a handicapping book that only the win bettor has a chance to retain an edge and that place and show were for amateurs and old ladies. He does not know who wrote this book or where it is today, but ever since he read this information he has never bet other than to win. He is not sure whether or not this has made much difference but intends to draw up some statistics, sooner or later. He keeps a careful record of his struggles; the fact is that he never totals. (For those who are interested I say that Simmons has lost slightly less than he might have otherwise lost had he bet place and show, but the difference in percentage terms is infinitesimal and the psychological benefits of having more tickets to cash would have well outweighed the minor additional losses.)

Simmons has, then, blown the first race. He has, for that matter, lost seven races in a row, going back to his score on the second race yesterday, a dash for two-year-maiden fillies that produced a seven-length victory for an odds-on favorite. Simmons collected $7.50 for his $5.00 ticket on that one; before then there is also a succession of losing races, although here, perhaps, Simmons loses his sense of precision. He is not exactly sure how many races he has lost recently or how long the losing streak has gone on. All that he can suggest at this moment is that he is deeply into what he has popularly termed a Blue Period and that his situation will have to markedly change for the better shortly or he will be forced to the most serious and investigatory questions about his life and career. Such as, what is he doing here? And what did he hope to gain? And why did he make the famous decision some months ago to have it over and done with the horses once and for all and to make them pay for his psychological investments? And so on. Simmons will phrase these questions to himself in a low, frenetic mumble, somewhere midway between sotto voce and a sustained shriek, and those people in his presence at the time the inquiries begin will look at him peculiarly or not at all, depending upon custom or interest. If he chooses to ask them of himself at the track, he will incite no response at all. There are, after all, so many questioners at the track. The churches—and I know a little bit about this subject—have nothing to compare with the track in the metaphysical area.

"Sons of bitches," Simmons says, but he says this without conviction or hope; it is merely a transitional statement, in the category of throat-clearing or manipulation of the genitals, and means, hence, absolutely nothing. The fact is that Simmons is not clear as to the identity of the sons of bitches, and if he were confronted by them incontrovertibly now or several races in the future, he would not quite know what to say. Manners would overcome reason. "You could have helped me a little with that four horse in the first," he would probably point out mildly, or, "Gee, I wish that the kid on my eight horse in yesterday's starter-handicap had tried to stay out of the switches." Overall, an apologetic tone would certainly extrude. The fact is—and it is important that we understand our focus at the outset—that Simmons is both mild and polite, also that he expects little beyond what he has already received and that when he is talking about the sons of bitches ... well, it would be naïve and simplistic to say that he refers mainly to himself; but as one who is extremely close to the situation, I can suggest that part of this is valid. (Part of it is not. Everything is irretrievably complex. This must be kept carefully in mind. The distance between a winning and tail-end horse in a field, any kind of field, is at the most ten seconds. Ten seconds upon which rests the ascription of all hope and, in certain cases, human lives. One must be respectful of any institution which can so carefully narrow the gap between intimation and disaster.)

"Sons of bitches," Simmons says again and opens the copy of the *Morning Telegraph* which he is holding to full arm's length and begins to look, with neither anticipation nor intensity, at the experts' selections for the second race. Because this is both a Tuesday and cloudy, Simmons is able to perform this gesture, articulate his feelings in isolation and quiet. There is no one within several yards of him in any direction, and Simmons, in addition, having long staked out exactly this spot at the upper stretch, feels that he can conduct himself here exactly as he would in his own home. The fact is, although he would find it painful to admit this, that Simmons despises company for private reasons and is able to find his fullest sense of identity at the race-track precisely because it both heightens and renders somehow sinister his sense of isolation. He knows that he would never be able to get away with his rhetoric in a social or subway situation, and he would not dare to do it at home because he has long been conditioned to the belief—alas— that any man who talks sprightly to himself in his own quarters is probably insane.

"Ah, God, there's no percentage," Simmons now mutters, a favorite expression, as he looks at the selection pages of the *Telegraph*. As always, this ominous newspaper renders him little comfort, since its selectors, like all selectors everywhere, are oriented toward favorites or logical choices and tell him only what a sane, conservative advisor (Simmons envisions him as a portly, rather puffy man who inhabits the clubhouse, has a mild cardiac condition, and calls all trainers "Willie") would offer if this advisor were, for some reason, to take an interest in Simmons and his plight and attempt to turn the situation around. Simmons, who once wanted exactly such a friend, now hates the specter of the Advisor, feels that the Advisor—like Clocker Lawton, Clocker Rowe and Clocker Powell—simultaneously embodies and parodies everything about successful followers of racing that he has come to hate and feels that he might as well kill him on sight. He has, therefore, transferred his revulsion to the selector pages, which he now turns away from with a moan. He goes instead to the past performances which he regards with a glazed and horrified expression as he comes slowly to realize that he has seen them all before, most of the night in fact, and that he knows less about differentiating the horses than he did at the beginning.

For the first time this afternoon, it occurs to Simmons that he might be losing his mind. Meanwhile, the bugler walks to the front of the paddock a hundred yards down the track and blows that call to indicate that the jockeys are to mount their horses. It is almost time for the field in the second race to come out.

Simmons has lost twenty dollars on the first race. He has lost two hundred and sixty dollars during his most recent losing streak. He has lost fifteen hundred and eighty dollars and forty cents (plus expenses) since he made his Career Decision some three months and sixteen days ago. I offer these statistics without prejudice, and only because, unlike Simmons, I am in a position to amass them, reconcile them with a larger scheme of possibilities, and see them in what might be tastefully called a metaphysical perspective. They cause me neither pain nor pleasure to recite: fifteen hundred, eighty dollars and forty cents is, after all, less than the total war budget for some sixtieths of a second, and can be considered in a relativistic sense (by which I do not strictly abide) to be an insubstantial amount. Simmons, on the other hand, confronted by these figures, would be unable to speak them distinctly. It all depends, as you see, although I am not saying that my position is necessarily superior to that of Simmons. Unlike him, I take no emotions from event, this being, I am led to understand by the philosophy I have studied, a serious defect. I hold my own judgment in abeyance; certainly, over the past few months, Simmons has taught me a great deal.

Now he sighs, mutters, stretches, curses. He wishes, of course, to make a bet on the second race (he always bets on every race, being unable to cope with the fear that he would otherwise know of missing out on the Ultimate Coup) but has no firm choice, cannot, pity him, arrive at that careful, judicious balance of speed, windage, condition, manipulation, desire, weight, and intrinsic class which is the key to approaching the variables of even the cheapest claiming sprint. Or, as he would put it, he cannot seem to find an angle. It is at this moment, therefore, that I decide to make my entrance, seeing little enough profit in delay and realizing that the Simmons who needs my help at 1:46 may have a definite superiority over the Simmons who could reject it at 3:10. For the fact is that I see already the pattern of the afternoon, and it is not pleasant. (Which is not to say that it is unmanageable. Only Simmons would think that the unpleasant is necessarily disastrous.)

"Look," I say without introduction. "Do you want a play in this race? Because I think I can give you something interesting."

"Oh, boy," Simmons says, looking up and then rapidly down toward his newspaper. (I should point out that this is not the first time I have approached him so abruptly.) "Oh, God, it isn't you again, is it?" Simmons' initial resistance toward my appearance has been somewhat blunted, but the fact remains that he finds me almost unacceptable. While his hold on sanity (I can attest) has never been in the least precarious, Simmons thinks that it is and that I am a manifestation of his breakdown. I have made progress in this area but not quite enough, and now, of course, there is not enough time. "I just don't want to listen," he says and covers his ears. Perhaps he is thinking of blinkers. "I don't want to hear any more of it. Losing is one thing, but this is another."

"Nonsense," I say and then address him with enormous tact and personal force. The covering of the ears means nothing. "We don't have time for overlong discussions and besides that I must warn you that unless you take some good advice quickly you will be verging on a truly massive disaster, one with overtones of violence and a sense of intrinsic loss more acute than any you have ever known. I am afraid that I must get to the simple gist of this. Bet the seven horse, win and place."

"Oh, God," Simmons says again, but obediently—there an enormous and satisfying submission to all horseplayers because the fact is that they need to be told exactly what to do—he opens the newspaper to the past performances and looks at the horse in question. "Salem? The number seven horse, Salem?"

"That's the one," I say and let my finger join his against the newsprint. The faint impression of the type slides against skin with an almost erotic smoothness. I can understand what is erroneously called the power of the printed word. "Win and place. Place and win." I try to speak distinctly. My time, after all, is not unlimited.

"But that's ridiculous," Simmons says. "This horse is already thirty-five to one on the board. He's the only maiden in the race, he hasn't shown anything since February at Tropical, and that was in a claimer two thousand dollars cheaper than this one. The jockey is a bad apprentice, the trainer is a known stiff, and the weight is the heaviest in the race. I don't see it. I just don't see it." It is well known that with such rationalizations about his marriage, Simmons walked out of his home four years ago and never returned. For this reason and others, I do not take his rationalizations seriously.

"Reason enough," I say. "He doesn't figure. That's the point I am trying to develop. It wouldn't be a good tip if it were logical, would it?"

At this moment, the bugler blows the second call and our conversation is halted. We stand in almost companionable quiet then while the announcement is made (I have always been suspicious of the involvement of the track announcer in the events he is describing, but that is another issue altogether), and the horses come onto the track, some of them with a curious skipping gait which indicates incipient lameness, others with a somnolent prance which might indicate either good spirits or the presence of undetectable drugs. The seven horse, a brown six-year-old gelding, moves somewhat ahead of the field and comes toward us, turns at a point in front of our section of the rail, and then, with some encouragement from outrider and jockey, both of whom are singing, breaks into a sidewise gallop which quickly carries him past the finish line and out of sight along the backstretch. The other horses follow less eagerly and at a cautious distance.

"Front bandages," Simmons says, "Front and rear. And he seemed a little rank, too. I don't know. I just don't know. Look, look, he's fifty to one." In his rising excitement—this is, to be sure, the very first tip I have given him, although on previous occasions I have sometimes gone so far as to offer advanced-handicapping advice—his hostility has vanished and his very disbelief seems to wave like a sheet between us punched with enough holes for random communication. "Ah, it's crazy, it's crazy," he says. "I mean, I'm willing to listen to anyone, but I just don't see it. Fifty to one, though." The tote board winks. "Sixty to one. Do you think?"

"I do not think," I say. "By the way, I can't stay any longer," and add something about probability currents and cross-angles of time which Simmons is expected to find obscure and to ignore. I leave him rapidly and in such a state of elemental self-absorption that I know he will hardly detect my absence and then only with an abstracted glare. For the fact is that I have put Simmons on to something.

I know that: I see all of the signs. As the horses gather in the upper stretch to talk things over a bit before getting into the dreaded starting gate (I am also privy to the emotions of horses, limited creatures but none the less poignant, at least to themselves), Simmons turns and begins to move at his own sidewise canter toward the pari-mutuel windows. Gasping slightly in my hurry to keep up—I am in rather poor physical condition as a result of my contemplative existence—I follow him, managing to join him only at the window itself, where Simmons joins a short line of ragged men, most of them pallid, who shuffle their feet and clutch their wallets while their twins ahead pass the window and scurry by, looking at the tickets they have bought with wonder. It is the ten-dollar win window, an excellent sign, because Simmons does almost all of his business at the two- and five-dollar slots. He does this, as he once explained to me, not because he wagers little but because he simply feels more comfortable at these more modest windows. Perhaps it is a question of his heritage or only the class system at work. In any event it is a fact—and I have witnessed this—that once Simmons bet fifty dollars on a horse to win and did so at the two-dollar window in the form of twenty-five tickets. He simply feels more in place there, the clerk's glare to the contrary. In that case, incidentally the horse won, profiting Simmons fifty-five dollars, something which he considered an excellent omen as well as a sign that his humility had been observed and respected in Higher Quarters. Nevertheless, he is now on the ten-dollar line.

"Got anything?" the man behind him asks. He does so in response to a certain stimulus which I have implanted midway between the medulla oblongata and the vas deferens, since I am curious about the confidentiality which Simmons feels in our relationship. But I have not been cautious technically, and there is a terrifying moment during which I fear the questioner might faint. Fortunately he does not, but the reasons he has worked out for betting his selection are now and will be irrevocably wiped from his mind.

"Nothing," Simmons mutters. "Oh, all right, the six, the six," he adds, "just got a tip out of the infield, but don't know if it's worth a damn. I'll stab, though." For an instant, I feel a jolt of horror. Has Simmons misunderstood me? Or already forgotten the advice? But then as he comes to the window, I understand that he is only being what he takes to be very cunning, and as he leans over, he makes the clerk lip-read the word seven. He has decided then to posture as a deaf-mute in order to protect his information, and this is safe since no ten-dollar clerk at this track has ever before seen him. As he now mouths *seven ten times*, the clerk returns that timeless, embracing nod of one who has seen everything—this look is also available in whorehouses but then only on reservation and for special customers—and punches out ten tickets. Simmons, the new deaf-mute, puts down a hundred-dollar bill (leaving him with only a few dollars and change) and takes the tickets, cupping them so that the man behind can only see his fine backhand, and then moves to the rear of the line. Pausing there, he verifies the number (something he always does, although his losing streak has now reached such proportions that when races are over he finds himself reaching for his tickets and praying that the clerk has made a mistake or that he, Simmons, has begun to lose his vision and did not verify properly) and then returns slowly toward his place on the rail, pausing for a brief cup of coffee, which he does not taste, although he can distinctly hear the clerk cursing him for not leaving the change from a quarter. I understand with disgust that Simmons will not visit the place windows, preferring to back up his bet with insistence rather than circumspection. It is an old failing.

He then goes on to his place on the rail, slightly more crowded now with only two minutes to post, but sufficiently uninhabited at the edges that he is able, without difficulty, to cleave out the yardage which he feels he needs as he prepares himself for the running. As he curls his hair, wipes his forehead (it is a cool day), runs a left hand absently over his genitals (his inner wrist catching the comforting bulge of the ticket in his trouser pocket), he begins a thin, shrieking monologue which he believes to be private although, of course, I am privy to every word. I listen to it with relish, delighted as always to see that my effects upon Simmons have not been imperceptible and that now, as in the past, I have the capacity to move him. Of course I have had to change many of my devices and manipulations in order to do so, but I have never lost that path of connection, and it is this, along with a few other things, that gives me hope. If I have not lost Simmons, then there is absolutely no saying what I might not someday gain, and in the bargain I have been able to keep abreast of his development. This is no mean accomplishment since Simmons has been even more variable within the last couple of years than in the past.

"Oh, you bastards," Simmons is saying, "oh you bastards, *please*, please give me this one; it's so little to ask, so little to ask. A hundred dollars, seventy-one now, that's seven thousand, seven thousand dollars, what's the difference? Who cares? What difference would it make? Favorites can win, longshots lose, longshots win, favorites lose, everyone gets out sooner or later. Oh, God, give me just this one and never again. The seven, the seven, just once the seven, what difference does it make to you, you dirty sons of bitches? But think of the difference it makes to *me*; a new chance, a new life, well, maybe the old life but certainly a lot better, a *lot* better, I deserve it. Oh, give this one to me now. *Eighty* to one now, oh, God, eight thousand dollars, maybe more, never less. Oh, please, please, it won't cost you a thing but think of what it means to me."

(There are two aspects to this monologue which I find objectionable. The first is that the main thrust of Simmons' appeal is to the sons of bitches rather than to the one who gave him the tip—that is to say me—and the second is that Simmons knows as well as I that were he to win eight thousand dollars, he would have no more idea of what to do with it than as to what to do with the hundred he has just bet. It is various and peculiar, peculiar and various, as they say, but it is the very *perversity* of Simmons and, by inference, humanity itself, which has always so involved me and, yes, made them lovable in my eyes. Who, other than themselves, would have ever conceived them?)

In any event, Simmons is now barely coherent. "Oh, I picked him, for God's sake, let me know that I still have my wits about me!" he moans and this, as everything else, I find amusing ... it is not the fact that my tip has so rapidly been transmuted into judgment that titillates me. No, it is something else; it has to do with the certainty of Simmons' conviction that, large or largest, massive things now work in the balance. This is an emotion only fully apprehensible at the racetrack, though other situations occasionally come close. None of those situations are, however, at all accessible to what Simmons or I would think of as the "working class."

It is now post-time. Post-time. It is, in fact, some seconds after post-time, one of the horses in the gate having clearly, to Simmons' anguished but farsighted gaze, unseated his jockey. "Oh, God, not the seven, not the number seven," Simmons says, and the announcer says, "That's number one, Cinnamon Roll, unseating the rider," and Simmons gives a gasp of relief as the announcer adds, "that's Cinnamon Roll now running off from the gate." "Oh, boy," he says again (actually the acoustics are quite poor, and for an instant he had thought that the announcer was talking about *Simmons* unseating his jockey and not the crazed horse) as several patrons to his right and left begin to spew curses, at the same time extracting tickets which they regard with loathing. Cinnamon Roll is the 7-5 favorite, as one glance at the tote quickly affirms. "I really can't stand this," Simmons says to no one in particular and bangs an elbow into the mesh, giving him enough distracting pain to keep him functioning while the out-riders meanwhile recover number one, gently urge her toward the gate, stand guard while the jockey remounts, and then tenderly pat the horse into position. The grandstand mutters angrily. The horse is the favorite and they feel (*they* is a generalization, but I can do a great deal of research very quickly) that it should have been scratched for medical reasons. But Simmons himself is beyond judgments; he has moved into an abyss of feeling so profound that only the announcer's statement that the horses are out of the gate is able to move him to passion.

The effect of this is, however, galvanic and would surprise anyone in the vicinity of the ten-dollar window who had decided to take a tip from the mute.

"Oh, you bastards, here you come!" he says with conviction, a sidewise glance at the board now informing him that the horse is at least ninety to one. "Oh, boy," he says, "come on, come on, get me out of this, come *on*, please," his voice winding its way from a low rumble to a whining shriek during the final words and impressing me, as it always has, with Simmons' utter lack of obscenity under stress situations. It all falls away in the same fashion, I understand, that soldiers in mortal danger of their lives or with broken morale are apt to curse somewhat less than a cross-section of the Mothers Superior. Obscenity, according to those studies with which I am familiar, occurs only during the relative contentment of hope and tends to vanish when the stresses become evident. "Oh, please," says Simmons and clasps his hands prettily. "Oh, please."

(Once Simmons had made a resolve not to address horses or jockeys during the running of races. He came to this decision on the basis that he was trying to be businesslike and participating in an investment program not dissimilar to stocks and bonds. Did brokers or customers, he wondered, scream curses at the ticker and shake their fists when old IBM went up two in the middle of the track? Of course they did not, and he made no fewer demands of himself than he would if he had been in a more favored position. This resolve had lasted four races, until Cruguet had done something really disastrous with a longshot who was caused to bear in on the rail, and from that time on Simmons has comforted himself with the belief that without air-conditioning, all brokers would work in their undershirts.)

The horses come toward the stretch turn. It is difficult to pick up the call in the midst of the shouting and difficult as well to see the numbers of the leading horses as flashed on the tote board because of the angle. It is for this very reason—a sense of rising mystery during a race, all possibilities enacted until the deadly, final knowledge—that Simmons has elected this for his vantage point, but now, past all shrieking, his voice is only a terrified whisper as he says, "What's going on? What's going on?" Hurling himself half over the rail, he is able to see the race for the first time; he cannot spot the seven horse. Four is on the lead and two outside of it is coming on. The seven must be behind another horse on the rail; either that or it has adjourned from the gate because, as the horses pass, he is unable to see it. "Please," Simmons says as he watches the field scuttle from him, "oh, please." There are diminishing shrieks in the distance and then a silence so deep and white that it could be laid over acres of glowing bone.

Numbers come up on the tote which Simmons is unable to see. After a time—and it is a considerable time, for first all of the horses must return to the paddock to be unsaddled and the jockeys to weigh in, but for Simmons there is no sense of chronology whatsoever—the announcer says that the race is official and reads off the money horses.

The seven finishes third, which is, in my estimation and possibly the announcer's, a remarkable showing for a ninety-to-one shot. Only one ninety-to-one shot out of ten beats even a third of its field; this one has beaten fully three-quarters. I point this out to Simmons in a mild, apologetic tone. "It was rather remarkable, you've got to admit that," I say. "And you could have had the show bet, which incidentally paid only eight sixty due to the two favorites running in."

Simmons says nothing. He is beyond modest mathematical remonstrances or calculation. Instead he is shaking his head, up and down alternately, his neck constricting, his ears bulging, his eyes fluttering. He appears to be entering a period of sea change, or, at any rate, it seems to be Simmons Transmuted which I see before me, an older, wiser, infinitely altered Simmons who looks at me with compassion and loathing intermingled as, palms spread before me, I back away, apologizing for my faulty information, my old impulsiveness, my overextended and familiar desire to please. My suspicion is that I too have become a compulsive gambler.

But after a long time, Simmons does say something. He says it in a low voice, and it is difficult for me to distinguish it for a moment. Then, the words seem to explode through me with the force of a grenade, or perhaps I am thinking of a waterfall, my taste for metaphor being as faulty as my way with horses. Nevertheless, I find that I am drenched in knowledge, swaying, gasping, so moved that I am virtually inarticulate, and the silence deepens further as we plunge into the True and Final Disaster and the epochal and grim events of the deservedly famous Last Descent truly begin.

"You can't win 'em all," Simmons says.

AS BETWEEN GENERATIONS

I

I run my father. For months, years, I have wanted to do this; now I cannot stand it any longer and I push him through the streets of the town, waving the whip, screaming at him. His senile legs patter, his ancient mouth drools, he is pulling the cart to the best of his effort, he moans, could I please not hit him so often and so hard. But I am remorseless; I cannot bear any longer the culmination of all the things that he has done to me and now at last I am seeking retribution. It is not very nice of me but it is the custom.

People line the streets as I run him. It is not an unusual event. On a fine Sunday such as this, maybe ten or twenty sons or daughters will run their fathers, through the clear dry light of morning and into the dank afternoon but for the moment I am the only one; the others, perhaps, waiting until I have finished as a gesture of respect. After all, I have been so patient for so long. I deserve full attention, without competing interests.

The route is one mile long, down the main street and although I am not performing the major exertions, I am puffing when we are barely halfway through, probably with emotion and short-breathed as well because of the things I have been screaming at him.

"Come on, you son of a bitch," I bellow as we pass Third Street, "take that and that and that," and slash him deeply, watching the blood run in aged streaks down the dull surfaces of his back. He is 78 years old. "That's for the time you wouldn't let me go with you to park the car!" I say, slashing him, "the time you said that I should stay with Mother in the restaurant because it was man's work. And that's for the time when you cut my allowance, you cocksucker, cut me down to 75¢ because you said you didn't like my associations. My associations, damn you!" I shriek and bring the whip down fully, "when you have not known for thirty years the quality of my inner life, the quality of my dreams, the very rubric of my existence. You dared to say that to me!" He pants and increases his pace.

The crowd cheers thinly as we stumble by and once again I bring down the whip, urging him to greater and greater speed. "Remember when I was necking with Doris in our living room and you came in in your pajamas, you old son of a bitch, and told me to grow up! Remember that! I never forgot that, you evil old man," I say, clouting him once again, "and for all the times when you did it to Mother when she was tired and sick and distracted, for all the times you laid your hands on her and carried her away I give you this," and slash him the hardest one yet, a streak of pain that makes the blood dance and I hear his high whining moan. Oh it is wonderful, wonderful, the music of his blood, the singing of his cries, the harmony of his pain, the fullness of my release and it all seems to blend together: sun street, clouds, cart, whip, memory, loss and retribution as we go winding through the path of the city toward the climactic events that surely lie ahead.

II

I am driving my son. I have waited for this for thirty-six years, now at last my time has come, the loathsome spawn. He screams in agony in the cart behind me, moaning and sobbing as the whip joggles in his hand, his humiliation visible to all of those who have come to see us. Many fathers have driven their sons in this town: now it is my turn. It has been too long, too long. I can barely control shouting my release to the sun.

It was raining a little while ago but now it is clear. Everyone can see us; his torment, his guilt, his horror, its effort—and it is time, time that all of this happened because I could not have borne it any longer. He cries in rage behind me as the whip once again harmlessly grazes my flesh. "That's for you, you whelp," I murmur, "that's for the time when you called me an old fart right in front of your mother because I wouldn't let you go out in the rain. Because I wouldn't let you go to your disgusting movies."

Behind me, the cart sways and I know he is near unbalancing. "Good, good," I shriek back at him, "take it, choke on it! That's for the time you borrowed fifty dollars from me at college and said you only needed it for a week and then squandered the whole thing on pinballs and asked for more and never said thank you. That's for the time you broke in on your mother and me when you were seven years old, broke in on us at four in the morning and my lead full and heavy within me and you came in to say you couldn't sleep. Take it, take it you bastard!" and fling these words back to him, back to his teeth, knowing that behind me he has been impaled upon the sword of his humiliation, the very bleakness of his history, consuming him as he moans, crouches. tries to drive himself beyond guilt and mumbles in the clutches of his vulnerability. Oh I deserve it, I deserve it. It is high time.

Alongside, the crowd cheers. They wave at me, tip their hats, smile, teeth glinting in the sun. They share with me the power of the destruction I have brought upon him and I smile back at them, lift a hand, tilt an eyebrow, urge my legs to greater haste so that behind me the graceless sway of the cart, quickening, will toss him to the bloodless stones themselves and tear him, ungracious heart to spent limb and leave him empty, rolling, a darkening husk upon the pavement, waiting, waiting then in the night for the dogs of the prairies to come in from the South and scenting his imminent bones tear out the very core of him.

THE FALCON AND THE FALCONEER

Depositions taken after the event:

ROMANO, CHAPLAIN: The ways of the Deity are imponderable; the more intricate and vast the universe becomes to us, the more imponderable they must be. This is the kind of thing which must be understood; it has taken me forty years to learn it, and I cannot emphasize sufficiently how basic the point is. There was a time, I understand, at the advent of institutionalized science and the emergence of the rational ethic, when it was thought that the further and further we went, the more we learned; the longer we voyaged, the more the mysteries would dissipate until finally, ultimately, there would be a time when knowledge outweighed mystery totally and everything was controlled. It was only within the last few centuries, I think, that we began to realize it worked the other way; that we learned only to play out our madness and insufficiency on a larger canvas; that space-drive and the colonization of the galaxy only meant that the uncontrollable had larger implications. At least, this is what I insist. Therefore, I feel no sense of guilt at what happened on Rigel XIV; it was not my responsibility. I did all that I could, of course, to discourage the disgusting adventure, but how much influence does a chaplain really have, particularly with men who have had almost to deny God to get where they are? I don't like this testimony any more than you like taking it, gentlemen, but one must face facts. In a difficult age, you must abandon preconception, posture, even hope, and do things in a difficult way. I have found this a life-sustaining rationalization.

Certainly I cautioned against it. I said to Williams the moment I heard about it and was able to gain access to him, "Captain Williams, I urge you to put an end to these plans. They are sacrilegious, they are abrupt, they are irrelevant, and they might even be actually dangerous. We should celebrate Christmas in the hallowed fashion, or we should not celebrate it at all, but we are not in any way directed to make a spectacle which can only be apostate. Besides, some of the more irreverent may be led to make remarks and come to conclusions which could only be justified under the circumstances. The idea of the creche is bad enough, but populating it with living figures is even more disgusting. Besides, the atmosphere here is absolutely intolerable, and the men will be forced to don heavy space gear if the ceremony takes any time whatsoever. And the Rigellians, while certainly affecting creatures in their own way, are unfortunately not of an appearance or manner which should be included in any serious religious ceremony. Aside from all the jokes which have been made about their physical aspect, they smell badly and they have a foul sense of humor."

Williams didn't listen, of course. There was no way he could. By the time I had managed to secure an appointment with him—a chaplain, as you are finding out, has very low rank on these survey teams—it was only two hours before the ceremony. There was no time to cancel even if he had been disposed to do so anyway, which he said he was not. He said my ideas were laughable. He said that I was looking at things in a totally didactic and sentimental fashion. He said that the men in this far-flung outpost needed their entertainment any way they could get it, sex to the contrary, and that the fact that they had wanted to have a Christmas pageant indicated that they might even be able to take something serious out of it, along with the other parts. He got up and paced excitedly and finished off a bottle of whiskey, which he said he was drinking in his quarters to celebrate the occasion, and then he threw me out, politely, saying that he had to get ready for the ceremony himself since he had been enlisted to play the part of a Pharisee, a very great honor. I came in without hope and left without despair. There was nothing that I could do. To the best of my ability I had stated my warning. Beyond that it could not be my responsibility.

As to the grievous events which followed and which resulted in all of us being here, I have nothing to say about them. I could have predicted it. We voyage further and further into the darkness, only to see the universe cleave and shriek under us. Of course. Of course. I furnished what moderate spiritual counseling that I could, and as far as the ceremony itself is concerned, I saw nothing of it. All that happened I derived only at third hand. You need only take it up, then, with those that were there. Why bother me, anyway? I realize that you need a religious expert to make a deposition, but I simply cannot help you, gentlemen, I have my own problems.

HAWKINS, BOTANY TECHNICIAN: Well, I guess lucky is the word for it. It could have been me. I was originally scheduled to play the role, only I changed my mind at the last moment, and they slipped Cullings in. Boy, was I horrified when I saw what happened to Cullings! It was like everything that was going on was happening to me, only I wasn't there. I ended up with a small role, tending one of the donkeys, which was bad enough under all the circumstances.

The reason I backed out at the last moment was because of Dr.

Romano, the team chaplain, and I really appreciate everything that he did for me now, although I wasn't happy about it then. Just when the rehearsals were beginning, Dr. Romano came up to me and said he wanted to talk to me when I got a chance, and because I didn't want to get in any trouble—he was an officer, after all—I went to his room later on and we chatted a bit. He said he knew from looking up my record that I came from a religious background and under all the circumstances he wanted to know how I got involved in something like this. I told him that the reason I had volunteered to play the Child was exactly *because* of this religious background of mine; I had always taken this seriously and had had a good upbringing, and taking the role I did was like I was making a contribution to what I believed in. But then Dr. Romano explained to me that it wasn't so much of a religious thing as an apostasy, he called it, because the thing was being done only for entertainment and spectacle and not because most of the people involved believed in it at all, and I began to understand what he was trying to say to me. He said that in any situation at any time you were going to find people who were going to play upon faith and use its appearance rather than its meaning for purposes of their own, but the thing the truly religious man learned to do was to recognize it and avoid it.

Fight it with all his heart's might, Dr. Romano said, or to something like that. So I backed right out of playing the role; I felt bad about it, of course, because they had already fitted the garments for me and arranged things my way, but knowing what a fool I had almost been taken for, it was a guaranteed thing I wasn't going to do it. I took one of those small, supporting roles instead, and they slotted Cullings in because he was kind of the same size as I was and they didn't have to make too many changes. Actually, Cullings was happy to do it; the way it worked out it was a kind of an honor to play that role, which was another one of the reasons I was unhappy. But when I saw the way it worked out, I started being grateful, and I haven't stopped being grateful to this day.

No, of course I didn't understand what was going on there. What was there to understand? Who could know? How could it get over to us? It was just a game, a kind of game we were playing in that damned place because we were so bored and the natives there were so anxious to please and because Christmas was coming on. If it happened to me in some other way in some other place, I still wouldn't know what was going on. But it won't happen because I'm getting out of the service; my enlistment would have been up a week ago if it hadn't been for this hearing; and no matter what you do to us, I'm never going out there again. Even if I'm kept to somewhere for thirty years. Because you reach a point when you finally reach a point, you know what I mean?

I didn't know Cullings well at all; he was just a guy. There were a lot of us out there, you know; it was like a good-sized town and everybody had their own jobs and fitted in with the people who were working around them. I was sure sorry to see what happened, though.

XCBNMJY, NATIVE: The trumpet shall sound and the dead shall be raised incorruptible for behold I tell you a mystery we do not sleep but we shall all be changed in a moment in the twinkling of an eye at the last trumpet (transcript becomes illegible).

WILLIAMS, COMMANDER: I'll tell this as simply and straightforwardly as possible, and then I'll have nothing more to say. I think that a court of inquiry has been called on this sad incident is disgraceful. There is absolutely no reason for it, and were it not for the fact that certain elements of the bureaucracy felt their own positions to be obscurely threatened by the events, this never would have occurred. They're merely trying to hang us so they won't be touched. I was always a straightforward man, and I speak the truth. This is one of the hazards of command. What do those hacks and clerks know of responsibility?

Sure, I okayed the pageant. Rigel XIV is a dismal outpost, one of the worst assignments in the survey corps. The terrain is lousy; the view is impossible; the climate is intolerable; and to top it all off, the atmosphere, which seems perfectly benign on first exposure, turns out to kill you if you're exposed to it for more than thirty minutes. That was found out by trial-and-error, of course, a long time ago.

It's a lousy detail and the best types don't generally end up there; most of us didn't have a connection of any sort, or we wouldn't have been on the post in the first place. In my case, they were out to nail me for that mess on Deneb X years ago, where they still think I was responsible for the survey missing the uranium deposits. There's no truth in that at all, but they've been after me ever since.

The only saving grace of the assignment is the natives. Friendly little beasts; stupid as hell, of course, and almost ineducable, but cooperative. They can learn the language after a fashion, and they can be taught to perform simple tasks, but I do not believe that this in itself indicates human intelligence. Too, they look like asses, and it may just be my xenophobia, but nothing that looks like an ass can earn my respect.

But they're pleasant creatures, they make ideal pets, and even a man in the heaviest gear can ride on them for hours. They have an amazing tolerance and they're curious as hell in the bargain, so one way or the other I guess that you could say that it is possible to establish some kind of a relationship with them. I don't want to get into this business of telepathy at all; I know that it's being discussed here, along with all those other mysterious powers they're supposed to have. I never saw any evidence of it, and I should know. And the whole history of the survey, which I know as well as anyone, shows that there's never been any trouble between them and us. They just function on their own level.

I heard about the idea of the pageant only when it was presented to me by a group of the men. Hawkins, one of the botany detail, was the spokesman, more or less, which I found surprising because Hawkins has always struck me as a kind of nonentity, one of those civil servants who make up the bulk of these teams, doing their jobs with all the efficiency and imagination they might possess if they were working in a huge bureau back here. I suppose certain things are timeless after all, but Hawkins was really enthused. I had never seen so much life in the man.

"We want to have a Christmas pageant," he said. "We can build a creche right outside, and the men will take the various roles, and the Rigellians can be the donkeys in the manger and the sheep on the fields. The idea is to re-enact the Nativity and give us all something to think about in our pasts or back home. We want your permission to go ahead and build the creche."

"I don't understand," I said, which I truly didn't. "Do you mean to say that you're going to assign the various roles of the story to people in the crew and just go through with this thing outside, in that terrain?"

"Exactly. We all kind of worked it out on our own, the engineers and the science detail. We think something should be done for Christmas. We didn't always live out here, you know."

"But what's the point? Why all the enthusiasm?" and, indeed, Hawkins and the others were trembling with interest; I had never seen the men so involved. "And what's the point of it?"

"It's kind of a tribute to our history. To what we are as men and where we used to be and what we once wanted to believe and where we are going. It's a reconstitution of myth within a contemporary framework, an infusion of dreams into the reality so that in the blending the two, dreams and reality, must be known together."

"That's a strange way to talk," I said. "I don't believe I've ever heard you talk like that before."

"We kind of worked it out beforehand," Hawkins said and looked at the floor. "Is it all right? Can we go ahead and do it then?"

"I don't even know if you need my permission. This would come under recreation which you are permitted on your respective schedules. I suppose it would take place inside the project?"

"Well, no. We wanted to go outside. There's a nice depression, only a few hundred yards from here where the creche can be set up, and we kind of thought that it should be in the open air. I can't explain why, but it seemed nicer that way."

"And these roles? You've already selected the people to play them? Won't there be some embarrassment about—uh—some of the assignments?"

"I'm going to play the Infant," Hawkins said. "And the others will fall into place." He pointed to the three who had come with him. "They're going to be the wise men, of course."

Of course. Well, I had no objection. I told him so. It wasn't my place to comment on it one way or the other; a commander's duties are very strictly outlined under the general code, and they do not involve intermingling with the crew on projects or recreation of their own choice which does not interfere with duty. The idea struck me as being a little strange, of course, immature and a bit preposterous, but as far as I was concerned, that was none of my business.

"You can have your pageant," I said. "I wouldn't advise abusing the natives, though, in the performance."

"Oh, not at all," Hawkins said. "They're kind of the key to the whole thing. The pastoral element and so on. We'll treat them very carefully. Actually, they're quite excited about the idea. It will enable them to know us better."

That's as far as I went with it. It sounded a little crazy, of course, but men tend to get crazy on these expeditions anyway; it's a kind of fringe benefit. I know some who have invented variations of chess and others who have papered their barracks, ceiling to floor, wall to wall, with pictures of various anatomical parts; I know more than a couple who progressed from serious alcoholism to madness during a run. This is what is going to happen inevitably when you set out to colonize the universe: men have to occupy it, and men are going to bring what they are along with them. The idea of having a pageant was no more insane than my conviction, during my second tour of duty on Campa I, that I was regressing to an ape-like state due to boredom and would be able to write the first logical autobiography of a subhuman species. You have to go along with this kind of thing.

When I learned that Hawkins had bowed out and Cullings had stepped in, it was of no interest to me; and when I was invited and went, it was only a way of showing the men respect and killing a couple of hours. I didn't like what happened, of course, and in a general human way I feel kind of responsible, but there was no way that we could know. How could anybody know? Besides, in the long run, it probably won't make any difference anyway. Cullings, I understand from people who knew him, was a sullen, nonreligious type; maybe the experience will do him some good. On the other hand, I don't like this kind of inquiry, and I have nothing more to say.

STOCK, PSYCHOLOGIST: There is a perfectly rational explanation for what happened, but you will not obtain it from many of the others, particularly not from Williams, whom I diagnosed early on as a rigid, repressed, anal-oriented paranoid whose fantasies were an enactment and rationalization of his basic, latent homosexuality. Of course, my job is to deal more with alien psychology and social relationships, but that doesn't prevent me from making judgments.

You have to do something to keep the intellect alive, after all: these aliens—most of those I've encountered and particularly the bastards on the Rigel survey—are little better than vegetables, and there's hardly much stimulation in working out group patterns and social interaction on a survey team because anybody who's on these is half-crazy in the first place and then they proceed to get crazier. By the time I got wind of the pageant and the way it was going, it was my best opinion that Cullings, Hawkins and the whole batch of them had regressed to a subinfantile state where they were using magic and mysticism as a way of warding off any kind of threat; they were even below the polymorphous perverse stage. I could catch that right away by the peculiar details of the pageant which they insisted upon—the relationship of the Madonna and child in the feeding position, the way that the aliens were grouped just around, the use of special straw for the creche ... all of this was sheer compulsiveness. And the fact that a big, hulking man like Forrest was playing the role of the Madonna with little Cullings added another element to it. The implications were fascinating; it was the first truly interesting thing that had happened to me since I signed up for this cursed project. But then again it could get a thoughtful man scared.

Several things scared me: in the first place, as I began to make my investigations, then quietly checking here and there, I found that nobody would really own up to having originated the idea of the pageant. "It just kind of came up one day and we got to work on it" was what I heard time and again, or "a lot of us just realized that it would be a honey of an idea." The sudden imposition of a mass-obsession without clear, individual origin is one of the surest indications that something is going on. I didn't like it.

I'm aware that it's been brought up now that the idea might have originated with the aliens who were using their telepathic ability to plant it in the crew so subtly that the crew thought it came out of their own heads. It would be a good explanation, but it doesn't make a pack of sense: these aliens are idiots in every possible regard; they are animaline not only in appearance but in behavior, and the fact that they have a low mimetic ability and are thus able to simulate language is no clue whatsoever to intelligence. No, the men got this up on their very own—mass-psychosis if it ever happened—and what happened to Cullings was totally their responsibility.

When you take a group of hacks, boobs, oafs and civil servants, set them up on a bleak outpost somewhere near the center of hell— otherwise to be known as the outer arm of the Milky Way—leave them to their own devices sans sex, sans organized recreation, sans the inner resources to make things come out their own way and when this group of men ends up raving religious fanatics who perform a strange rite out of which comes death, disappearance and madness ... what other explanation do you need? It is not so much that I am an excessively rational man ... but after all, how far afield does one have to go? The simplest explanation is the right one; I learned that a long time ago. The simplest explanation is the right one here. I will not cooperate with this inquiry any further, and I care little what happens to me as a result of it.

MARTINSON, CREW: Well, I'll give you a simple account, as best as I can remember. I don't know why you're asking me; all those other guys who testified would be much better able to do it than me. I'm just a simple athlete. Haven't you heard? I'll just stick to the facts. The rehearsals went pretty well, although the time when Cullings and Hawkins switched roles set us back a little. The whole point was not to make a mockery of it. I was playing one of the people in the inn; I had only one line which was after the innkeeper said no room I was supposed to get up and say "but what of the child?" Just that, "but what of the child?" It was the key to the whole scene, but there was so much else going on that nobody listened.

The aliens worked into it just great. They not only played the animals, there were plenty left over to be in the tavern as well. There was nothing peculiar about them playing human roles; we just took it for granted. They really worked into it and they were good actors, too.

So, the night we did it, it went just like the rehearsals, all the way up to the end, when things changed a little. What we were supposed to do, as I recall, was simply to group around Cullings and look at him, and then the floodlights that we had set up would be switched off, and that would be the end of the thing. Cullings looked very peaceful; he took the role seriously. All during rehearsals, as soon as he stepped in, he was saying that he felt for the first time as if he had truly discovered himself. Recovered himself? Maybe; I forget.

But when the lights were supposed to go on out, they didn't. I have no idea what happened; maybe somebody at the controls wasn't there. Anyway, the lights just kept on glaring and there was the whole bunch of us, standing on the straw, most of us in robes and some of us sitting up on the Rigellians.

The words? Yeah. You want to know those. I don't know who it came from, one of the donkeys, maybe mine, maybe another, and they said *Thou Art My Own Beloved Son; I beckon unto thee and we are conjoined forever.* That was all. The voice sounded pleased.

Cullings ... he began to shake.

He shook and shook and then he was drooling and slobbering and crying. It wasn't like the rehearsals at all; it was as if he was having a fit or something, and he began to scream things like "I see, I see" and "what is going on here?" and "the thieves, they double-crossed me!" and it didn't sound like his voice at all, it was so strained and high-pitched. Then he started to throw himself around on the straw. Like epilepsy. Only more interesting.

The whole bunch of us were just so stunned that we didn't even go in to pick him up or try to help him. We just stared. It was kind of frightening because we hadn't counted on it, you see; we were just going to shut off the lights and go back to the ship and have a few drinks. And sing the old carols. All of a sudden, we have a situation. He was twitching and jerking like mad, Cullings; it was like he was trying to stand up but he simply couldn't make it. He would get to his knees and then it would happen again.

And then, of course, he said those words.

Well, of course, I was upset. Cullings wasn't exactly a close friend, but I knew him and when you live in close quarters with a guy, you tend to get involved. I was very sorry to see what had happened to him, but there just wasn't a damned thing I could do. There wasn't a damned thing anyone could do; we just stood there like a pack of fools. And the asses. After a while, when we realized that it was over and yet it wasn't going to stop, someone said that we might as well get back to the ship and have a few drinks anyway. Nobody wanted to touch Cullings, although someone suggested we drag him over there. We just couldn't bear to. So we left him there surrounded by the donkeys and we went back. Midway into the ship we saw the floodlights get cut, and then we went inside and got really stoned. All that I know is that Captain Williams said we should all leave the planet immediately, and that was some operation, you can imagine, with over half of us staggering drunk, trying to work on the ship. But we got it off, and we got back here in good shape, and then all of a sudden we found ourselves with this court of inquiry and like that. I don't know what's going on. I have great sympathy for Cullings, though. I sometimes think about what he must be doing now. If anything. But I try not to think about these things at all.

PETERS, FIRST SECRETARY: I think that the evidence, based upon what we have heard and upon the "statement" of the alien is pretty conclusive. Incidentally, that alien is going to die if we don't get him back there soon. We cannot simulate their environment; there are things about it we don't understand.

It is really conclusive, and I don't think there's much point in going on further. Our decision to make is simple: do we go back to Rigel XIV or don't we? Since I can see no basis for our returning other than to reenact a continuing madness, I think we should stay out.

I think we should stay out of a lot of places, I really do. There are forces in this universe which we are not meant to understand, and our attempts to make them conform to our vision of rationality can only make us cosmic clowns to far more than the Rigellians if we keep this up. I think that the Bureau will carefully have to review all of its procedures and policies now and that we are in for a period of regrouping and terrible reappraisal.

As for what may happen in the decades to come, this is something that we cannot possibly ascertain. Whatever happens, it is something that we will have to live with. I can only trust that religiosity for them, as it was for us, proves to be a localized phenomenon.

And I call upon the mercy of this court; I do not think that charges should be filed against the deponents. What did they know? What do we know? In similar circumstances, we would have done the same. We are that kind of people. Give them desk jobs and let them alone.

We cannot make a Civil Service adjunct of the universe. I think that this, at least, is pretty clear.

LAST WORDS OF CULLINGS, ABSENT: *My God, my God, 32 years to go—*

But I'd rather be getting crocked at the Inn!

JULY 24, 1970

July 24, 1970

Dear Mr. O'Donnell:

Your "time-machine" story has some merit and with revisions might be suitable as a "first" for one of our low-budget magazines; whether or not these revisions are anything you wish to undertake, however, must be your decision. The script, of course, is only 550 words and for $5.50 many writers would be inclined to apply their efforts toward better ends ... such as extraordinary theft. Still, this is a common problem in our branch of the market, and we hope to boost circulation soon through our "I want to go to the moon or beyond" contest; we'll then be able to install, perhaps a quarter of a cent raise into the system. At any rate, I'd be most happy to see this one again if you, in turn, will have another look at it.

The first problem is that the basic device has become as despicable an editorial chestnut as those deals-with-the-devil stories, all authors of which an editor-friend of mine once promised to shoot in the future on sight. (I, however, deplore violence; we have too much of it.) Any script that begins—as yours does—with an editor rejecting the first-person story of a writer who notes in his journal that he has begun the day by going into a recently-invented time machine and murdering his grandfather, and which terminates in the middle of a word is apt to be nestling in your thoughtful return envelope before it has fully gleaned the dull light of day that sifts into these offices. Nevertheless, I do like your twist in the middle, here, when the editor takes note of the fact that the writer, in a covering letter, states that the editor is a distant relative. This intimation—that the editor, his magazine and the submission itself might all vanish simultaneously because of temporal paradox is mildly provocative. In short, you demonstrate the paradox operating on more than a single level of negation and this is somewhat promising.

What I suggest you do, therefore, is to rewrite the story from the point of view of *the editor of the magazine to whom the story is sent,* using his sensibility rather than the epistolary method. Show, if you will, the increasing dismay of the editor as he realizes—in the process of rejecting the script—that he is possibly looking at the roots of his own causation.

Imply, thusly, that the editor finds himself in a *terrible dilemma*: the story is hackneyed and the writer undoubtedly that inept crank who always, under whatever name, pops up in some corner of the day's mail load; nevertheless, he (the editor, that is to say) has spent his entire life muddling in nightmare and must, against his will, accept the possibility—the existence, I mean—of that which he has exploited. Indicate, then, that the editor wishes by all light of critical knowledge to *reject* the script *insultingly* yet fears to do so on the horrifying possibility that he is rejecting *himself.*

So, the editor returns the story not with a form rejection slip but, instead, with a request for rewrite so surely tortuous, unrewarding and beyond the writer's limited skills as to make the possibility that he will ever see the script or author again distinctly limited. Try to indicate that under his businesslike facade, however, the editor feels anything but businesslike; to the contrary his backbone is pressing against his sensitive spinal cord and his *delicate hands* even as they type the letter, crawl with dread; any moment he expects the keyboard, the backbone and his own offices, perhaps, to vanish and ... well, what then? What then indeed?

If you will do this for me, Mr. O'Donnell, I think tha

PACEM EST
(with Kris Neville)

God, in his heavens, was lonely.

I

For four days the dead nun lay under the barbed wire in a cold luminescence that seemed to be candlelight. In a stricken way, she seemed at peace; she seemed to have located an answer.

II

Hawkins was himself obsessed with answers at that period and he passed her twice each day, admiring the way she had taken to death: the cold frieze of her features under the stars, the slight, stony chasms of her cheek coming out against the wide brown eyes. Someone, probably a detail sergeant, had clasped hands over the chest after she died and so there was a curious air of grace and receptivity to her aspect; almost, Hawkins thought, as if she were clutching the lover, Death, to herself past that abandoned moment when he had slammed into her. His reactions to the nun comprised the most profound religious experience of his life.

She lay there for four days and might have been there a week if Hawkins had not taken up the issue himself with the company chaplain, insisting that something be done because such superstitious and unsettling events could turn the platoon under his command into demoralized savages.

The chaplain, head of the corpse detail, carried a large cane and believed in the power of the cane to raise the dead and create spells.

The next morning, when Hawkins took his men out on a patrol, the nun was gone and the barbed wire with her; in her place they had put a small block of wood on the fields; it gave her name and dates of birth and death and said something in Latin about being *in memoriam*. Hawkins felt much better, but later, implications of the bizarre four-day diorama exfoliated in his thoughts, and he decided that he didn't feel so good after all.

III

SISTER ALICE ROSEMARIE, etc., etc., the wood said. GONE TO HER REST, 2196. BORN SOMETIME, AROUND 2160, WE THINK. *IN QUONIBUS EST HONORARUM DE PLUMUS AU CEROTORIUM MORATORIUM.*
Caveat emptor.

IV

The nuns were always there, administering comfort to the men and helping the chaplain out at services and even occasionally pitching in on the mess line, although the men could have done without that part of it nicely. Someone in the company who was Catholic said that it was one of the most astonishing displays of solidarity with battle the Church had ever given anyone. Hawkins imagined, like himself, that the nuns were simply moving around on assignments. When the next one came through, they would get out.

The nun who had been killed had, apparently, wandered out for some private religious ritual and met stray silver wisps of the enemy gas which traveled from the alveoli of the lungs to become exploding emboli in the roiling blood of the ventricle, leaving her outward appearance unchanged. The other nuns, Hawkins supposed, had wanted to pick her up but feared to defy the hastily erected signs saying AUTHORIZED PERSONNEL ONLY PERMITTED INTO THE KILLING AREA and that had led to the whole complication of getting rid of the body. All of it still would not have been so particularly distressing to him if these events had not come in his period of religious revival.

He had never been much for religion: men who become captains of reconnaissance patrols in major wars were not, after all, profoundly religious types. They accept what they are told, and seldom, if ever, think beyond the conventional wisdom of their *milieu*.

But Hawkins had begun to feel twinges of remorse and fear from the moment he landed on the planet—probably helped along by his first view of the caged alien at the entry port. Just as indoctrination had warned, the aliens looked exactly like our own troops.

Then, too, the more he became aware of the death rate, to say nothing of the fact that the aliens were out to kill all of mankind, the more he began to feel convulsions, succumb to dim, vague fits of gloom in which he visualized himself taking complicated vows of withdrawal. It had some subtly demoralizing effect upon his work. Still, he might have reached some fragile accommodation if it had not been for the business of the dead nun which coalesced all his thinking and began to lead him to the distinct feeling that he was going insane.

On the sixth night after the removal of the body and the erection of the wooden block, Hawkins cleaned up after he had returned to the area and, in what was the best approximation of dress uniform he could make in the terrain, wandered to the rear where the nuns were; stood idly outside the huts for a time, holding his helmet in one hand; and wondering exactly what he was going to do.

V

Remember, they had been instructed; *the fate of mankind depends upon your showing here, but do not feel in any way that you are under pressure.*

VI

The old nun's face seemed strangely dull and full. It passed from one of the huts toward another and then, for some reason, stopped and asked him what he wanted.

"I want to pay my respects to the dead one. To the dead ..." In his embarrassment, Hawkins was unable to think of the word. "To the dead female priest," he said, finally.

"That would be Teresa," said the nun. "She never understood what was happening—she always talked of flowers and trees; but she had wanted to come so badly because it was the decision of the order that all of us were to come, without exception. She said she was afraid, but all things could be part of heaven if they were observed so; and then, of course, she died. You were the one who arranged for her removal?"

Hawkins nodded dumbly.

The old nun touched him lightly, two fingers spread to accommodate his wrist, and then led him toward the hut. "It was quite kind of you," she said. "We wanted to send for Teresa, but they wouldn't let us. They said it wasn't permitted. We had to think of how she lay there in indignity—and then you returned her to us."

"Well, I tried," Hawkins said.

"We couldn't manage stone, so we used wood. We had to sneak the marker in. She was very unlucky, Teresa. No luck at all."

"Unlucky?" Hawkins said. He had always believed that religious people made their own luck, uneven but connected.

They were at the door of the hut now, that door being comprised of a series of burlap sacks which had been strung together, and she pushed them aside to lead him in.

"Sit down," she said, pointing at some spot in the flickering darkness where he could sense a low-slung chair. "You'll want to talk to the Mother Superior."

"That wouldn't be necessary."

"It's the way we do things. But she isn't prepared yet."

"Do you think I could pray here?" Hawkins asked pointlessly. "Would you mind?"

"If you want to. It doesn't do much good, though. But we can give you a book."

"No books," Hawkins said. "No *books*. I want to make up the words all by myself."

"Of course," the nun said, and went away. Hawkins clasped his hands and began to mumble words like FATHER and KYRIE ELEISON and HOLY MARY, which were about all he could remember of the things he had picked up about it; but even in the murmuring stillness, with the effect given by the one candle on the shelves above him, it wouldn't quite take.

It occurred to Hawkins for the first time that he had absolutely nothing to say to God, and for some reason this cheered him; if that were the case, then God probably had nothing to say to him in return. And he would undoubtedly not be in the kind of trouble he had been fearing. There was no question of interference from forces or people with whom you had no communication.

He thought about the dead nun then, and for the moment it was without horror; perhaps the calm of her features had been an utter resignation rather than a lapsed attention caught by the fumes. It was possible, in fact, that she had died in knowledge, and if that were so it made this more the bearable—although not entirely so, of course.

After a while the curtains parted again and the old nun came out. She was dressed in what Hawkins took to be a Mother Superior's outfit and she looked very well indeed. He was not surprised in the least; he had expected it from the start.

"So, then," she said. "Now I am Mother Florence and I am prepared to properly sit by you. That was a very fine thing you did for us, and you are blessed for it."

"But why did you come out here?" Hawkins said. He was being matter-of-fact about the identity question because it was, of course, the Mother Superior's business, and not his.

"We in this order believe that the revelations of St. John are most fully realized, or to be realized in the events of these particular days.

We wish to hold out, for you, against the Apocalypse."

"There are no revelations of St. John," said Hawkins, the refutation holding only a private meaning for himself. "There is no Apocalypse, either."

"We feel otherwise," she stated, calmly.

"What about your Teresa? Does she choose to believe? Dead nuns are deader than dead men. I'm sorry; there was no need for that."

The nun touched his shoulder. "We have borne worse. We come, and we observe; we hold, and we pray. And we give what comfort we are able."

Later, away from the hut, Hawkins wandered toward the center of the encampment. Drifting around him were strange night odors and within him his rage, and he guessed, as he picked up his pace, that when the two of them combined—the outside and the inside—they might make a kind of sense; there might be something to his feelings, his being. And in that hope he burst free, still moving, through the area itself and out to the other end, to the fields. Unswerving, poised with the grace of insistence, he plunged toward the wooden block in the distance. When he got there he caved it over with a sigh, feeling its edges rolling against him; he pivoted on his back to look at the sky, wondering from where and from when his brothers the aliens would place their special silver stake in his heart.

To combat his loneliness, God invented religion.

THE NEW RAPPACINI

I

Carefully, lovingly reconstructing his wife Glover has a sudden intimation of fright, at the moment that he applies the generating spark to the corpus it will lift from the sheets, lean toward him on a propped elbow and with a tone of perfect, level accusation say: *it doesn't make any difference, no difference at all, I still hate you, it was all a lie, the whole thing was a lie from the beginning and you should have let me sleep* and nailed by this somewhere between remorse and fulfillment he will stand frozen forever, unable to cut the power, unable to deal with the resurrection. But along with so much else he has put this out of his mind; the thing to do is to get her walking and talking again and then they will work it out from there. He busies himself with the organizer, the synthesizer, the power grids, the cellulose acetate blender, the entire intricate apparatus which would be an object of amazement to him if it was not purchased on credit and tries to keep in mind only one thing: when he is done she will come toward him with mingled gratitude and knowledge in her eyes and he will do nothing but stand for a long time and hold her, the breathing spaces of her body, the opening crevice of her necessity under his and past that there are no thoughts at all, only the old tattered admixture of dream, anticipation, loss and revulsion which seized him from the onset of this mad decision.

II

Under him in bed (he chose to remember) she had been gentle and ferocious by turns, pulsing with his body, muttering words into his ear, telling fragments of her history to him as he yanked himself toward orgasm; a good wife, a cooperative partner, a hint of scatology in her own devices which had matched some devilish stroke of prurience in his own nature or was it only perversity which had guided him in those nights, nothing else. It was very hard to remember, all of this receding from him; the point was that she was the most important thing in the world to him by virtue of permanence if nothing else and thus he had taken her death very hard, the more so because, when you came right down to it, it was all very inconsequential. Perhaps he had never needed a wife in the first place, only something accessible and socially approved to masturbate against but there was no time for that kind of consideration now, what he wanted to do was to put her together again, reconstruct her with the Kit which would surely be adequate if he were only careful and patient and mixed the materials well. The instructions had been very positive, almost cheerful in their tone. *You will be thrilled by the renewed energy of your relative.* Only this, only this he wanted: that when she was free from it and activated she would come slowly toward him, her eyes merging mystery and madness in the old merry light and she would say, "Why, you old bawd, you old son of a bitch, I didn't know that you cared that much, what a surprise, what a pleasant surprise, why I'm just tickled to death." It didn't seem too much to ask but, of course, he had long since resigned himself to the fact that even in this simplest of relationships there were no easy answers.

III

Putting the last filaments together, within three or four hours of completion according to the booklet, Glover has an idea: he will improve upon the original model. There is no reason why he cannot; the booklet, of course, is slanted toward reconstruction—this is an amateur's piece of equipment—but on his own he can suspect innovations, adjustments, possibilities. Whistling in the depths of his basement laboratory he widens her nipples, extends the droop of her breast by some two or three inches, imparts an arch to her eyebrow which he believes will, in nightheat, inflame him like a swordsman. Also, he makes certain modifications on the cerebral cortex, induces some subtle acids into the thalamus which will improve her intellectual potential by, perhaps, some 20%, not enough, not enough—she was never a very bright woman—but a beginning. He thinks as well of doing something to the pelvic muscles to tighten her vagina but decides against this: it would be sheer weakness and, in the bargain, would impart to his almost sacramental set of tasks an overlay of self-indulgence which he cannot accept; he is not reconstructing his wife for a better fuck but only because he loved her deeply. This he assures himself, singing a Hebraic chant in an odd, off-key tenor, the creaking of his voice moving at some bizarre off-angle to the high boards under which he works, the sound of his solemnity working toward the very heavens or at least some facsimile of them he hopes he hopes, he surely hopes.

IV

It had been a peculiar accident, having something to do with a twisted ankle, an object on the steps, a wrong angle of bones and joints, a slow slide, a sickening fall, poor luck, who knows? He had found her that way when he came home, her face perfectly white, stretched taut like an eggshell, seemingly pasted, from that angle, against the deader white of the ceiling and his first surge had been one of remorse because he was not absolutely sure that in some mad corner he had not plotted out all of this, even to the angle of the patella when it missed stride, flung her outwards, but he put that out of his mind immediately, only leaning, gathering her in his arms, raising her, putting his lips against her fine, dead neck. "Don't worry about a thing," he had said to her, "don't worry about a thing, I'll get a kit and make it up to you. I'll prove to you that it wasn't my own fault, it wasn't anyone's fault, it only just happened." And indeed he would not be willing to swear, even at this penultimate moment, that his prime motivation for all of this madness, all of this unalterable work has been not love, not grief, not remorse, but only the slender, raving, wholly insane voice of reason, talking levelly in a small room somewhere, trying to establish that there is no culpability to be understood and therefore no history, never any history, not even possibility; no, there are other things, other things with which he must be concerned he is not sure that he is feeling very well.

V

Pausing before the moment of activation in the stillness of his cellar Glover has a dream: in his dream his wife awakens and rises, turns toward him in an opening fullness like a flower, the cords of her neck distended like vines and says, "you son of a bitch, it was only vanity, vanity and technology that drove you through this, if it had been for me I would have let me sleep, let me sleep the sleep of the damned or just but nothing else, not between, never, I tell you that technology alone can never keep us from meeting our ends but can only cloak them in dread and waste," and then, with a perfect solemnity, perfect grace, perfect control, she will lean back on the table, close off the switch and for the final time, the irrevocable instance, she will die and he will awaken but to the colors of what he knows he will never understand.

BAT

The point I must bring out is that all through it, I was so coked with speed I could hardly breathe. Even in the aftermath of the jag, I could still feel the slight compression, the energetic, pulsing connection that is the essence of speed itself, moving toward the discovered center, charging capillaries and corpuscles and arteries with lunging, distant heat; making the brain itself stir in reaction. Speed, God bless it, heightens, broadens, deepens, but it also does peculiar things to the psyche above and beyond the allergic reaction stuff; not for nothing is the freak playing a risky game. Only by luck, I figured, had I lasted this long on it without running into real complications.

But I was still in the flush, then: easy days, easy speed, easy life with the goddamned gawkers passing by almost unnoticed in the streets, now; the found body tuning itself like an orchestra to the A of the drug and all the parts gliding, oozing, blending together; easy dreams too, then, and a feel of weightlessness at the edges. The hell with the gawkers; I had it beat. Suspended high in the cavern of self, those caverns suspended high above West 84th Street with the sun making the brass glow I thought of little, eating what little I needed off the streets and paying my rent with the compensation check and letting even the papers slide while the speed went on its merry way. My connection was Alfie; one of the truly important men on the second floor of the tenement and Alfie could be trusted; appeared every day at 10 A.M. with the spansules glittering on his paw: money in the left, speed from the right. Otherwise, we had no relationship at all except for those occasional evenings when, centering myself slowly, I would edge downstairs and find him on the landing, playing solitaire on his haunches, his face drawn with abstraction. He and his wife weren't getting along and she locked him out often. On evenings like this he would tell me that the cops were bugging him for a speed-merchant when all he was doing was contributing to keeping the human race sane, and I couldn't have agreed with him more. The cops—some of whom were remaining on the job—had no idea of the complexity and delicacy of the balance at that time. *The man that brings the speed doth serve our need.* I would comfort him and move out, peripherally, in search of occupation, hoping that I would miss the gawkers. I didn't want dinner in those days and I did damned little drinking but the streets themselves were endlessly interesting, wide-open: an inverted tent or bowl if you will, full of wonders disunited by the sun. The bomb within me, fed by some correlant twitching in the New York dusk, would light its last fires at about that time and it was difficult to remember what I did between seven and nine any evening. I was doing *something* of course because later I had dreams.

I was wanting to tell you, though, about this thing that happened to me in the very center of my speed-jag; not wanting to get bogged down in the usual rhetoric and social analysis which while always interesting is usually irrelevant. What I wanted to tell you is about the time I met the ship full of gawkers in Central Park while I was on the bridle path, and what they said to me and what I said to them which convinced them not to liquidate our planet, at least not for a while.

They were lovely aliens; unusual types, all of them, not like the run-of-the-mill bastards. The usual run-of-the-mill alien these days, of course, is a bore and a drag; after you've talked to them five minutes you know everything you could possibly want to know about them and despite the fact that they come from distant segments of the universe, they all sound pretty much the same. Planet to planet, star to star, the variations, as you know, aren't much greater than those between Bronx and Brooklyn. But we've all been through that before: it is no secret what a disappointment the aliens have been to all of us during the three years they've been jaunting by and you'll have to pick up other studies which get into that. I sure as hell hope that when Earth goes off the bargain list—which we understand will be in a few more months now, our time—they'll find other, equally interesting places at the economy level and they'll decide we're not worth retail. This is not an unusual sentiment, of course.

This group of aliens that I was talking about was in the process of debarkation when I passed them, moving slowly with my hands folded behind my back, looking carefully for pieces of flop on the sides of the bridle path so that I could check them out for unusual sparkle. I didn't even look at them, of course. There's no point in looking at them because it all comes to the same thing and, besides that, there's so much of it now that it isn't exceptional, even for the specialists. All things being equal, I would have wandered along the path and speeded out of the park itself and gone home without even thinking about them further, past the thought that they were making more sounds in their group than aliens usually did. But things weren't equal because something unusual happened. For the first time in my experience, an alien talked to me.

This is highly unusual, as you know. All of the aliens are similar, and they are most similar of all in that they never speak until they are spoken to and, even then, not too damned much. This led to a great deal of embarrassment with the scientists at the beginning, of course. There is nothing quite so frustrated as a scientist who has been denied the kind of opportunity he has been trained to think is his entitlement and these particular scientists—I mean all the ones that commented about the aliens when the thing started; wrote for the supplements, appeared on television, gave out the interviews—were one damned stricken bunch, you can be sure. What can you do with interstellar visitors—they *say* they're interstellar visitors—who have absolutely no interest whatever in humanity? *None at all.*

As I was saying, however, on this one highly unusual occasion, an alien spoke to me. He was perhaps four feet three inches high with peculiar mottled skin and dismayed eyes that crawled around the ridges of his forehead; an average alien, in short, except for the coloration which was a kind of frozen yellow, or so I later described it in an interview. I am absolutely jammed on the speed-fit. I wish to make this clear again. Even at the levels of diminution, it does not leave you without a considerable struggle.

"Greetings," the alien said. "This would be your 'central park' wouldn't it?" I could hear the quote marks ramming into place. I was astounded, of course, to be addressed.

"Well, yes," I said, "that's what it is. Haven't you ever been here before?"

"Not recently," said the alien and came over to me, his hands clutched tentatively before him, his behind waddling. He was a very intense alien, there was no doubt about it. "Not in our generations anyway. Are you simply taking an airing, here?"

"Like that," I said. "Just easing some of the steam out of the system, trying to unthrottle."

"You have this 'nervous energy'?"

"You would call it that. I call it amphetamine. I'm one of your speed freaks, if you want to know the truth. I've got a habit and I've got to expend some of the excesses."

"Ah," said the alien thoughtfully, unclasping his hands, and making motions behind him at the ship, perched like a painted rock behind him on the grass. Two more aliens came from inside it and walked slowly toward him, flanked him, looked at me. It was an interesting scene, aided for me greatly by the fact that the stress was bringing the speed to life again; a series of slow charges, blendings and bubbles seemed to be working pleasantly in my intestines. Meanwhile the aliens looked at me. I hadn't seen so much interest for a long, long time; certainly it went back to a time before aliens had come here.

"What do you think?" the first alien said to the others. "How does he strike you?"

"Drugged," said the second. "He told you that himself. Not compensating normally. Pull him out of the fit, he'd faint."

"Not so," said the third who had the highest pitched voice of all and, it seemed, the most positive manner, "drugs are pretty common these days; the stress reactions are pretty high. Any time of social dislocation is going to institutionalize escapism one way or the other. The drugs are probably decreasing his ability to confront the reality; that is, the reality of us. I would suggest no interference at this time."

"Well, that's just fine," said the second, rather petulantly, I thought. "So what in hell are we supposed to do, pack up and fly away?"

"There are others. They're all over the place. Eventually we'll find one totally receptive."

"Rejected," the first and senior alien said. "We'll have to deal with this one on its own terms. I'm the leader and that's my final decision I've just made. I wanted the two of you around to study him, though."

"It's too dangerous," the second said. "Look at his eyeballs. They're limpid. We could—"

"Forget it," said the third. "He's the leader and he made the decision. He's right. And if he isn't right, they'll hang him, not us. We're just consultants, remember?"

The other one remembered. They turned and waddled back to the painted rock; a small hatch flipped open and they crawled inside. That was better, from my point of view, than the sudden materialization with which they had come. It restored rationality to the situation. Or at least to the speed-fit.

"Good enough," the alien said, and winked at me. His manner became confidential, as if he had passed some kind of crisis with me and was now entitled to familiarity. "I have a question to ask you now. Think carefully and don't be rash because the whole history and future of the human race are at stake. Why shouldn't we exterminate you; dissolve the planet on the spot? Earth goes off the economy package in two of your hours and we doubt if any of us will be coming here for a long, long time to come. Why not vaporize and be done with it? It's not a bad resort area but it's not worth more than the economy-rate and you people don't seem very happy, anyway. What say? Do you want us to? Consider me the full and final representative of all of us and take your time."

I thought about it for a few moments. He was right, it was a tough question. The speed rippled, smoothed the edges of myself. His eyes blanked as the sun passed over us but he failed to show the slightest kind of impatience. He was right, it was a very serious issue.

"Oh, I don't know," I said, eventually, "it hasn't been much fun since you people started passing through here anyway, you know. Life has kind of lost its meaning; it's been very humbling you know not only to be visited by alien crates but alien creatures who use everything you've got and don't even talk to you and are absolutely invulnerable. I guess I'm one of the lucky half; those that took up the drugs. On the other hand, once you leave we'd probably pick up our megalomania again and carry on; society isn't all that damned broken down. I guess we deserve a chance at that. We might fit into a tour package ourselves, some day."

The alien shrugged and looked back at the rock. He already seemed to be at a distance. "That's it?" he said. "You have nothing more to say on the question?"

"Not really. I mean in the long run it doesn't make any difference at all but you've got to carry on as if it did, that's all I know. You might as well let it all stand, I don't know why."

"That's reasonable," the alien said, after a short pause. "I can understand that. I like what you say. Of course, the fact that anyone in your position might have said it doesn't change factors. I wonder too if you would answer in the same way if I asked the question excluding all but you and your packet of drugs for which we could make courtesy provisions of our own."

"Probably not," I said, honestly enough. "Speed is pretty important to me and I'm pretty important to myself, but there just isn't that much outside that matters."

"I appreciate the honesty. Well," the alien said, "I think we'll let it stand for a while. Next cycle, next time, who knows? But we'll let it go. Perhaps you people will turn out useful after all, although from your behavior since our arrival, Lord knows how."

He nodded at me and did what might have been the equivalent of a tip of the hat, and went back into the rock ... merged into it this time. After a few instants, the rock glowed and vanished. That was pretty useful. I looked at the space where it had been for a while but except for the characteristic smell, nothing was there.

I walked back slowly, letting the last of the speed edge through me, taking a long look at the hotels and tenements of the West Side as I made it back, watching the sun cast its last shadows as it dropped behind the river. There was a block juice party going on at 83rd but I passed it by having, for the moment, lost interest in the drugs.

By the time I got back to the brownstone I was practically cold sober and when I got up to the second landing the first thing I did was to tell

Alfie—he was still there—that I had just saved the world, at least for a millennium or two. He told me that he thought that was pretty interesting and be thanked me a lot but before I could go into the facts of the case, he had passed out on the carpet, his face drawn in a light smile, facing the ceiling and it was obviously pointless to continue. It would have been nice to do so, though: it would have been nice to have been listened to for a change.

So what I did, after it all was over, was go up the two more flights to my room and lock the door and as soon as I got there, I went for the speed. To be saving about it, I shot it cold, no popping or sniffing, let alone digestion. A shoot was for special occasions and as the first lights and colors swirled into that old acuity, I figured that this was the most special of all.

Nothing beats speed. Sometimes I think the aliens just gave us the right excuse.

A QUESTION OF SLANT

Midway into the central confrontation of his science-fiction novelette, the baby screaming in the next room, his wife muttering pointless comforts as she rattles furniture, midway into the Encounter of the Aliens, Constantine finds himself seized with an idea more genuine than he has ever known and rolls the story out of the typewriter, throws the seven accumulated pages of the script cursing into the corner and embarks instead upon a portion-and-outline for a sex novel. "It doesn't pay," he says, referring to science-fiction, "two cents a word, three cents a word, markets, requirements, editors, slants, concepts, the hell with the whole thing, I'm going to make some of that easy money instead." Forty-five years old, the winner three years ago of a convention "old-timers" award for services to the field above and beyond the cause, he types the title I'M COMING SWEETHEART below his name and address and begins with some facility to write an extended sex scene between a middle-aged college professor and a coed who is trying to persuade him to give her a passing grade. "This is more like it," Constantine sings as the first conjoinment of genitals takes place before him in the clean second paragraph. "Simple, simple, basic forms, no question of ideation, just hustle and scurry in the dark. Fifteen hundred dollars cash on the line. Should have done it years ago."

Constantine, forty-five years old, blazes through the first four pages of his sex novel in a high dreamlike state, now unconscious of the moans of his firstborn, the sniffles and curses of his wife, the sound of plastering two floors below in his west side tenement. Never a sex writer (one of the citations of the old-timers award had noted his "integrity") he is surprised by the easy skill of his writing, the quick, twitching lurches from scatology to moans of which he is capable, the energy of his two characters which more than any he has ever created seem to be above and beyond him. "Now I got it," he says in falsetto as he double-spaces and begins a long transition into the impotent past of the professor, "now I'm swinging, now I'm getting into some kind of decent bag, now I know what it's all about." He feels ennobled, sanctified. It is hard for him to know exactly how long this impulse, these talents have been generating. In any event it seems to be worth it.

Pulp, pulp, it is all interchangeable, all of it on the same level. With sanctified ease he converts rocket boosters to breasts, engine pumps to surging genitals, alien dialectic to the cracked screams of love. He is so deep into it that he is barely aware of his wife's presence in the room until she strikes him sharply on the shoulder with a plank of wood left over from the baby's hastily-constructed crib and says, "I can't stand this anymore. He cries and cries all the time. We had no business getting into this, I'm too old for it. What do you think I am, fourteen years old?"

"I'm busy dear," Constantine says and tries to get back to his scene (the Professor was unable to make it with a whore on his seventeenth birthday and this failure has polluted all of his life) but his wife is insistent, the baby is hysterical in the background and even as he types he begins to feel it all go away from him, the motions of generation now only fervid twitches as his fingers slow on the keyboard and then he is at a dead stop. "Don't you understand!" he screams, "I'm just trying to make us a living! You've got to have some goddamned respect for what I'm trying to do."

"I can't stand science-fiction," his wife says. It seems that some kind of confrontation is on the way on this of all afternoons. "I can't stand anything about it: I don't even understand what you're writing and all of the people in it are crazy and it pays about six thousand dollars a year. How can a grown man your age devote himself to—"

"You don't understand," Constantine says with what he hopes is a winning smile but he suspects that it is only a stricken grin, the same stricken grin, perhaps, with which he greeted his wife's pregnancy or the announcement from the Association of Science Fiction Writers that one of his major markets was now being blackballed, "you don't understand, I'm not writing science-fiction just now. I'm doing a sex novel. Now if you'll just leave me alone and let me be, I'll be able to knock down an easy couple of thousand—"

"Sex novel!" his wife says, "sex novel, you're not going to publish *that* stuff under my name," and before Constantine can explain that the sex market is invariably composed of pseudonyms, that none of the writers of sex paperbacks ever puts his real name to his work, that the question of identities in sex novels is completely interchangeable, his wife takes the manuscript from his desk, original and carbon, and tears it in half, dumps it triumphantly into the wastebasket and before Constantine can say anything whatsoever leaves the room, leaving the door open behind her. "I would think," she says, "that you had had quite enough of sex by now. Wouldn't you?" He hears a series of high-pitched shrieks which can only indicate that the child, being raised abruptly from its crib, has noticed the absence of a bottle.

"Oh God," Constantine says, "oh God, I really can't take this anymore," but there is no time for any of that of course so he only allows himself to sigh heavily once or twice more (and that is a question of gesture rather than otherwise) and then he picks up the last page of the manuscript of SURVEY STARLIGHT and locates himself, puts it back into the typewriter and begins where he left off, right in the middle of the alien captain's speech. *You Earthers do not understand, this is a colonial investiture,* the Captain says, *we are linked to the Galactic Mindlords by a cosmic and complex chain.*

Constantine feels the cosmic and complex chain. It seems to be about three feet long and is bound around his chest. Nevertheless, as he works into the expository sections a slow smile works itself unconsciously around the thin corridor of his mouth; one would think (if one did not know better) that he has the aspect now, typing, of a Man Who Has Had His Fling.

WHAT TIME WAS THAT?

Some prefatory notes: the time machine could not be invented, of course. For that reason, it never was invented. Go look it up. The paradoxes negating the possibility of the device are too prohibitively profound. Consider: the jaunts, the murders, the alterations of the past, the assassination of the inventor's ancestors by a disgruntled legatee. That kind of thing. Because it could not happen, it did not happen. There never was a time machine. Was there?

Time is a constant. Think about it. (Planck and Einstein had some thoughts on the matter, as well as myself.) It moves forward, only forward, creating chains of purposeless causality, tearing at everything that resists it—making shreds and pulp of endeavor, creating what becomes known in retrospect, then, as "memory" or "loss." Turn it around, stumble to the imploding mouth of time and you'll only get a sound, wrenching bite on your meddling fingers. So there.

You can't fool around with time.

As I said, think about it. Max Robin did. He couldn't think very well, of course, having been deprived of the educational advantages of secondary school, undergraduate school, graduate school, professional school. Nevertheless, and within certain crude limits, he tried. He was a born thinker. So much so that he even ended up in the library now and then and struggled with microfilms of obscure professional journals—not that he was sure he understood what they were all about. He went through the almost unbearable exegesis of men who probably looked much like himself—he did so with loathing but nevertheless driven. Eventually, of course, the effort drove him even crazier than he had been in the first place.

Consider Max. He is one of those dim, anonymous men you find eating lunches from paper bags at the Automat, steaming cups of tea somewhere to the left of the numb, stricken, stunned gaze. Or—oh, yes—going through microfilms and ancient newspapers at the public library. Wide, staring eyes slammed into a face emerging almost indifferently from a drab checked shirt, uncashed unemployment check nestling in the breast pocket. That kind of thing. Now and then he cursed strange young women on the subways for displaying their bodies. But Max had (or has) this one enormous obsession. It redeems him. It even purifies, as great obsessions have been known to do. He wants to travel in time. All the way back. All the way forward. What's the difference?

The important thing is to punch through to the end and get some damned answers. Probably looks the same at either end.

Never mind why. Who knows? Why do some men go to the West Coast, some become touts; still others yearn to be published writers—these are the really dangerous ones—or absconding stockbrokers. The analysis of selection is not within our compass. This is a fiction piece. Max Robin wanted to move in time.

It would be really great to know the way everything is—put me one up on the sonsofbitches.

Unlike potential writers or absconders, however, Max's possibilities were not clearly defined for him. He lacked precedent, a sense of history. The writer always has the rejection slip, the stockbroker the SEC.

The potential time traveler, however, is in a bind. As you know, time machines do not exist at present—neither do time travelers (this proves the point that it was never invented—surely we would otherwise have been visited). Not even what we might call prevailing literature exists on the subject, let alone a how-to kit. Oh, there are science-fiction stories and novels, of course, but for Max at least these did not count. They deal with extrapolation, speculation and so on, usually with an almost apologetic air of clinging disreputability. Despite the increasing popularity of these works in the Speculative Sixties, Max Robin found himself repelled by the category.

It ain't got nothing to do with reality ...

Consider him now more specifically if you will, please. Max Robin, forty-eight years old, more than a little battered on the top with white patches which would be less ominous if they were simple baldness, the familiar dull eyes now suspended openly in his skull as he looks at something—a contraption—he has constructed in his room.

I did it. And I ain't even got no degrees. I built it myself, by golly!

He means this to be a recollection but since you and I are already in the room the thought comes out rather as an announcement.

The something we are looking at is about four feet high and wide, six feet in depth (the proportions, then, very much like Max's own), made of coils and wires and dangerously frayed electric cords of some sort. Power must be on because static leaps from one coil to the next but it does so without purpose, without even that venom and air of danger which can be associated with bad machinery in abrupt decline. Suspended at the heart of the network is a pocket watch which dangles from an uncoiled paper clip. It ticks feebly. It indicates to us—we have excellent eyesight, the two of us—that the hour is two-thirty and we make the inference that it is morning from the absence of light through the uncurtained windows. Then again thanks to certain architectural innovations, it is almost always dark in Max's two-room, furnished. He prefers it that way.

"Son of a gun," Max says reverently. "I think I've gone and invented it. It really looks as if it's going to work. It's my time machine, all mine." He can be excused, after all his months of struggle, a little megalomania. "No one else would have had the guts to do it," Max says. "Only Max Robin could work it out."

He would prefer, of course, to address these remarks to an audience. Max, like most creative geniuses, is not above a little human contact applied in small doses used sparingly. Unfortunately he has no companions in these rooms. There have been no visitors since the day several months ago when Max, taking his ease in customary fashion, was interrupted by his landlady's demands for rent. After he subsequently took her firmly by a heavy arm, threw her out of what he called his "chambers" and stated that if she ever returned he would evict her, his rooms have been without guests. Since the lady at issue is something of a sadi-maso (I hope I am using these terms correctly; I am not a specialist) she accepted this dictum without wonder and their relationship, such as it is, has more recently devolved around Max's occasional, convulsive payments of rent. At the moment, locked in his regret, Max would even have settled for his landlady.

Since you and I are already here, however, we may suffice. Ordinary fellows, both of us, but in the "right place at the right time" as they say, and therefore the best of all alternatives. It is necessary, however, to introduce ourselves.

I do so in the most graceful—if abrupt—manner possible. Max is not a man interested in social intricacies. Stepping forward the few necessary inches to bring Max's attention to me, I say, "Congratulations? Is that the time machine? Did you just invent it?"

All questions. I am not sure of anything.

Max considers us with mild approbation, satisfied that we exist and not interested in pursuing the matter beyond that. It would be strange if he did. Max takes most things in his life—there being so very, very few—for granted.

"Yeah," he says, "that's mine. I did it."

"Does it really work?"

"I'm pretty sure it does. I don't know for a fact, though. It's never been tested. I'll be making a trial run in just a minute, now, just as soon as I knock off this cigarette."

I note that Max's eyes, during the last part of this, have wandered over and set on you, without eagerness, but with that slow, dawning suspicion which is, perhaps, Max's most characteristic manner of confronting the universe. Anxious to avert a scene—which for reasons I will not go into would be highly complex—I say hurriedly, "He's a friend of mine. He just came along with me."

You nod to this, beam and try in your various ways to verify this statement for Max. Like me—although speechless in your case—you do not wish to involve Max in an extended analysis of your presence. But he averts all this by shrugging and turning away. It is difficult, at times, to maintain the fiction that important inventors maintain their own fiction of involvement.

Max knocks out the cigarette, considers the machine for some time and says, "Well, I guess I'd better get going if I want to take it for the trial run."

"We'll be watching," I say.

"It's geared to send me back fifteen minutes in time and leave me there. Just for the trial run, that is. I figure if I'm lucky I meet up with myself and we have a conversation or something—then I vanish. Or go away. I ain't gone any further than that. I don't have that kind of mind."

"That's perfectly all right," I assure him.

"I mean, how much can a man do?" Max asks rather sullenly, I think. "I invented the damned thing. That's enough. How do I know how it's going to work or anything like that?"

"Sounds all right to me," I say. "Doesn't it?"

I indicate that you should nod and obediently you do, round-eyed. With a sharp, covert gesture I indicate to you that you are on the point of sucking your thumb and warn you to withdraw it, sir.

"Of course," Max says, "it could go completely haywire. Nobody ever done this kind of thing before. How can I make any guarantees? I don't know if I should be on the trial run. I invented it, after all. I'm too important to waste. What if it blows?"

"I'm sure it couldn't," I say.

I consider him with what I hope he interprets as high admiration, even trust. For reasons which will develop shortly I am not interested in crossing Max.

"You want to go?" he asks.

"Can't do it," I say regretfully. "Wish I could but I have a bad stomach. I can't take conveyances of any kind."

"Oh, you really wouldn't be traveling, you know. You'd just sort of be moving along in—"

"I'm sorry," I say delicately. "All the same principle. Terrible nausea. I might spoil your machine if you put me in there."

That stops him.

"That's a point," he says. He tilts a finger to his chin, considers the ceiling. "That makes sense. What about him, then?"

He points to you.

"Oh, he's just along to keep me company," I say. "Here for the ride, so to speak. I don't think he'd make the right subject for an experiment. He can't talk, you see, and he couldn't tell you any of his impressions. He came out that way. He just couldn't—"

"Well," Max says cunningly. "Well." The cunning is manifested as a subtle flush which cleaves his face in half, gives those halves the preternatural appearance of gloating cross-eyed at one another. "It doesn't matter that he's a dummy or something. The important thing is that he breathes and we'll know if he keeps on breathing."

He reacts in an explosion of agility, a series of motions too rapid to follow even if I have any interest in following them, which I certainly do not. When it is all over you have been hurled into dead center of the contraption, a belt winched loosely around your waist. Max rubs his hands and moves toward a switch.

"Look, Max," I say, trying to explain, even though there is nothing after all, to discuss. "You shouldn't have bothered doing that. You see, you'll only—"

"Too late, brother," he says with some satisfaction. A switch is closed and there is a sound of breaking glass, a dispersion of smoke. When I recover my vision it is quite obvious that you are gone. I take this with regret, if without surprise. It means that I must go almost all the rest of the way alone, now.

"Well it does something," Max says, considerably subdued by that knowledge. The ultimate pity of his condition is that he did not believe the machine would work. He had not fully realized this truth about himself until this moment and the resultant depression was strong, even for Max Robin. "Now I guess we have to wait and see if the guy comes back in fifteen minutes. If he does, I guess I got it made. I'll get a patent."

"No, you won't," I say sadly. "He's never coming back."

"How can you say a thing like that? Just tell me how you come off saying something like that!" Max shouts. Suddenly, he is completely discomfited, riding on the raw edges of his Automat-nerve, back with the microfilm. "If it works he'll come back."

"They never come back. Because time moves ahead," I say, still feeling the pointless sorrow. "So his fifteen minutes will never catch up with yours. You'll run in a straight line forever, like blind cross-country runners. We could have told you all of this if you'd listened. That's what we came back here for, as a matter of fact. To tell you. But now it's entirely too late and things will just have to work themselves out."

"What work themselves out? What cross-country runners? What coming back?" It is a little too much for Max. "Listen, I don't really have to listen to this. I'll go out for a drink or something and leave you here. The hell with you."

"You can't leave. You see, you can't get out. Max," I say, hoping that he will listen, spreading my arms to convince him of my utter sincerity. "Max, you're already in the machine."

"Me? In the machine?"

"Whom do you think you put in there?"

Max blinks, shakes himself slightly like a confused dog. "This is just like science fiction," he says. "I told you, there's no such thing. I figured it all out. Time is time—you can't fool around with it. You never meet yourself and you never change the past, you just kind of move around in it all the way back and forth. I know that."

"That's your theory. Now, if you'll excuse me, my fifteen minutes are up. I really can't stay, you see. Not any longer."

I leave. Actually it has been extremely close. I clear Paradox by only a matter of seconds. But clear it I do and now I am gone.

Quite alone in his room, then, the inventor Max Robin stands in the silence, looking at his machine. It hums peculiarly and there is a sawing noise, then a sound of distant plopping.

Max stares with wonder.

It is happening now. Right this moment, it is happening. But there is no one to warn or even to audit him so Max can only watch it occur.

And so, then, from all corners of the mighty time machine—from all the crevices and interior spaces—Max Robin is coming out. There are five of him, ten of him, eleven, fifteen and a thousand and they are all falling on the floor, struggling against one another to wizened, tiny feet, trying to stagger toward him. Their eyes are wild. They are almost as wild as his own. The mouths—wee, gaping mouths—are saying words. They are trying to make some kind of a point.

Unfortunately they are barely coherent.

"I told you not to mess around with this, you bum," is what they are trying to say. "If you had stuck to your rolls and your sex-dreams none of this would have happened. But now, look. Look—"

Since they are all Max Robin himself, however, this fails to come out with the necessary forcefulness. Max never had much self-respect anyway.

Then they turn on him and begin to strike.

That works.

It should.

He is, after all, severely outnumbered.

A SOULSONG TO THE SAD, SILLY, SOARING SIXTIES

Dear Joe:

I really can't stand much more of this now but it is difficult to explain what it is like but I can only tell you that it is a sensation of LOSING CONTROL and then reenactment, perpetual reenactment of the simplest, most horrible kind, known again and again in that kind of timeless banality which perhaps can be ascribed too to sex and death but it isn't that simple: I'm telling you it's crumbling fast and

MEMPHIS: He stood out there in the fading wash, watching the grayness above intersect with the gray below, all of it melding and muddling toward the colors of night, feeling the strain inside his collar, gasping for coolness, looking absently toward the balcony: from this depth it was impossible to get any kind of perspective, it was only a kind of diminution, fading really, the sense of figures at some vast remove and then in the midst of all this scurrying, he felt the sense of it moving away from him, graceless, toward some dark conjoinment of its own and he was falling, falling, into a centrality so persuasive that

Dear Natalie:

You see the reason it didn't work out had nothing to do with emotional factors or that question of "reluctance" which you ascribed to me. I was not reluctant and again and again women will project their worst sexual fears and tensions on men. No, Natalie, it was a question of simply not being able to function anymore; I have no idea whether you can understand the level at which I was operating last summer, perhaps on the outside it all seemed the same to you: the same weariness, the same charade, the faithful old gestures but inside there was this feeling of sliding imbalance, all sensation, memory, trundling merrily, madly down a hillside to fall with a dim clatter it was still within the bounds of reasonable control then you understand but by September it had become and I able to leave but it was nothing personal oh God it is so impossible

CHICAGO: There was nothing, in the center of the fire then that high, dead stricken silence so common to disaster at the point where it begins to turn past occurrence toward inevitability and he thought at that instant then that he could see all of it laying out before him; perhaps it was only the history of the nation that was at issue but it seemed to go beyond that, seemed in fact to be his own vision: he was lying on a table and they were beating him, methodically, carefully: it was all a question of surgery and what they were doing was for medical purposes only; they were, then, eviscerating him carefully, tenderly, lovingly, all a question of health but he screamed and screamed anyway, doubtless inattentive of their skills and at that moment the vision broke and he was running, running; there were stones in the air, fire in the dusk, screams in the center and he held onto the shoulder of a young girl, running, running, all of the threads of disaster seeming to spiral out from him, bright with meaning, foul with blood, circling through all the corridors of meaning as the club caught him neatly at skull center and imploded consciousness, reason, memory, possibility in a thick grinding spray that leaped toward darkness.

I must try to make some sense of this diary, not really a diary but notes to myself; I do not know what is happening. I must try to set it down right. What am I, a microcosm? Am I supposed to re-enact it personally? But I really had nothing to do with it, I watched half of it on television and the other half I only heard about and that it would come to focus in me it's too complex to be insanity, I didn't think that there was such *corporeality* in madness. Maybe it's just the job, just a question of too much pressure coming down on me but if this is because of pressure then what I'm trying to say is that it's obviously gone too far

DALLAS: Oh his wife was beautiful, he had such a fine wife for all her faults—she was a little vicious and stupid but then they all were and she had her reasons too—and her smile so fine amidst the roses, her body good and warm inside the nestling pink and at that moment he could have fucked her for joy the bitch up on the front seat saying how much they loved him and he reached out to touch her, just a twinkle, just a brush but before he could get his bearings he was moving forward with astonished speed, diminishing gnome and then they caught him in dead-center with the spray and he knew the sonsofbitches had him, they always cut down outlanders when they came in without the proper credentials. And fell, fell, into the absorbing blackness, curiosity his only emotion as he tumbled into the swelter of the night, the screams and squeals of his wife punctuating the heave and billow of his mortality.

Dear Mr. Simmons:

I am truly sorry to tell you in response to your note that I do not think I will be able to return to my job as an investigator for the Bureau. I have had a slight illness which is not serious and is in fact very slight but has made me realize that a number of things in my life must change and I am still too indisposed to go out. Perhaps at some time in the future we will be able to discuss this; in the meantime, if you would simply mail me my check I

ARLINGTON: Ah the bastard, he had him lined up good in the sights, the revisionist son of a bitch, always talking and talking about his plans, his meaning, the new order but at heart a jew-lover like the rest of them, that was the whole thing; the bastards were in such control that they could even hire the anti-semites to keep the Americans at bay with their easy platitudes but enough of that; he had him dead-center and pulled the trigger with a flourish, seeing the bastard tumble and fall, a Chevrolet, no less, a cheap Chevrolet was the only thing he could drive and in the clear, dead space which the bastard had left vacated he saw a vision then and the vision was of a cross, a cross of fire on which the Enemies would be impaled and so he knew then

DALLAS: Leveled the bastard right in his sights, the roses, the pink, the bitch in the front seat and imploded his brains with a precision so intense that it could have been a knife and he felt good, he felt good, he felt

All right, I mean, I might have taken this all a little bit more, uh, *intensely* than the average; there's no question but that the papers and the news can fill something of a void and I admit that during most of the decade I haven't lived the most exciting, rewarding, personally satisfying life imaginable and too often I ate dinner with a newspaper instead of a girl and too often I was writing letters to the editor instead of trying to get a day's work done but even so, I thought that most of this essentially was for laughs. I mean, wasn't it for laughs? I always thought that it was a freak show, a comic book brought around in black-and-white and packaged for commercials but if deep inside on some interior level I was taking it

NEW YORK: Oh God he was falling, falling, the sound of the machine guns like giant bees in the air and she was pinned there, pinned by the fire; wanting nothing more than to run to him, to clutch him, to tell him that it was all right but she was afraid, that was the thing; she was afraid too, afraid that the guns might get her and then what would happen to the children her breasts hurt. Oh Malcolm, Malcolm and the blood was moving out over the raised surfaces in enormous rivulets, gleaming and yet dull and still the fire went on; now they were screaming to the right and left of her and finally she could take no more; she got up, began to move there slowly but it was all a weight within her: his death (she knew that he was dead), his blood, her fear, her loss, their terror, the evil and the loneliness and knelt beside him, his eyes closing like doors in his face and took it then, took it as she knew it would look thirty years from now and her cold and old and closed the eye, closed the other eye: the prophet, stoned.

Dear Sirs:
I am interested in obtaining psychiatric treatment at your clinic. I am 31 years old and have been a resident of this city all my life. My life. Recently I have had "spells" and fits during which

LOS ANGELES: Moving briskly, all purpose, some vindication too; no recrimination, however, not for me, other things to be done, deeds to be won, corpses to be kissed, time to be known and then, OH GOD THE FEELING! the head splitting open, the feeling of seeds spilling from the filter of self, all heartspumpings moving the blood toward death and I fell, the floor a blanket, the stones a void and knew then as I had always known what it would be like, a feeling of familiarity, catching the lover death, the brother's shroud, picking it up and falling falling and knew then that

Something has happened to my brain I think

MOBILE: Oh boy we got the bitch.

JACKSON: Look at them twitch. I swear to you they almost look alive.

Dear Sirs:
My previous letter in relation to clinical aid has still not been answered and I fear now that

VIETNAM: The hot rockets, the

THE MOON: One small forward step and then I thought the whole thing was for laughs

THE MOON: And dropped the bomb to make the dead bitch lurch.

ADDENDUM

THE COMMANDER: The circumstances of Dean's flight from our expeditionary force, his random explosion in the community itself prior to his apprehension and the heroic actions taken by our enlisted and adjutant personnel to apprehend and segregate the villain having already been passed on to a grateful but alarmed population, it is now time for my own brief comments to be delivered. I must emphasize to you gentlemen that absolutely no damage appears to have been the outcome of Dean's convulsions; the time-cycle itself remains snow-white, uncorrupted, and the visible consequences in our own delightful continuum appear to be restricted to a few isolated cripples appearing amongst us, one unattractive new species of flora and, of course, a moderate alteration in the business cycle which has made a "boom" out of a "bust" as the economic council has so jovially put it. My own modest savings have tripled in purchasing power, not that I would have it thought by anyone that I seek to profiteer by misfortune.

I point out, then, that there is no reason for panic and that those dissident elements screaming for "explanations" or "a change" are merely capitalizing, inexcusably, upon minor difficulties demanding instead that reaffirmation of loyalty which our nation has always responded to in the past. I am not on this platform, then, to reassure those elements nor to lend my prestige to their appeasement, heaven forbid. I seek only to complete records already complete and totally clearing all of us from those scurrilous charges the "opposition" find itself so inevitably indulging.

Let us talk only of the record, then; the record will show that Dean's instability and unpleasantness under the pressure of the voyage was by no means indicated in the personnel records or psychiatric tests but, instead, only manifested itself under situational stress; something which, despite all our cautions and procedures, will occasionally occur. Lord bless us for being human, gentlemen! for not being wholly contained by "profiles," "examinations," or "duplications," and may we always be so! The alternative is the stricturing of the soul itself into fascism; from the totalitarian soul emerges nothing other than the totalitarian state! (I will tie this into the matter of the "opposition" somewhat later.)

We were talking of the situational emergence of Dean's recklessness. Let it be known that our efficient and loyal crew instantly took all reasonable measures to contain and quarter the scoundrel; minimized all possible demoralizing effects he might have had upon marginal passengers. He was placed, at enormous expense, in a private cabin, given warm meals and the best of medical attention, and received the undistracted energy of our morale officer for the last 3/5 of the voyage. Our ship's log will definitely prove that. We could, of course, have returned the unfortunate to the original continuum—we were always aware of this option—but we were determined, at all costs, to remain within the expedition's original budget, and because the situation was so well under control, this never occurred to us as either a serious or necessary step. I must further point out that at no time during the voyage did Dean's condition seem to be of the communicable type; rather, he was completely withdrawn and even benign under the unflagging consolations and advice yielded him by the morale officer. Other passengers were not even aware of the unusual events occurring in the first hold and since Dean had shipped alone, there was no question of relatives or friends making difficulties which would have made recycling credible. I do not think I have to apologize for my actions further. As a senior officer with many years' experience, my judgments under the line of fire, so to speak, must exceed in value and pragmatism the hysterical speculations of amateurs whose sole relation to the important duties of the Expeditionary Fleets are to share in their benefits.

Dean in control, then, we arrived at our check-in point without incident and, noting that our error was less than 14 minutes (thank our Minister of Technology for having such centering devices routinely installed on all our ships, now) we perceived that everything else was completely in accord with the charts and data as supplied. We proceeded, therefore, to make arrangements. Crewmen were stationed in various strategic posts while others were infiltrated carefully with the populace, the better to amuse the passengers when landing and observation began. Garbing, dialect, and physical appropriateness were checked in within a variation of .0002 per cent, quite negligible even for the highly volatile political events under inspection. Dean, of course, was under guard in his cabin and the morale officer, most unselfishly, volunteered to remain with him rather than to take up his normal duties at sittings which consist, of course, of amusing passengers with witticisms and social comments. The ship was cloaked for invisibility and placed some 50 yards from center, on a point of slight elevation where it was reassuringly within view of passengers although not, of course, of populace.

I must emphasize that everything was under such control that under normal circumstances, everything thereon would have proceeded without a "hitch." Contrary to the seditionists belaboring all around, the errors cannot be ascribed to any of us, or to any failure of duty but only to simple failure of sustaining luck and an overgenerosity of motive. Dean, using up an inhalator, requested another of the morale officer and he, generous to a fault if not aware of the effects of the pernicious drug (morale officers must be non-inhalators in order to qualify for their position, as you know) speedily left the cabin to obtain a new supply from the stockroom. He should not have done it, of course; with that there is no argument, although the "opposition" contention that he did so deliberately is yet another seditious lie. (Exhaustive investigations have failed to unearth the slightest connection between the morale officer and Dean, other than that of professional services administered in that context.) By the time the officer had returned, Dean had vanished, which is to say, as subsequently proven, that he had made a "break" from his cabin, from the ship itself, and from the delimitation of territory which the crew had accomplished through wiring and radio signals. Seizing some of the observation tools, in fact, he had made his way into the general scene some fifty yards below where automatic tracking devices lost him and the crew, become stunningly aware, made chase.

All right, the point is conceded: *Dean broke out.* He was, however, apprehended *almost immediately.* Security forces collared him instantly; the total time he was out of range could not have exceeded more than a few milliseconds, our time, during which moments the ritual under observation itself proceeded without any apparent interference.

It is true—I hasten to admit that it is true—that there was a momentary flurry in the procession and that there was a reassembly some short distance beyond, *but this must be ascribed to intrinsic causation.* It is impossible that Dean could have had anything at all to do with these events. Found by the security forces cowering on the sixth floor of the building, Dean had already put aside his illegally acquired observation tool and went willingly into custody, stating to us that he had "seen everything he needed to see; done everything that he had to do" as comments were relayed to me by the now frantic but properly exonerated morale officer. This comment, consonant as it was with the illness evoked through prior stress, was obviously of no significance.

As per policy, of course, Dean was sequestered for detailed observation and remanded instantly to hand upon our return. The reports of his regression and terminal outlook, of course, dismay me. But I am happy to nevertheless reassure you distinguished assemblymen that there can be detected absolutely no changes of significance; neither in our lives, customs, nor habits is alteration observed. Indeed, our cycle continues unaltered on its merry, uncomplicated fashion; granted random deaths here and there and the obliteration of an unneeded territory or two, granted the new genus of flower and accelerated economy: what a small price it is, nevertheless, to pay for our minor mistake in fifty years of successful recycling; that marvelous technological institution which carries the bodies of our dead back to fragrant implantation in the fields of our forefathers, thereby guaranteeing us constant renewal, connected always to our history, as we move forward to better outcomes, better gestures, better purges, and always more colorful, costlier deaths!

THE IDEA

It came to me out of the blue that Thursday morning. The conception, I mean. Its coming had absolutely nothing to do with the top-level meeting that was scheduled upstairs later in the day. If I had remembered the meeting, I'm sure the idea would never have come in the first place. I function poorly under pressure, an old predicament.

"Educational," I told Miller after I had sketched in the outlines to him. Miller is my immediate superior so he deserves the courtesy, up to a point. "That's the hook. It's educational."

"Not enough," said Miller. He is one of those bleak, desperate men in their upper forties who remind me now and then that even I am mortal. Sometimes I consider his history, which so approximates my own progress through network to date as to be distressing.

"It's more than enough. Would I lead you wrong? The atmosphere, the times. The social tension. Everything's ready for it. Would I lead you wrong? Trust your instincts. Think of your children. Wouldn't they understand?"

"I won't propose it, Howard. I won't get before that meeting and present this. We'll be slaughtered. I'm thinking of you more than of myself."

"Did I ask *you* to propose it? I will. All I wanted was to clear with you." This was after Miller had reminded me of the meeting which he had done as soon as he had told me that he had no time for ideas, but too late for me to give him mine.

"I refuse to clear it."

"We've never had a serious disagreement. Must I go over your head?"

That made him think, as it was meant to. I could see him playing off the one thing against the other thing: an official complaint from a subordinate against the question of approval. It was a difficult decision. Part of the immediate beauty of the idea was that it made decisions difficult for everyone. Right away, it vaulted us into a new world of possibilities. Everything had implications beyond the simple dilemma of *need money; hate job*, which was the ordinary key to existence. "I can't put up with it, Howard," he said finally.

"Then I should go higher?"

"Not exactly. No. Just bring it up. At the meeting. As something you were discussing. Not as a recommendation or anything, though. Just as an idea. That's as far as I can authorize you to move on it."

"No good. A full presentation or nothing."

"You haven't got the material for a full presentation." Then he said it. "I think you're crazy, Howard."

"No, I'm not. Besides, we're all crazy. What I do is think; think all the time. It beats response, beats precision, it even beats competence. No substitute for original human thought."

"You can pose it but just as a curiosity. Say that you had this silly way-out idea and here it goes up the chute for laughs. No more. I'm a desperate man, Howard, you can see that, but I won't go beyond that."

"Fine," I said, having satisfied himself. "That's fair enough. I wasn't even thinking of the meeting to tell you the truth. If I had remembered the meeting before I came in here I wouldn't have thought it out. Pressure, you know?"

"No," said Miller.

So I pitched it to them and it went over fantastic. I had figured it would. Bald men, wigged men, old men, young men ... all of these responded as one by the time I finally got out the full sense of the idea. I had help, of course. Several of them were bright enough to catch the implications right off and Miller himself, once he saw the drift, had a few angles himself. The meeting broke up at about five after five—which meant that half of these guys had missed connections of one sort or another and would have to rearrange the whole evening if not most of the next day—and a whole group of them wanted to go out to a restaurant and finish the discussion. They couldn't get off it, were on the point of arranging for a private room in Sardi's until I said that I had an important previous engagement and would have to personally bow out.

Well, for some reason, that killed it. None of them wanted to go out or stay with it without me. They said that I was the guiding star or motivating force or things like that but it took me until a long time later that I finally figured out the real reason. Not that it matters anymore, of course.

The pilot went up for production four weeks after that, and it was terrific. They had hired the two best bodies available, big show business names as well, to do it, and it quickly became something of a classic. The price was right for those kids and they were glad to have the work. I was there at the filming and they got everything, didn't miss a nuance. About that time or shortly after, Miller had a mild heart attack and was put on leave for three months and it was just natural to move me into his spot. Just temporarily, of course. So I was able to add a few little personal touches to the pilot.

It glided right through network approval, of course, because this was one of the few pilots in history which had network money in it from the start, which kind of gave us a break on coverage, not to say the decision-making process. The go-ahead orders came right through, but it was decided to hold up production for the fall until the pilot itself was slotted as a one-shot midsummer special and we could get some reactions. If they went as we hoped they would, it could then be full-speed ahead. It was about that time, that the first glimmers of trepidation seemed to come around. Until then it had been a real spin, a voyage toward destiny conducted in as full, frank and comradely a way as I had ever seen in television—because all of us, at last, felt we were beating the biggest rap of all—but now, with the pilot in the can and actually scheduled, things began to break the other way. Rumors: too many party girls hanging around outside board meetings, stuff like that. Nothing definite.

About that time, too, was when it became "Howard's idea." Not the "fall spot" or the "turn-around gig" but "Howard's conception." I began to be asked about a lot of things which really weren't my responsibility, placement angles and sustaining spots and stuff like that. And which we wanted to tie into primarily: Nielsen or Arbitron. These were all landing at my desk and it was at about that time that I realized the fix was being put in. I remembered what Miller had said to me the only time he called from the hospital. "It's going to work, Howard," he said, "and they'll eat all of us alive for having shown them how badly they wanted it."

Prophecy from an oxygen tent. I began to find my evenings booked solid with receptions, interview shows, guest shots. Of course I couldn't come out and really say what was going to happen—we had decided to keep as tight an official lid on as possible—but the point was to hint a lot. The more I did, the more the applause meters went up.

August 3rd was pilot day. I watched it in my own home surrounded by my own family from 8:30 to 9:00 and it was like nothing that had ever happened before in the history of the world. The thing took to the tube even better than it had to the screen. The closeness, the *compression* fitted it. It was impossible not to be moved by it.

When it was over, my wife cursed me and took the children upstairs and left me to have a drink all alone and when I came out of the kitchen they were gone. I haven't seen them since, but I get messages.

About five minutes after the third drink, the phone started ringing and it hasn't stopped since. Not for a moment. Outside, inside, all I am is a message center, all clogged by grief. Right? Right.

The final trial will begin this week and I wish that Miller were here to see it, only Miller is still in this spa in Arizona. Anyone else you can think of will be there, though. As they say, they want to see Howard get what's coming to him. Howard being the man who almost destroyed America.

"Educational," I try to tell my lawyer. The first thing was, it was educational. How can you knock the accretion of knowledge in this highly technologized age, I ask you.

And my lawyer, an old friend, very short, smart guy who used to bail T & T out of all kinds of trouble before they dropped below 50 and the trouble stopped says, "What you got to understand, Howard, is that the world is full of guys all as unique as you and when it thinks that the time for something has come it is going to make one of them do it but then the world, not liking the great man theory of history, is going to lay it on the one who did it. So it can say it never happened. So it can go on its way and blame the Communists or the drinking water for the kick. But if it's any comfort, Howard, the next time it's done—and thanks to you, it will be very soon—it will be a lot easier and in the meantime I promise you that I will charge you a very small fee, nothing that the company policy won't be able to pay in full if the ultimate happens which, of course, we don't want it to."

THE END

Barry N. Malzberg Bibliography

FICTION (as either Barry or Barry N. Malzberg)

Oracle of the Thousand Hands (1968)
Screen (1968)
Confessions of Westchester County (1970)
The Spread (1971)
In My Parents' Bedroom (1971)
The Falling Astronauts (1971)
The Masochist (1972, reprinted as Everything Happened to Susan, 1975; as Cinema, 2020)
Horizontal Woman (1972; reprinted as The Social Worker, 1973)
Beyond Apollo (1972)
Overlay (1972)
Revelations (1972)
Herovit's World (1973)
In the Enclosure (1973)
The Men Inside (1973)
Phase IV (1973; novelization based on a story & screenplay by Mayo Simon)
The Day of the Burning (1974)
The Tactics of Conquest (1974)
Underlay (1974)
The Destruction of the Temple (1974)
Guernica Night (1974)
On a Planet Alien (1974)
Out from Ganymede (1974; stories)
The Sodom and Gomorrah Business (1974)
The Best of Barry N. Malzberg (1975; stories)
The Many Worlds of Barry Malzberg (1975; stories)
Galaxies (1975)
The Gamesman (1975)
Down Here in the Dream Quarter (1976; stories)
Scop (1976)
The Last Transaction (1977)
Chorale (1978)
Malzberg at Large (1979; stories)
The Man Who Loved the Midnight Lady (1980; stories)
The Cross of Fire (1982)
The Remaking of Sigmund Freud (1985)
In the Stone House (2000; stories)
Shiva and Other Stories (2001; stories)
The Passage of the Light: The Recursive Science Fiction of Barry N. Malzberg (2004; ed. by Tony Lewis & Mike Resnick; stories)
The Very Best of Barry N. Malzberg (2013; stories)
Ready When You Are and Other Stories (2023; stories)
Collaborative Capers (2023; stories)
Collecting Myself (2024; stories)

With Bill Pronzini

The Running of the Beasts (1976)
Acts of Mercy (1977)
Night Screams (1979)
Prose Bowl (1980)
Problems Solved (2003; stories)
On Account of Darkness and Other SF Stories (2004; stories)

As Mike Barry

Lone Wolf series:
Night Raider (1973)
Bay Prowler (1973)
Boston Avenger (1973)
Desert Stalker (1974)
Havana Hit (1974)
Chicago Slaughter (1974)
Peruvian Nightmare (1974)

Los Angeles Holocaust (1974)
Miami Marauder (1974)
Harlem Showdown (1975)
Detroit Massacre (1975)
Phoenix Inferno (1975)
The Killing Run (1975)
Philadelphia Blowup (1975)

As Francine di Natale

The Circle (1969)

As Claudine Dumas

The Confessions of a Parisian
   Chambermaid (1969)

As Mel Johnson/M. L. Johnson

Love Doll (1967; with The Sex Pros
   by Orrie Hitt)
I, Lesbian (1968; as M. L. Johnson)
Just Ask (1968; with Playgirl by Lou
   Craig)
Instant Sex (1968)
Chained (1968; with Master of
   Women by March Hastings & Love
   Captive by Dallas Mayo)
Kiss and Run (1968; with Sex on the
   Sand by Sheldon Lord & Odd Girl
   by March Hastings)
Nympho Nurse (1969; with Young
   and Eager by Jim Conroy &
   Quickie by Gene Evans)
The Sadist (1969; with Flesh by Max
   Collier)
The Box (1969)
Do It To Me (1969; with Hot Blonde
   by Jim Conroy)
Born to Give (1969; with Swap Club
   by Greg Hamilton & Wild in Bed
   by Dirk Malloy)
Campus Doll (1969; with High
   School Stud by Robert Hadley)
A Way With All Maidens (1969)

As Howard Lee

Kung Fu #1: The Way of the Tiger,
   the Sign of the Dragon (1973)

As Lee W. Mason

Lady of a Thousand Sorrows (1977)

As K. M. O'Donnell

Empty People (1969)
The Final War and Other Fantasies
   (1969; stories)
Dwellers of the Deep (1970)
Gather at the Hall of the Planets
   (1971)
In the Pocket and Other S-F Stories
   (1971; stories)
Universe Day (1971; stories)

As Eliot B. Reston

The Womanizer (1972)

As Gerrold Watkins

Southern Comfort (1969)
A Bed of Money (1970)
A Satyr's Romance (1970)
Giving It Away (1970)
Art of the Fugue (1970)

NON-FICTION/ESSAYS

The Engines of the Night: Science
   Fiction in the Eighties (1982;
   essays)
Breakfast in the Ruins (2007;
   essays: expansion of Engines of the
   Night)
The Business of Science Fiction: Two
   Insiders Discuss Writing and
   Publishing (2010; with Mike
   Resnick)

The Bend at the End of the Road
(2018; essays)

EDITED ANTHOLOGIES

Final Stage (1974; with Edward L.
Ferman)
Arena (1976; with Edward L.
Ferman)
Graven Images (1977; with Edward
L. Ferman)
Dark Sins, Dark Dreams (1978; with
Bill Pronzini)
The End of Summer: SF in the
Fifties (1979; with Bill Pronzini)
Shared Tomorrows: Science Fiction
in Collaboration (1979; with Bill
Pronzini)
Neglected Visions (1979; with
Martin H. Greenberg & Joseph D.
Olander)

Bug-Eyed Monsters (1980; with Bill
Pronzini)
The Science Fiction of Mark Clifton
(1980; with Martin H. Greenberg)
The Arbor House Treasury of Horror
& the Supernatural (1981; with
Bill Pronzini & Martin H.
Greenberg)
The Science Fiction of Kris Neville
(1984; with Martin H. Greenberg)
Mystery in the Mainstream (1986;
with Bill Pronzini & Martin H.
Greenberg)
Uncollected Stars (1986; with Piers
Anthony, Martin H. Greenberg &
Charles G. Waugh)
The Best Time Travel Stories of All
Time (2003)

Made in the USA
Columbia, SC
05 November 2024

45526211R00100